Shalom
India
Housing
Society

The Reuben/Rifkin Jewish Women Writers Series
A joint project of the Hadassah-Brandeis Institute
and the Feminist Press

Series editors: Elaine Reuben, Shulamit Reinharz, Gloria Jacobs

The Reuben/Rifkin Jewish Women Writers Series, established in 2006 by Elaine Reuben, honors her parents, Albert G. and Sara I. Reuben. It remembers her grandparents, Susie Green and Harry Reuben, Bessie Goldberg and David Rifkin, known to their parents by Yiddish names, and recalls family on several continents, many of whose names and particular stories are now lost. Literary works in this series, embodying and connecting varieties of Jewish experiences, will speak for them, as well, in the years to come.

Founded in 1997, the Hadassah-Brandeis Institute (HBI), whose generous grants also sponsor this series, develops fresh ways of thinking about Jews and gender worldwide by producing and promoting scholarly research and artistic projects. Brandeis professors Shulamit Reinharz and Sylvia Barack Fishman are the founding director and codirector, respectively, of HBI.

Other Books in the Reuben/Rifkin Series

Arguing with the Storm: Stories by Yiddish Women Writers
edited by Rhea Tregbov

Dearest Anne: A Tale of Impossible Love
by Judith Katzir

Dream Homes: From Cairo to Katrina, an Exile's Journey
by Joyce Zonana

Shalom India Housing Society

Esther David

Afterword by Jael Silliman

THE
FEMINIST PRESS
AT THE CITY UNIVERSITY
OF NEW YORK
NEW YORK CITY

Published in 2009 by The Feminist Press at The City University of New York
The Graduate Center, 365 Fifth Avenue, Suite 5406, New York, NY 10016

First published in 2007 by Women Unlimited as *Shalom India Housing Society* by Esther David, New Delhi, 2007.

Library of Congress Cataloging-in-Publication Data

David, Esther.
    Shalom India Housing Society / by Esther David.
        p.   cm.
    ISBN 978-1-55861-596-0
    1. Jewish sects—India—Fiction.   2. Jews—India—Fiction.   I. Title.
    PR9499.3.D39S53 2009
    823—dc22
                                                            2008049190

Cover design by Drew Stevens
Illustrations by Esther David

13 12 11 10 09   5 4 3 2 1

Contents

For Nathaniel
my son-in-law

Prelude

Who is Prophet Elijah?

Before you start reading *Shalom India Housing Society*, I would like to introduce Prophet Elijah or Eliyahu Hannabi. Maybe you know him, maybe not. If you have read Kings 1 and 2 in the Old Testament or the Jewish Torah, you might know him. But before you start reading this book, it is important that you know him, because he is the main protagonist of this novel.

I have always been intrigued by Prophet Elijah's appearance, because idol worship is taboo in the Jewish religion. So there are no pictures, references, or descriptions to help us to conjure up images of the prophet. Yet Indian Bene Israel Jews know what he looks like and I will describe him exactly the way they know him. For us Prophet Elijah is real. The Indian Bene Israel Jews are remarkable as they not only know what the prophet looks like but have taken the liberty of giving him a face, breaking all rules against idol worship.

When I started researching for my novels *Book of Esther* and *Book of Rachel*, I was fascinated by the prophet.

Most Bene Israel Jewish homes have his poster, a large rectangular picture, which shows the long-haired, white-bearded prophet in a rose-pink robe with a blue mantle, riding a chariot of fire drawn by two powerful white stallions, rising upwards in a cloud surrounded

1

by cherubs and angels. Down below on earth you can see the silhouette of Jerusalem—or maybe it is Alibaug, where the Bene Israel Jews first landed in India.

It is said that Prophet Elijah ascended to heaven from a site near present-day Haifa in Israel. Bene Israel Jews believe that on his way to heaven, the Prophet flew over India, stopping at Khandalla, a small village near Sagav, Alibaug, in Raigadh district on the Konkan coast, leaving behind the imprint of his horses' hooves and the chariot wheels on a rock when he departed.

This rock is known as Eliyahu Hannabi cha Tapa. It is revered by Bene Israel Jews as a pilgrimage site. They invoke the rock and make vows asking the prophet to fulfill their wishes. When a wish is fulfilled the prophet is offered a malida, a platter of poha or flaked rice, with dates, fruit, and biscuits. This custom is followed by no other Jewish community of the diaspora. The malida is followed by a community dinner at the synagogue, or if possible at the rock site.

It is said that some two thousand years back when they were fleeing Greek persecution in Israel the Jews were shipwrecked in India. They lost their books in the Arabian Sea, but preserved an oral tradition of Hebrew prayers like the *Shema Yisroel* and the prayer to Eliyahu Hannabi. They circumcised their sons and followed strict dietary laws, like not mixing milk with meat and not eating pork or shellfish. Known as Bene Israel Jews or Children of Israel, they made their home in India. But they soon realized that it would be difficult to remain Jewish in India, a land with many gods. So the elders must have created the cult of Prophet Elijah to help them preserve the Jewish ethos.

The Bible tells us the story of Prophet Elijah's ascension to heaven in a chariot of fire, which is connected with the belief that he will eventually return to earth with the Messiah.

Prophet Elijah also plays an important role in the Jewish festival of Passover or Pesach, which celebrates the exodus of Jews from Egypt. All over the world, Passover is observed by eating unleavened bread or matzo for seven days to remind Jews of their days of slavery. On the first two days of Passover, a chair and a goblet of wine on the seder table are kept aside for the prophet Elijah. When the prayer to the prophet is recited, the door of the house is opened as it is believed that the prophet visits Jewish homes on this particular day. Unseen, he sits on the chair allotted to him and drinks wine from the goblet. I had always been intrigued by this part of the Passover prayers, more so when I saw how Jews all over the world believe that the prophet is present amongst them and seated at their table.

Almost like Krishna, Elijah has ensnared his believers in the web of his Maya. For this very reason, I decided to make Prophet Elijah the protagonist of *Shalom India Housing Society.*

For me, Prophet Elijah is a fun-loving mischievous character who enjoys watching the theater of human follies and good heartedly intervenes when necessary. But when his duties on earth are over, he prefers to retire to his heavenly abode and soak in a spiritual bubble bath!

1 The Prophet Arrives

It was the first day of Passover or Pesach, when Jews all over the world await Prophet Elijah's visit.

He often found it hard to cope with travel, jet lag, indigestion, and the inevitable hangover. He was expected to visit Jewish homes unseen, sit in the chair allotted to him, and drink from the special goblet kept for him on the Seder table. To prepare himself for his night of global drinking, he had a leisurely bubble bath in his heavenly abode. Immersed in the pink foam, he dozed, forgetting all those earthly problems the Lord had burdened him with.

He then combed his curly silver tresses with an ivory comb. Carefully, he removed the intricate knots and applied a shining gel to match the color of his hair.

The prophet dressed slowly, in a flowing purple robe tied at the waist with a gold girdle. He fastened the buckles of the new sandals he had picked up in Jerusalem during his last trip there. They were similar to the sandals worn by prophets for centuries. It was part of their dress code. Looking at his reflection in the gilded mirror, for a second he did not recognize himself. As he pinned a blue mantle to his shoulders with brooches and put on his gold bracelets, Prophet Elijah was satisfied that he looked exactly like the poster he had seen in most Bene Israel homes of India.

Prophet Elijah then descended to earth and landed at the gates of Shalom India Housing Society in Ahmedabad, stopped next to a car, saw his reflection in the windscreen, pulled out a pocket comb, and combed his windswept curls.

Before the prophet started his act, he had some chores to attend to. The chariot had to be transformed into a pumpkin and the stallions into little white mice which he kept in a small mousetrap inside the pumpkin, so that they were not up to mischief, running here and there, excited by the matzo leftovers they relished. His winged angel with the sword of fire and the cherubs who flew around him showering flowers were transformed into flies and pinned to the mousetrap.

Prophet Elijah, also known as Eliyahu Hannabi, needed everything to be in one place so that whenever he decided to leave, his flying machine was handy. He had found this theory of transformation in *Cinderella*, a tattered children's book he had picked up from a garbage bin during one of his sorties to earth.

There were no instructions for the parking of chariots in the prophets' flying manual. He had to work out his own devices. Actually he was paranoid about losing his chariot and not being able to fly back to heaven. The prophet loved zooming around the earth in his flying chariot.

Eliyahu Hannabi knew from experience that he could not possibly leave the chariot unattended in the parking lot. There were pranksters everywhere who would jump over the chariot and pull the horses' tails. He was afraid the horses would bolt and then, where in the universe would he look for them?

Not many people know about a prophet's worries.

Once transformed into a pumpkin, the chariot had to be packed into the perforated box he always carried with him. He flew upwards with the box and left it with other boxes in the room next to the terrace. From experience, he knew it was the safest place in human homes, as it was often unused or used only as a storeroom.

Elijah then flew downwards and prepared to make a dignified entry into Shalom India Housing Society.

He tucked his magic wand into his waistband and stood whistling a tune from the film *Fiddler on the Roof*, gauging his surroundings, and making sure nobody was around. Of course they were all at home, waiting for him to visit them on Passover night, when the summer moon was like a circle of matzo bread.

The prophet Elijah was supposed to enter Jewish homes when the Haggadah was being read out, which told the story of the flight of Jews from Egypt.

The timing for his entry was halfway through the Haggadah, when, after pouring the third goblet of wine and reading Ani Ma'amin ("I believe with perfect faith in the coming of the Messiah; yes, though he tarry, I await his coming . . . "), the leader of the Passover services pointed to the cup of wine reserved for the prophet Elijah and requested a child to open the door for the prophet and invite him to drink. Jokingly, Elijah often referred to the cup as his e-goblet.

Just now the doors were closed, as it was not yet time for his entry. Anyway, each family expected him at a different time, depending on when they started the prayers. From habit, he looked for the ritual palm print on the door. Some families still dipped their palms in the blood of a fowl and left an imprint on their doors, in memory of the night of the tenth plague, when God commanded Moses, " . . . and the blood shall be to you for a token upon the houses where you are; and when I see the blood, I will pass over you, and the plague shall not be upon you to destroy you, when I smite the land of Egypt."

The Jews of Shalom India Housing Society were rather diffident about observing such an ancient tradition. All except Salome, who came from an Orthodox family and lived on the ground floor. She marked her door as she believed it protected those living in Shalom India Housing Society from harm. Everybody noticed it, but nobody commented, so she did not speak about it. In their silence, she sensed approval. What with earthquakes and riots, they needed their own voodoo against evil forces. And if sometimes her non-Jewish friends asked Salome the significance of the palm print on her door, she would smile secretively and say, "Isn't it an age-old Indian tradition?" She never let them know it was blood, not sindoor. The day before Passover, Salome collected a little blood for the ritual from a fowl or animal made kosher by the cantor Saul Ezekiel.

Prophet Elijah pulled out his magic wand, twirled it seven times about his head, transformed himself into an invisible column of swirling smoke, flew up the staircase, and heard the chant of Passover prayers.

The prophet was satisfied.

Shalom India Housing Society was a fairly recent event in the lives of the two-hundred-odd Bene Israel Jews of Ahmedabad.

Until the riots of 2002, they had lived in houses scattered around Bukhara Moholla—next to the synagogue, on the way to Jamalpur Gate, Rani Sipri's mosque, and the Ahmedabad Municipal Corporation at Khamasa Gate. In little congested lanes, close to the Parsi fire temple with its shops of sandalwood sticks, these old houses stood next to shops selling sindoor and peacock feathers at the corner of the tall gates of Teen Darwaza, three of the fourteen gates that stood like sentinels around the city.

For years, they had lived in these bustling streets with Hindu, Muslim, Parsi, and Christian families.

Then the riots had struck like the plague.

The screams, the weapons, the blood, and the dead bodies had revived memories of violent persecution which they thought they had buried with their ancestors in Alibaug.

What a long journey it had been for the ancestors fleeing Jerusalem to find themselves shipwrecked on the twin cliffs of Chanderi-Underi on the Konkan coast.

How many years ago was it, one thousand? Two thousand?

Much later, in the 1950s, when a hundred thousand Jews left for the Promised Land, there remained behind in India perhaps a thousand Jews.

During the riots, some of them saw an angry mob armed with spears and swords stripping a young boy to see if he was circumcised.

He had been burnt alive.

The Jews had been terrified, as they were also circumcised. It was a pact between God and the patriarch Abraham. They had read in the Torah " . . . this is my covenant which ye shall keep, between me and you and thy seed after thee. Every man-child among you shall be circumcised. And ye shall circumcise the flesh of your foreskin; and it shall be a token betwixt you and me."

They knew it was time to move from a predominantly Muslim moholla to a safer part of the city.

After the riots, Ezra, a contractor by profession, had decided to build apartments exclusively for Jews.

"Just Jews," he had specified when inviting tenants at the synagogue, "so that people know we have a separate identity from other minority communities."

Whether they liked it or not, it was the truth.

It was in this mood that the foundation stone of Shalom India Housing Society was laid in posh Satellite in west Ahmedabad, where they lived in harmony with Hindu, Christian, and Parsi families. The Muslims were far away in the suburbs near Chandola Lake. The ghettoization of the city had begun.

The Jews felt safe in Shalom India Housing Society, but were often guilt-stricken at having betrayed their Muslim neighbors by shifting to a safer location. Yet what if the men were mistaken for Muslims because of a missing foreskin?

Shalom India Housing Society had two blocks, but Ezra could find Jewish tenants only for Block A. Block B had been allotted to Parsis and Christians, as their food habits were similar to those of Jews.

In fact, what others believed about the food habits of Jews was a myth, as Indian Jews were vegetarian for the greater part of the year. This was because, in accordance with the dietary law, they did not eat meat unless it had been made kosher at the synagogue. Yet some of them, like Hadasah of 114, Ezel of 109, Opher of 112, and Ezra, bought meat from Muslim butchers at Vejalpur Circle. It was an open secret.

The residents of Shalom India had left behind their homes, dilapidated buildings around Magen Abraham Synagogue in Bukhara Moholla, where they had lived with Hindu and Muslim families for over three generations.

The cool mosaic courtyards, the carved, stained-glass windows with star-shaped grills, and the roofs laid with terracotta tiles still reverberated with the Hebrew chants that had in the past mingled strangely with kirtans and the call of the muezzin.

They had left Bukhara Moholla with heavy hearts and fixed the mezuzahs on the doorposts of their new apartments, hoping it would ward off the evil eye.

For the devout Jew, it had been convenient to live around the synagogue during the Sabbath, a circumcision, a Bar Mitzvah, an occasional wedding, festival, or prayer to Eliyahu Hannabi.

The high-domed building of Magen Abraham had smooth marble flooring, glass windows, ancient crystal lamps, flame-shaped electric lamps, a wall with yellow stained glass in the women's gallery, old fans with enormous wings, tube lights, tall chipped Grecian pillars, an ornate menorah, and a brass mezuzah carved with stars and affixed to the door. The velvet curtain of the ark was embroidered with Hebrew letters; there was an old wired-glass screen and a thunderbolt design in the railing; there were sturdy wooden benches and tall chairs covered with ornate textiles, one for the prophet Elijah, the other for a rare circumcision. The marble plaques of the Ten Commandments written in Hebrew and Marathi shone in the glow of the old chandeliers. The house of prayer, Magen Abraham Synagogue, resounding with the chant of the Sabbath prayers under the evening star on Friday evenings, had always comforted them.

Shalom India Housing Society had a big board at the entrance, with an enormous blue Star of David painted on a white background and the name of the society written in English, Marathi, Gujarati, and Hebrew. Ezra had also designed a special wrought-iron gate at Laxmi Welders, spending three full days there to design four interlinked stars painted black, white, silver, and blue, copied from a book of Israeli artifacts.

Until now, the new tenants of Shalom India Housing Society had celebrated Passover at the synagogue with the entire community. But at the time of this, their first Passover after the riots, there was still tension in the walled city. A man had been stabbed in broad daylight at the crossroads between the synagogue, the fire temple, the Hanuman temple, and Rani Sipri's mosque. The army was called in and the city declared under curfew. Life was almost normal where they lived, but every stabbing in the city made the Jews feel afraid and insecure. It was in this tense atmosphere that the Jewish families of Ahmedabad decided to celebrate Passover on their own, within their own homes, as they felt they were about to pass over to a new phase of life. In fact, the whole city was passing through difficult times.

In normal times, the cantor Hazan Saul Ezekiel conducted seder services, which were followed by a joint dinner in the courtyard of the synagogue. For the first time, they were on their own and found it difficult to go through the services. Some had written down the entire ritual in Marathi with Saul Ezekiel's help. Ezra had photo-copied and distributed English and Marathi manuals for conducting Passover prayers. He had also received two packets of matzo from Israel and earned a mitzvah for himself by distributing this among the families of Shalom India Housing Society.

Yet most women had spent a whole morning making their Indi-an style chapati-matzo with the cantor's wife Elisheba and Salome.

Some families had American Haggadahs, the books with the Passover prayers in English; others had Marathi versions; and some just recited the prayers, in keeping with their oral tradition.

It had not been easy to organize Passover prayers at home, and they prayed for the coming year to be peaceful so that they could join the congregation at the synagogue.

Only one person disagreed, and that was Hadasah of A-114, as she practiced her own style of Passover services. She invited friends from all communities for the seder service and they said the prayers of the religion they followed. This included the Muslim and Chris-tian versions of the crossing of the Red Sea.

The other families of Shalom India did not approve of her indi-vidual style of practicing religion, but did not comment. They allowed her to follow her own path. If the prophet Elijah accepted her prayers, they had nothing to say in the matter. They knew that had Elijah disapproved he would have let her know. But it was obvi-ous that the prophet not only approved of her, but also admired her, as nothing really untoward happened to her. In fact, he appeared to give her a lot of masala for the stories she wrote.

The prophet and Hadasah appeared to have made a pact, as long as she did not criticize him, all would be fine between them.

As swirling smoke the prophet Elijah passed under the door of A-101 and entered the apartment of Daniyal the Shamash.

A mousy man of sixty, he was Ezra's distant cousin. He had never stuck to any job and so Ezra had appointed him Shamash, the tradi-tional messenger of the synagogue. Daniyal informed members of the community about births, deaths, engagements, weddings, mali-das, and festivals. At first he went from house to house by bus and by foot, then the community bought him a bicycle, which was replaced by a moped and finally by a secondhand scooter.

A-101 was allotted to Daniyal because it was a ground-floor apartment. He had the additional duty of acting as chowkidar of the housing society. He looked after security, and received all courier and registered mail. He also did odd jobs for the women like buying soda, milk, and vegetables. He also helped Saul Eze-kiel to make the meat kosher at the synagogue and brought it back in neat packages. Hadasah was the only one who never ordered kosher meat, but bought it from the Muslim butcher at Vejalpur Circle.

Daniyal was paid wages in bits and pieces for being the commu-nity Shamash, chowkidar, occasional waiter at communal dinners, and everybody's Man Friday. He lived mostly on charity. The resi-dents gifted clothes to Daniyal and Salome and made sure their kitchen was well stocked with food and provisions. The prophet showered Daniyal with benign smiles; he was pleased that the com-munity took good care of him and his wife.

Yet Daniyal always wore a worried look on his haggard face, which resembled that of an old horse.

Prophet Elijah sniffed; the apartment was not cleaned for Pass-over, nor were the dishes washed. As usual Daniyal's home was clut-tered with utensils and furniture. Clothes were piled over each other, pushed into corners, and hidden beneath dusty old bedspreads.

The apartment was hot and pungent like the curry boiling in the kitchen. Salome was shuffling between the kitchen and the dining table. Somehow, even if she wore the brightest of colors, she always looked grey and tired.

As a habit, every evening Salome prayed to Prophet Elijah and told him all her problems.

In her younger days, she had even begged him to bestow a child on her. Feeling guilty about not having fulfilled her wish, he tried to concentrate on the seder table and the glass of wine they had kept aside for him.

In contrast to the apartment, the seder table was arranged with care. A wine-colored glass was filled to the brim with rum and lem-onade, and rubbed at the rim with salt, sugar, and a squeeze of lemon juice exactly the way he liked it—that is, whenever he was in India.

Perhaps in gratitude he could grant a child to Salome?

Like the matriarch Sarah she could become a mother at a ripe old age. Then, suddenly feeling helpless, he left them and went over to the next apartment.

The Hyams lived in A-102.

Hyams worked as a clerk in the railways. He was a man of principle and made an offering to the prophet as ritual demanded.

Prophet Elijah knew Hyams would have something pure for him. He looked into the white ceramic goblet which had his name painted in blue with a bunch of grapes. He sniffed and took a deep breath. There was nothing liquorish about the drink, yet he could see that Sheba Hyams and her daughter Rachel had worked hard. They had made the traditional Bene Israel sherbet with black currants that had been soaked overnight, boiled, strained, cooled, and poured into an old wine bottle. He was bored with homemade drinks. He wondered why women slogged so hard to give a personal touch.

He left through a crevice in the door, telling himself that he needed something strong for the special Pesach kick.

A-103 appeared to be quiet.

The prophet applied his ear to the door and smiled. It was the home of the rather autocratic Samuel. Even without entering, he knew the scene inside.

Everything was picture perfect like an Israeli greeting card, because they had lived in Israel for a long time.

The heavy beige curtains with deep brown tassels were drawn, the sky-blue walls looked clean and untouched. There was a painting of a landscape on the wall, a decorative plate from Jerusalem, a Hannukah stand, a Sabbath candle-stand, portraits of three generations of twin males of the family, Samuel's wedding photograph, and a family photo with his own twins. The identical twins sat quietly opposite each other, not daring to touch the clean tablecloth.

Samuel was reading the Haggadah in a monotonous voice.

Elijah was annoyed and would have liked to shout at him for being such a killjoy. He was making the parting of the sea sound like a dull scooter ride on Gandhi Bridge over the river Sabarmati.

Irritated, he looked down at the e-goblet and saw that his drink looked colorless.

Elijah felt like hitting his head on the wall. But after all, what does one expect in a land of prohibition? He planned to fly over to wetter pastures like Bombay, Calcutta, or Cochin. And if he was not satisfied there, he planned to hop over to Jerusalem for a chota peg.

He looked at the watery liquid in the glass and decided to give it a try.

He dipped his finger in and licked it.

It hit him like a bomb.

It was a glass of straight gin, which was why they were all swaying genie-like.

This was something to look forward to!

Happily he glided into A-104, the home of Ruby the widow.

He wasn't expecting much from her except music. She was wearing a walkman and listening to Beethoven instead of reading the Haggadah.

The prophet knew she was thinking of the Christian violinist she had recently befriended in Block B. She was lonely and he knew that she would have preferred to play the piano but did not want to offend the others.

The table was set for one person with the traditional spread. Everything was sparse and neat and his glass, although small, had run over. It had a deep red color. Elijah watched suspiciously, perhaps it was homemade black currant sherbet.

He turned to leave, but stopped, as he knew he would regret it if he did not check it out. Though he was sure it was a sherbet, either plum or pomegranate.

The prophet then looked up at the still-beautiful woman and whispered, "This cannot be true, this cannot be what I think it is, but it is!"

Elijah danced wildly and almost toppled a side table on which she had placed a photograph of her late husband with a table lamp behind the frame, so that it gave the impression of light glowing in his heart. Sensing a disturbance in the room, Ruby turned around to see what it was, then decided that it was perhaps a tremor, as often occurred after the earthquake of 2001. She closed her eyes and adjusted the headphones of her walkman.

The prophet hoped she would ask for a favor so that he could grant it, but she did not ask for anything, not even a solitary meeting with the violinist.

He left gleefully; this was something to really look forward to, real Ruby-red wine.

What fun!

Elijah floated into A-105.

There was an air of festivity here.

And the reading of the Haggadah had gone awry.

They were singing and dancing, passing around plates of samosas, chips, and peanuts. It was never easy to ask them, Now where in God's name is the matzo?

This was not the normal atmosphere in the home of Noah who ran an English medium school.

When Noah was in one of his rare good moods, his family was boisterous; else they sat around quietly, watching television as though they were in mourning. But today, besides Noah and his family there were many others in the apartment.

Holy pee, what was that, the e-goblet had a questionable color like pale straw. He was furious and stood sniffing from a distance, hoping to catch a whiff of the drink. How was he to explain to them that he was a man of taste and was particular that his drink have a good color?

He wondered why he could not catch the fragrance, had he by any chance caught cold while flying between continents?

But there was no catch in his breath; in fact he had never felt better. So the prophet inched closer to his e-goblet. It was only half full. Somebody was telling Noah to fill it to the brim, as the prophet liked a pucca Parsi peg.

Elijah saw Noah pick up a bottle of Chivas Regal and noticed that he was pouring it haltingly, asking the prophet to forgive him because he was going to mix it with soda.

His words infuriated Elijah, and he held Noah's hand in his and tilted the bottle towards the glass.

The whisky flowed into the glass, guided by the prophet's invisible hand. It overflowed onto the plate and a discolored stain formed on the tablecloth. Noah looked up, worried, and asked his wife Leah to help him, as he was sure he had frozen shoulder and could not control his hand.

Suddenly there was silence, everybody was watching him, but nobody offered help.

Noah looked terrified and Leah gave him a look which said, "Serves you right, how could you even think of cheating the prophet! He could be amongst us at this very moment." She looked around nervously. There was no sign of the prophet, so she took the bottle from Noah's hand and placed it on the table and did not see Elijah standing at her elbow, watching the e-goblet with a satisfied look on his face.

Noah was shivering, wringing his hands, cracking his knuckles and saying, "I don't know what happened to me, for a moment I felt paralyzed. Maybe I am developing arthritis." Then, looking at the stain, he moaned, "Imagine all that precious whisky gone to waste."

"Waste!" sniggered the prophet and floated towards A-106.

This seder table had a sumptuous spread, and everything was according to rules. Perhaps this was the best table in the entire housing society, even though he had never answered Shoshanah's prayers and helped her locate her daughter Miriam.

Yonathan and Shoshanah had lived in Israel for years. They knew how to follow rituals according to the Book. In fact they always knew more than the others at Shalom India and their e-goblet looked perfect. Although he could not figure out what was in the stoneware goblet.

Elijah did not particularly like arty glasses. He muttered to himself, "Why on earth couldn't they have had normal transparent goblets and if they did want something fancy they could at least have got themselves simple wine glasses." He went closer to the goblet and dipped a finger in the amber liquid. It was beer! He did a little jig like a Bollywood actor and went up to A-107.

Eliyahu Hannabi was livid when he saw that A-107 was locked. Perhaps the Jews living here were non-believers or had been invited elsewhere. Or had Ezra allotted the apartment to a non-Jew?

The nameplate had a mix of names—Juliet, Priya, Rahul, Romiel, Abhiram. They did sound in a way like Jewish names, but his prophet's ear told him that some had a false ring. So he concentrated only on Romiel and Juliet to assure himself that it was a Jewish home. But then why was there such a big lock on the door?

He entered the locked apartment and felt strangely sad. His heart sank and his spirits fell. Eliyahu Hannabi sat down on an empty packing case and worried about the fate of the Bene Israel Jews in India.

How was he to protect them from outside influences?

He was particularly fond of Indian Jews and they were particularly fond of him.

His heart went out to them. As the last few Jews in India, they were lost, never quite at home in India, in Israel, or anywhere else.

The Bene Israel Jews of India were a constant cause of worry for him.

There was no light in the apartment.

Imagine, he told himself, this is a good Jewish home but there are no candles, no light, just some light reflected from the neon lights on the road that falls through a ventilator. The prophet was sad.

Suddenly, light from a car backing up on the road below filled the apartment and the prophet saw his own reflection on the wall.

At first he thought Romiel and Juliet had left a mirror behind and he was seeing his own image.

Or else how could there be two Elijahs in one home? Was the good lord playing tricks on him or was someone impersonating him?

The prophet was still in the form of a cloud of smoke and needed a breather, so he pulled out his magic wand, twirled it around his head, and became his normal self all over again. He stretched and noticed his poster in the half-light. The usual one showing his holy self riding a chariot of fire, dressed exactly as he was at that very moment.

Satisfied, he smiled, so Romiel and Juliet believed in him.

The prophet touched his forehead and felt his third eye throbbing.

He had covered it with a transparent sticker-bindi. He removed the sticker and opened his eye. It was his Maya, which let him move without effort from one country to another, from one world to the other. With his third eye he saw Juliet and Romiel in an apartment in Lod, Israel, near Ben Gurion airport.

It was a small apartment like any of the innumerable honeycomb apartments which dotted the Israeli landscape. The Passover table was too small for those present in the room, so they had pushed it against the wall and spread a Rajasthani bedspread on the floor. It bore a circular design dotted with camels, elephants, horses, peafowl, and deer. Little India, smiled the prophet.

Then he started looking for Juliet and Romiel.

Perhaps they were fresh from the boat, and it would not be difficult to spot them. Immigrants wore a special hunted look.

He floated around the bright electric chandelier and studied the group below and noticed a young couple holding hands and generally looking uncomfortable.

He was sure they were Romiel and Juliet from A-107 of Shalom India Housing Society.

Juliet-Priya was wearing a shiny pink synthetic salwar-kameez with a matching dupatta, and a green bindi pasted like an exclamation mark on her forehead.

Romiel was sitting cross-legged in a three-piece suit.

Juliet had a square determined face and curly hair combed with a center parting and tied in two long braids. Romiel was thin and tall, but had massive shoulders, a V-shaped face, and long black hair tied in a ponytail. It was hot and Elijah wondered why he was wearing the suit. They were observing the others and following them. Elijah felt sorry for them but was happy that they were sipping his favorite Carmel wine.

The e-goblet was filled to the brim with wine, but he had to refrain from touching it, as it was not yet time for him to enter for the ceremonial drink.

But then tonight he was hard pressed for time. So why not take a sip just to give that extra kick across countries? Anyway Shalom India had very little to offer in terms of really good wine, so why not?

He stood there, wondering, To drink or not to drink? Then suddenly throwing all caution to the winds, Elijah sucked in his breath, took a sip, and felt the warm wine hit his chest.

As the prophet turned to leave, he heard Juliet's uncle Rahmim ask, "Ralphi, did you drink from the prophet's goblet?"

Ralphi looked embarrassed, "No Uncle," he said, "I would never. Perhaps someone spilled it, there are so many people in the room," he said, looking irritably at the young couple. Ralphi was angry that he had lost Juliet to a convert. "Black Jew," he hissed and Aunt Hannah looked at him resentfully. He whispered spitefully into his father's ear, "Must be Romiel, he does not know anything."

Romiel flushed angrily as he stood up saying, "I know the meaning of the prophet's goblet, I would never . . . " and walked out.

Juliet rushed after him, stopped him at the landing, pacified him, and brought him back to the apartment, where he sat neither drinking nor eating. All he wanted to do was return to India.

Uncle Rahmim tried to resolve matters by apologizing, "Sorry Romiel, I was just wondering if someone had touched the prophet's goblet as there is a stain on the bedsheet."

The prophet smiled, wiped his mustache, turned around, closed his third eye with the sticker-bindi, and returned to Shalom India Housing Society, satisfied that Romiel and Juliet were observing the Passover ceremony. Had they been in India, they would have surely offered him a good drink like vodka, rum, or a Bloody Mary, why not?

In A-108, he saw the lights were dim and the prayers were being said like a Kaddish for the dead.

This was where Yehuda and Rivka lived.

Their young son Leon was saying the prayers all wrong in a shrill voice and Elijah was irritated. He wanted to tweak Leon's cheek and teach him to read the Haggadah correctly.

He also wanted to tell Yehuda to give more life to the words. The parting of the Red Sea was dramatic, like a Kiddush, it was about life, l'chayyim! On a day like this, Jews remembered their freedom from slavery. Elijah hummed, "To life, to life," a song from *Fiddler on the Roof.*

Elijah was annoyed that the lights were dim and he could not see what was inside the e-goblet, a tall flute-like champagne glass.

The dim lights gave the drink a questionable color.

It did not look familiar. He guessed it was Mahuda, but he was not sure. So he decided to nose-dive into the glass. Like all prophets, he hated suspense.

Hovering over the drink like a hummingbird, he saw that it had the color of wine, but was not wine. Then, resting his nose on the rim of the glass, he inhaled, and fell back, shocked. It was rose sherbet! He looked down disdainfully at Rivka, who had tried to cheat him into believing that all that was red might be wine.

For the Passover, he expected each and every home to be lit up like a Christmas tree, flowing with food and wine . . . not rose sherbet.

Elijah was surprised. Rivka was particular about ritual and took great pains to make the matzo herself, lay the seder plate as prescribed in the Book, and always had kosher food at her table. But when it came to the matter of the e-goblet, she had faltered.

Suddenly, the prophet was suspicious. He saw that their own drink looked different from the one in the e-goblet. He dipped his little finger in Yehuda's drink and almost hit the ceiling. They were drinking brandy diluted with warm water and honey.

Suddenly Elijah was hopping mad and wanted to remind them it was Passover, not the flu.

He saw Yehuda reaching for the brandy bottle he had hidden under the table. Elijah removed his bindi from his third eye and mesmerized him.

Yehuda became like one in a trance and could not control his hands.

Elijah forced him to pour the rose sherbet from the e-goblet back into the jug and the brandy into the e-goblet.

Rivka was fluttering around him, asking, "What are you doing?"

Yehuda shook his head, saying nothing. He felt his hands weighed a ton of bricks.

When the prophet closed his third eye with the bindi, Yehuda stood up, flexed his arm muscles, and said, "Perhaps I had a cramp, I had no control over my hand. Must go to the gym tomorrow."

Smiling spitefully, the prophet slipped out of Yehuda's apartment and entered A-109.

Elijah saw the door was open and Ezel was alone in the apartment.

The prophet noticed that Ezel had lost his hair since last Pesach. The apartment was a mess and Ezel was sitting on the balcony, legs resting on the railing, a glass of beer in his hand, chanting,

"Eliyahu Hannabi, Eliyahu Hannabi, come drink with me . . . "

The prophet was flattered. The table was not set—there was no food, no matzo, not even an e-goblet, nothing but a plate of non-kosher mutton samosas from Famous Bakery and a bottle of beer.

The prophet smiled and forgave him; after all, Ezel was going through a tough time. Since his wife left him he had been lonely and had aged overnight.

Ezel had six bottles of beer in the fridge and it did not really matter that there was no sign of the e-goblet. Even if he tried to look for it, Elijah knew he would never find it in the mess.

A home without a woman is like a barn without a cow, mused the prophet.

If there was no woman in Ezel's apartment, there was no man in A-110. The two sisters, Abigail and Lebana, lived there with Abigail's young daughter Yael.

Abigail was a widow and Lebana had never married.

Everything was picture perfect in their apartment, and to his surprise they had tequila for him. He wondered how they had swung that one.

It was possible that someone had brought the bottle for them as a gift, and, as they had not known what to do with it, they had respectfully offered it to the prophet, who noticed that the three women were daintily sipping chilled limbu paani.

Heartened, the prophet slipped into A-111, obviously a lucky number. This was the abode of Ezra, builder, businessman, and president of the Jewish community of Ahmedabad.

He had four children, two boys and two girls, and his good wife, Sigaut. The Lord had given him health, wealth, and happiness. So the e-goblet was brimming over with strong Golconda wine and stood amidst boxes of matzo—square, corrugated, and perforated—recently flown in from Israel.

Jauntily, Eliyahu Hannabi looked into A-112 and saw Sippora in the apartment, where she had set up a beauty parlor. Her husband Opher worked in Surat and returned home on weekends. They had three daughters and were always making plans to emigrate to Israel.

They had a bottle of Indian whisky and had filled the e-goblet with watery whisky. He forgave them, as they had more problems than one.

Jacob the electrician, his wife Leeraz, and their ten-day-old son Israel lived in A-113. The Bombay-based Yohan Daniel, the official moel of the community, had circumcised little Israel when he was eight days old. Jacob felt deeply indebted to his neighbors as they had contributed to the moel's airfare from Bombay to Ahmedabad and back.

Jacob was a little awkward at the circumcision ceremony, as the prophet had blessed him with a son seventeen years after his daughter Diana was born. With little Israel in his arms, Jacob had sat on the special circumcision chair, as Yohan Daniel had removed Israel's foreskin with a blade. Leeraz and Diana had distributed the traditional boondi-laddoos to the community.

Nobody wanted this particular apartment because of the number. So it was allotted to Jacob on condition that he would pay the installments at his convenience.

Dressed in a red tunic, Israel was crying as there was dressing on his pee-place. So Leeraz was behind time in setting the Passover table. The prophet was touched to see Jacob mixing gin and angostura in the e-goblet.

Pleased, he turned towards A-114, the last apartment in the building.

It belonged to Hadasah, the author who wrote Jewish stories.

She lived alone, and would often shock her neighbors by inviting friends of all communities to her seder table. From the aroma in the apartment, he guessed she had cooked the best non-kosher meal for Passover. And of course her silver e-goblet had the best of French wine. Sometimes she annoyed the prophet by wearing a bindi bigger than his Maya-bindi and leaving her white tresses open like his. Even her kurtas were cut like his robes. Once he had seen her in a sari, her hair in a chignon, and had planned to tell her that he liked her in saris. But her dress sense somehow unnerved him. He had planned to whisper his thoughts to her by entering her dreams, but hesitated, as he knew she was stubborn and would laugh it off. She would also embarrass him by writing about him, hardly realizing that prophets are shy by nature.

Eliyahu Hannabi felt honored that she had made an effort to please him although she was not particularly religious.

And he appreciated the fact that she invited friends from other communities to her Passover dinner and introduced them to the Jewish way of life.

The prophet Elijah knew he had to wait till the Jews sang the Ani Ma'amin. The head of the family, man or woman, would then point to the e-goblet and request a child to open the door. It was symbolic of their faith in Elijah's arrival on earth. When the door opened, the e-goblet was supposed to be filled to the brim, accompanied by the chant:

This cup of wine is called Elijah's cup. The prophet Elijah is the messenger of God, appointed to herald the era of the Messiah, an era of perfect happiness, when the Jewish people and all people throughout the world will be free. Let us sing together the song of Elijah and pray that we may soon see the happy world. Soon may he come, bringing with him the Messiah.

The doors of all Jewish houses were then opened with the chant of, "Eliyahu Hannabi . . . Eliyahu Hannabi . . . "

Whenever the prophet heard the chant of Eliyahu Hannabi, he had goose pimples. He felt excited, loved, honored that they waited for him, keeping a chair for him, filling the e-goblet, believing that he was present in the room with them.

Then, unseen, Prophet Elijah would enter Jewish houses, sit on his chair and drink from his e-goblet.

It did not matter that the cocktail of all those innumerable drinks would give him a hangover the next day.

Day two of Passover would start with a splitting headache and the cherubs would have a hard time looking after him, holding out pans if he wanted to throw up, giving him hot and cold presses, often helping him to the toilet, rubbing his brows with Tiger Balm, pressing his feet, making innumerable cups of black coffee and if that didn't help, giving him aspirins dissolved in a concoction of milk and soda.

If none of this worked, they called the special medical unit of the Lord to give him a vitamin injection.

To add to the hangover, the prophet had shoe-bite. So, one of the cherubs attended to his feet, applying cream, powder, and a Band-Aid to the blister.

After the second night of Passover, Prophet Elijah changed into his linen nightdress and slept on his ornate four-poster bed till the sixth day. He woke up on the seventh day, groggy and irritable, to conduct the prayers for the last day of Passover.

That was for later. But he was known for performing the ritual of entering Jewish homes to perfection, always entering at the right time. His time management was his secret Maya and nobody understood how he managed never to let down his devotees.

He often flew back and forth between countries, always arriving at Jewish homes in time for the prayers.

When the prayers ended, the prophet would again transform into his original self, sit in the special Elijah chair with legs stretched out on the table, and drink from his e-goblet.

He estimated that on Passover nights he drank thousands of gallons of wine or whatever it was that was offered to him. As long as it was offered with love.

When the lights of Block A of Shalom India Housing Society were switched off, feeling lightheaded and giddy, Prophet Elijah staggered up to the terrace. He stood there laughing, till the heavens resounded with the chant of Eliyahu Hannabi which he sang to himself.

With so much wine inside him he knew it would be difficult to release the horses and chariots from their charm. But that was one point on which he never faltered even when he was tipsy. He always remembered to keep his magic wand carefully tucked in his waistband. He saw to it that his chariot was handy, so that however drunk he was he could quickly escape from the fetters of earthly life.

Flying in the chariot and looking at the problems down below, he knew he did not want to get stuck on earth. It was better up there, no problems, no worries, no anxieties about trying to fulfill the impossible wishes of his devotees.

On earth there were too many demands on him, and so he needed the space up there to blank out.

2 Leon

As Leon danced, the death's head moth appeared in the synagogue from nowhere. It hovered over him, dancing, then flew up to the Ten Commandments and settled for a while on the chair of the prophet Elijah. The chair was covered with blue velvet and the moth decided to settle exactly on the Hebrew words.

Leon's mother Rivka appeared agitated. He did not know why, for she knew he loved to dance. Was it because the moth had a skull-shaped design on its wings? Suddenly he touched his head and realized that he had lost his skullcap.

Even as he was dancing, he looked all around, but did not see it anywhere on the marble floor. Anyway, he decided, it was too small to be noticed. Somebody must have trampled on it.

He was upset for a second, because his uncle Shimshon had sent him the star-spangled blue silk skullcap for his bar mitzvah. He did as his father had taught him, "When you do not have anything to cover your head, not even your handkerchief, put your hand on the head." So he danced with one hand on his head.

It was not easy to dance like that and felt as if someone had tied his hand. To add to the irritation, the moth circled over his head, almost as if reminding him that he was not wearing his skullcap. He jumped higher to drive away the moth with his free hand, but it soared higher and higher, resting for a while on the enormous glass chandelier above the Teva.

So he pulled off his mother's red dupatta that he had worn as a waistband and tied it round his head like a scarf. He saw his mother twist her mouth in distress. From a distance he looked like a woman, and she did not approve of his antics. She also worried about his father's reaction.

It was the festival of Simhat Torah, the celebration of receiving the law, when the silk curtains with the Hebrew letters were pulled aside, the doors of the ark opened by the highest bidder, and the ornamental caskets of the Torah brought out, cleaned, aired, and carried around the synagogue by men dancing around the Teva. It was a night of fun, frolic, and food, which usually ended with a fancy dress competition.

Leon was dressed as the patriarch Moses.

He had worn a long white satin robe, actually Rivka's dressing gown. The red dupatta was also hers. He was wearing a Santa Claus wig and beard to look like Moses from the film *The Ten Commandments*.

For effect, he had also powdered his eyebrows, drawn wrinkle lines with his mother's eyeliner, and used a dash of red lipstick.

Leon stood in the doorway of the synagogue when his name was announced. But before he could step forward he saw his father climb the Teva and introduce Leon to the congregation.

He hated it when his father embarrassed him. After all, he was grown up now, accepted as a Jewish adult ever since his bar mitzvah, and part of the minyan, the ten Jewish men needed to conduct prayers.

Leon stood frozen and waited; he knew what was to follow.

His father Yehuda, with his bespectacled, lean, lined face and trimmed, dagger-shaped mustaches, was wearing a white full-sleeved shirt over his standard synthetic coffee-brown trousers. He was telling the congregation the story of Moses.

Yehuda dramatized everything. He had always wanted to be an actor, but had ended up as a bank officer. Leon suffered him for a full ten minutes, standing in the stance of the prophet, leaning on his grandfather's staff.

Standing frozen in the doorway, Leon felt as though his father was playing "statue" with him. He felt ridiculous waiting for his father to release him from the charm, but he knew from experience that once his father started talking not even the appearance of the prophet Elijah could stop him. After what felt like ages, his father finished his speech, and with a stern glance nodded at Leon, giving him permission to start his act.

Leon heaved a sigh of relief and marched into the synagogue as the prophet, stamping his staff on the ground and saying, "I am Moses." Then suddenly his voice was snuffed out as he felt the hard horsehair mustache slipping into his mouth. He would have liked to spit it out, but knew his father would disapprove of such an act. He had already made a fool of himself by giving a lecture and it would be too demeaning if his son were to spit out the mustache, after all, he was playing Moses. Leon could not do anything as he was playing a role and his hand was not free to put the mustache; back in place, so he let it slide over his lower lip. He could hear giggles.

The beard was sliding down to his chest, lifting the wig higher, so that it rested on his eyebrows and he looked more like a langur than Moses.

So he stood in front of the judges, pulled off the wig and said, "Respected judges, you saw me as an old man, but this is what Moses looked like as a boy." Everybody laughed and the judges gave him the second prize.

Later that night, Leon received a spanking from his father.

Yehuda had noticed that in the absence of a skullcap Leon had tied his mother's red dupatta round his head.

When the tempo increased, Leon had grabbed little Elezier's turban, unrolled it and danced like one gone mad, shaking his hips and waving the cloth around his head. Elezier was dressed like an Indian king and the turban was made with his mother's blue dupatta. When Leon snatched his turban, he was so upset that, like the moth, he started to chase Leon, running behind the dancers and crying.

Leon was so carried away by his act that he did not notice his father, sitting still, hands on knees as though posing for a photograph. His eyes were shining like red-hot flames and if looks could kill, Leon would have died that very minute. But Leon so loved dancing he did not once look at his father.

Leon was the center of attention and the others stood around him clapping. He danced, he pranced, he jumped, and did all the filmy jhatkas he knew so well. And the death's head moth kept following his hand movements. But whenever Leon jumped to grab it, the moth flew higher towards the marble plaques with the Ten Commandments.

Yehuda did not speak to Leon for a full two days, nor was he allowed to touch his bicycle or play football for a week. Meanwhile, his mother was worried that the moth with the skull design on its wings that had hovered over his head had spelled doom for him. She prayed to Eliyahu Hannabi, asking him to protect her son against all harm.

Leon was such a good dancer that even the women stopped to watch him, thinking, "He is so graceful, so handsome."

Leon knew Yael was watching him spellbound.

She was always staring at him as if he were an overripe banana, ready to be swallowed in one gulp. She was older than him by a year or two, and pretty in a delicate sort of way, but her voice always startled him. She had a loud voice, so loud that it shocked people, as they expected a delicate girl like her to have a silky-soft voice. Her mother and aunt often scolded her, because "Girls should be seen, not heard."

If by chance Leon and Yael met in the elevator or passed each other on the staircase, she gave him a longing look, while he removed his sports cap, stylishly bowed, and said, "Hello Yael, how's life?"

She would turn red, lower her eyes and smile, feeling weak at the knees. But at that point Leon was not attracted to girls; all he had was a passion for dancing and dressing up like a woman. As a child, his favorite place in the apartment had been his mother's dressing table. It was like a perfumed garden of lipsticks, rouge, eyeliners, mascara, powders and, of course, foreign perfumes.

Rivka did not take it seriously, assuming these were childish games.

Later, when even as a teenager he continued experimenting with his mother's makeup, she assumed he was interested in fashion, because he also wanted to wear his hair long in a ponytail. But she did panic when she returned home one day and found him wearing one of her printed churidars over her katori-shaped sari blouse which he had stuffed with rags, fully made up like a bharatanatyam dancer and sitting with his feet in a bowl of soapy water doing a pedicure.

Rivka had pushed him into the bathroom and shouted at him for being so silly, what if somebody saw him like that, what would they think, was he a girl or a boy? She had been very upset about Leon's attraction to her things. It was still worse telling her husband anything. At first he listened quietly, his eyes crazed, and then he caned Leon.

Holding the battered child in her arms, Rivka suffered silently.

Rivka was not really surprised to see Leon dancing like his favorite film star at the synagogue. Biting her nails, she watched the others, worrying what they would think of her son, but they seemed not in the least bothered; in fact they were enjoying Leon's show.

Not comfortable with Leon's secret feminine fantasies, Rivka had forced him to join the gym and sent him for football and cricket matches. She had also bought him some very plain manly shirts, but Leon always disconcerted her by painting them, slitting his jeans, and writing all sorts of crazy things on them. And if she ever asked him to choose a shirt, he invariably chose something floral or colorful. She was even more disturbed when he suddenly took to wearing a fancy Lucknowi kurta over Pathani pants. He had saved his pocket money to buy the embroidered kurta, which looked very feminine. His mother had warned him not to wear it in his father's presence. Yet he had worn it for the Yom Kippur prayers, when it was compulsory to wear white for the Day of Atonement. Rivka was surprised that Yehuda had not even noticed the embroidery, being content that his son was dressed in white.

Leon had felt bolder and wore the kurta often, referring to it as his Yom Kippur kurta.

Rivka felt she was suffocating with her secret and had to speak to someone about Leon's love for makeup, saris, and skirts.

To add to her tension, she had seen a late night documentary on television about homosexuals, men with female tendencies who fell in love with each other. Since then she had wondered if Leon had developed some such inclination.

According to her, a child taking to drugs was bad enough, but this was worse.

Unable to find a confidante, Rivka whispered her problems to the prophet Elijah, imploring him to make a man of Leon; she did not want her son to have a female tendency. With a husband like Yehuda she could not possibly handle a problem like this on her own.

But she was surprised that Yehuda was least bothered about Leon's colorful clothes, perhaps because he was certain that beneath the clothes Leon was a real man, like himself. As all the men in their family had been he-men.

"Look," he said, "How he is growing, tall and big."

On the afternoon of the fancy dress competition, Rivka had barely averted a family catastrophe.

Leon had locked himself in his room to dress up, saying he wanted to win the first prize at the fancy dress competition.

After hours, he emerged from his room dressed as his favorite heroine, Madhuri Dixit. Unknown to his parents, he had been practicing a popular song of hers, wearing a bright pink flared skirt with Rivka's katori-shaped blouse and cheap padded brassiere. Under the skirt he had worn black stretch pants to hide his hairy legs. His hair was freshly shampooed, backcombed, fluffed, and tied with a bandanna at the forehead, just like the star. A sequined blue dupatta taken from his mother's cupboard was thrown over his shoulders and he wore bangles up to his elbows.

Rivka could not stifle her scream when he appeared in the doorway, shaking a hip and arranging his breasts.

Yehuda had rushed out of his room fearing the worst, but stood shocked at the sight of Leon dressed as a woman. As he reached for the cane, Rivka pushed Leon back into his room and locked the door from the outside. She had pleaded with Yehuda; he could not possibly cane his first-born on a holy day like Simhat Torah.

Rivka ordered Leon to remove his skirt, pull on a pair of jeans, and run down to the D'Souzas in Block B. Their eldest had a Father Christmas beard and wig in his room.

Yehuda was raving, and she tried to comfort him, saying Leon would make a perfect Moses and would leave home dressed as a biblical figure.

Halfheartedly, Leon removed the skirt, dressed as Moses, and left for the fancy dress competition.

3 Yael

Try as she might, Yael could not stop thinking about Leon. He looked like the film star, Charlton Heston, who played Moses in *The Ten Commandments*. She thought he looked even better when he was dancing with the red dupatta. He had not bothered to remove the white silk gown and it was flying all around him, exposing his strong legs. She watched, fascinated. He was wearing clogs and from the ankle up his legs looked so sexy that her eyes were glued to the lower part of his garment. She would have liked to throw all caution to the winds and dance the samba with him, the type she had seen on television. She was bored as she danced the slow garba with the women, not exactly a garba, but a fusion hora-garba.

Compared to the rest, Leon looked bold and happy.

She hated herself for being so shy and timid.

Yael was older than Leon by two years and till recently they had played together. But, after she started menstruating, her mother Abigail and Aunt Lebana became very strict about the games she played with boys close to her age.

Yael was expected to stay home when she came back from school. She had to fold clothes, help with the cleaning and cooking, finish her homework, and watch television.

In between, before dinner, she stood on the balcony, watching

Leon playing basketball or cricket with the boys. She suffered from flutters and cold sweats. She wanted to tell him how much she loved him.

But as soon as she came face to face with him she felt tongue-tied and silly. He was so smart and she was so simple. Would he ever like her? Perhaps she could try to catch his eye at the fancy dress competition?

Yael had been dreaming about the fancy dress competition for a year. She would dress like a Gujarati girl, wearing a backless choli over a flared red skirt with mirror-work embroidery, a transparent green dupatta, a long artificial braid with a string of pearls in the center parting of her hair, a nose-ring, chandelier earrings, a dozen multicolored glass bangles, a waistband, anklets, bright pink lipstick, and green mascara, with a beauty spot painted on her cheek.

The day they were to register their names for the competition, she returned from school to see her mother and aunt sitting at the dining table as usual with the tea things laid out on a floral tablecloth. Yael would have preferred coffee, but tea had been a ritual for her parents, and had continued even after her father died in a road accident. Her mother poured the tea and offered a cup to Yael, who accepted it politely, nibbling at a cucumber sandwich.

The sandwich tasted bitter to her, as she had her own ideas for the fancy dress competition, but her mother and Aunt Lebana were discussing it as though she did not exist. They were telling each other Yael was too shy and so she must participate in such events. "She needs to mix with other teenagers her age. She must become more outgoing. She is very shy, perhaps she will open up if she takes part in the competition."

Neither sister bothered to take her opinion on the matter. Lebana went to the balcony and called out to Daniyal who was repairing his scooter, inviting him upstairs for a cup of tea and asking him to put down Yael's name in the list of participants.

Daniyal bit into the sandwich and asked, "Will she dress as a biblical character or a Kashmiri girl?" Abigail and Lebana were confused and started thinking aloud, "A biblical character will be perfect for Yael . . . " They were not sure. Daniyal was about to write down Yael's name, but on second thought looked up at the young girl for her approval and noticed that she looked on the verge of tears.

He gave her a kind smile and asked, "Would you like to dress as a matriarch? Should I write Rebecca, Sarah, Naomi, or Ruth?"

Still nibbling at her sandwich, Yael answered softly, "Gujarati girl in garba dress." Daniyal noticed both mother and aunt choke on their tea.

Daniyal would have liked to have had a daughter like Yael. She looked so simple and sweet, how on earth was she going to dress like a Gujarati girl, especially when she had two witches for mothers? But he held his peace.

Yael was lost in thought. Ever since she was five, she had wanted to wear a full garba dress, but knew that her mother and aunt would never allow her to wear one. They felt it was a vulgar dress, which revealed the female anatomy.

Daniyal noticed that Yael did not look up as Abigail asked her rather sternly, "You do not have a chaniya-choli suit, do you?" Yael shook her head as though she had committed a crime, then lowered her eyes and started studying her nails. She had bitten them clean and small. Even if she painted them a natural pearl-pink color, she was sure Leon would not like her hands. What if they were ever to meet on the staircase and he held her hands, he would have one look at her nails and drop her hands like a hot potato.

She knew he was a man of class and always wanted the best.

Feeling the blood rush to her face, she made a resolution that very moment that she would never again bite her fingernails. She would grow them long and paint them a bright purple, for somehow she had a gut feeling that he liked bright colors because he was always wearing red, blue, green, and purple.

Yael had noticed that even if Leon left the house in a plain white tee shirt in the morning, when he returned it would be covered with stickers and paint and have all sorts of funny things written on it. She sighed as she told herself that Leon was an artist at heart and she was not artistic enough to attract him. She had neither color nor wit nor humor, while he always had something funny to say. She had noticed that the only time he was quiet was when his father was around, but as far as his mother was concerned, he had her wrapped around his little finger.

So Yael always made it a point to smile at Aunt Rivka and say, "Hello, Aunty."

Yael was tall, slender, had straight shoulder-length hair and was always dressed in plain jeans worn with plain shirts. And because of her plainness, she was always in awe of Aunt Rivka, because she looked smart in her stylish Punjabi suits, short curly hair, and red lipstick.

Her mother and aunt were very simple. Abigail always wore polyester saris in pastel shades, with her hair tied in a neat chignon and a little kohl in her eyes. Aunt Lebana, a retired nurse, wore outdated Punjabi suits of the sixties, embroidered at the smock and worn with sequined georgette dupattas.

Yael yearned for her mother to dress like Rivka and immediately felt guilty about having such thoughts. She had been taught to respect and love her parents and did not want to go against the law.

As her face turned cherry pink in the afternoon light, her mother touched her asking, "Are you all right, my poor little thing?"

Yael smiled and said, "Nothing, Mama, I was just thinking about the fancy dress competition."

Her aunt held her in her arms and asked, "What would you like to wear?"

"A Gujarati dress," said Yael with a straight face.

She looked so sad that Daniyal felt his heart go out to her, but the women exclaimed, shocked, "No, not a Gujarati girl."

Yael felt suffocated as she watched Uncle Daniyal sitting with his pen suspended over his notebook, not knowing what to write.

She suddenly silenced them with her unusually loud voice, "Yes, I want to wear a Gujarati dress."

"But, sweetheart," Aunt Lebana argued, "You do not have a chaniya-choli suit. Look, it is already 5:30. By the time we finish cooking, it will be too late to go to the Law Garden night bazaar. That is the only place where we can find a reasonably priced mirror-work dress. Besides that, tomorrow morning we have to get up early, so we cannot possibly go now, can we?"

Yael knew she was facing a wall; the two women would never allow her to expose her body, even a bit of the back and tummy. It was forbidden. Abigail and Lebana wore their clothes like bandages, only exposing face, hands, and feet. The body had to be properly covered in the right places. Since Father died they had become even more paranoid about wearing revealing clothes.

33

They had double doors, grills, and double locks everywhere, even on the balcony, and the house was like a cage.

"Why can't we borrow a chaniya-choli suit from a friend?" asked Yael.

"What?"

"Borrow," repeated Yael in a voice loud and clear.

Abigail placed her hands on the table and said, "Dear child, have some sense, borrow from whom?"

"Radha," said Yael.

"Radha who?"

"Radha my school friend."

"Where does she live?"

"Shahibaug."

"Do you know the distance between Satellite and Shahibaug?"

"Yes."

"Then how can we go so far just to fetch a skirt for you, do you know the time?"

"I could phone her, she can bring it to school tomorrow morning."

"Well . . . "

There was so much tension in the room that Daniyal stood on the balcony while he waited for their answer. Not knowing how to handle the situation, Lebana switched on the television and sat with arms folded, watching the film *Return of the Mummy.*

Suddenly she stood up and called out to mother and daughter, "Why not become a mummy? Nobody would have thought of such a brilliant idea. Daniyal brother, please write down Mummy with a capital M. Yael will dress as a Mummy for the fancy dress competition."

He gave them a quizzical look and wrote down Yael's name as a participant and left wondering how on earth they were going to dress a young girl like that as a mummy. He was not sure of the meaning of the word and asked his wife Salome, "Is mummy ever written with a capital M?"

Salome was confused, "Look it up in the dictionary in Ezra brother's house," she said.

Yael's jaw dropped as the sisters planned her dress.

Once upon a time, Yael's father had fractured a leg and they still had rolls of bandage in the house. Also, Lebana was a retired nurse and had great expertise in bandaging people. So that was it.

Yael listened to them, her dreams shattered. She had been looking forward to wearing a tiny backless choli and showing off her midriff to Leon. Now, showing even her little toe seemed impossible.

Suddenly Yael was very angry and threw her bag on the floor with a big thud. Stunned, the women looked up asking, "What is the matter, Yael?"

She bent down, picked up the bag and said, "The bag fell from my hands," then paused and asked Lebana, "Aunty, why can't I dress like Nefertiti? She was also an Egyptian like a mummy, I saw a program about her on Discovery Channel."

Yael imagined herself dressed like Nefertiti in a white shift with a slit at the knee, beads round her neck, a huge conical crown, strap sandals, ruby-red lipstick, and blue eyeliner round her eyes like a bharatanatyam dancer.

Abigail and Lebana turned a deaf ear to her and said they did not know anything about Nefertiti, anyway they rarely watched channels like Discovery or National Geographic. Instead, a mummy sounded perfect. Aunt Lebana sealed the matter; no more discussion was encouraged as she started rummaging for the bandages stocked in her cupboard.

Yael would have liked to say, "If I participate in the fancy dress party, it will be as a Gujarati girl, nothing else." Instead all she could whisper was a meek, "Yes."

"Good girl," they said in unison.

Yael thanked the prophet Elijah that her aunt had not asked her to dress like the scorpion king from the same series of films.

The next day, after school, Yael stood in the middle of the room in her jeans and a long-sleeve tee shirt, her hands spread out like Jesus Christ nailed to the cross as Abigail and Lebana bandaged her.

Rolls of bandages were neatly stacked on the dining table. Systematically, they were covering her and mummifying her. Yael felt they were making her shroud even while she was alive. Abigail and Lebana started with her armpits and shoulders and flattened out her young breasts and continued in the same way with her slim waist, almost saying "Thou shalt not show your breasts or your tiny belly button. It has to be preserved for the eyes of your husband." They wrapped the bandages round her hips like a chastity belt. Her virginity was being protected like a jewel for her future bridegroom. The women were working on Yael's legs: each leg was wrapped in bandage and it looked as though she had fractured her limbs. Task completed, they helped Yael to pull on a pair of socks to cover up the loose ends, then bandaged her arms, "Thou shalt not touch any part of your body or that of any other person until your wedding night."

Yael felt like screaming, but the bandages had snuffed out her voice, "Thou hast no face, no eyes, no lips, no voice."

Considerately, they had tied the bandage a little loose around her eyes, nose, and mouth so that she could breathe.

Yael was thinking, "If they could, they would monitor my breathing and release doses of oxygen in small quantities so that I remain alive till the night of my wedding."

For a moment she wondered, if brides had to be virgins, were the grooms also expected to be virgins on the first night?

Lebana had seen *Return of the Mummy* twice, and remembered the scarabs. She told Yael that the mummy would be incomplete unless she pinned some beetles on Yael's body.

She rushed to the kitchen and quickly retrieved some water chestnut shells she had thrown into the garbage bin, washed them clean and pinned them on the mummy, telling Yael she believed in detail and that from a distance the shells looked exactly like beetles.

Yael felt like throwing up, at least that would have released her from the curse of the mummy, but after the hours of work the two women had put into the creation of the mummy, she did not want to spoil their evening.

Yael did not want to look into the mirror, but Lebana forced her to look and she felt she had become a corpse and resembled her father's shroud. Again, she felt sick and prayed to the prophet Elijah to release her from these earthly woes.

And, as if matters were not bad enough, they even called the man who ran Alankar Photo Shop at the corner of Shalom India to take a picture of Yael for keeps.

Photograph taken, Yael just about made it to the door and wondered how on earth she would get into the elevator dressed in such a bizarre outfit, and if Aunt Lebana had called an ambulance to transport her to the synagogue. Yael was praying to the prophet Elijah to make sure Leon did not take the elevator at that very moment.

The prophet heard her prayers.

Both women helped Yael to the elevator and called a rickshaw to take them to the synagogue. The driver was worried and asked them to find an ambulance for the child, as he did not want to risk carrying an injured person in his vehicle. The women laughed and explained to him that she was just dressed for a fancy dress competition. He agreed to take them, but was sure that both women were mad.

All through the Simhat Torah services, Yael suffered and sweated and felt Saul Ezekiel was reading the mourners' Kaddish.

As soon as her name was announced, Yael went through her act in a daze, arms spread out and walking like a zombie, saying exactly what Aunt Lebana had taught her to say, "I am an Egyptian mummy." Her voice sounded muffled and she was sure Leon was laughing at her.

Actually she had blanked out and felt there were two Yaels in the mummy; one was Nefertiti, the other was the Gujarati girl in a backless choli.

While she recited the mummy piece, Yael was praying inwardly to Eliyahu Hannabi, imploring him to transform her into a Gujarati girl.

Yael had noticed the moth flying ahead, was it the prophet sending her a signal that he was there and would fulfill her wishes?

She was not sure.

In her dreams the night before she had imagined that she was transformed into a Gujarati girl in a garba dress.

Yael could see her other half dancing in front of her, with the mummy just following like a corpse.

She was asking herself, "Why couldn't I have asked Radha to leave the dress with Elisheba the cantor's wife, changed in the women's gallery upstairs, and given them a surprise?"

Yael was seething with anger and tears, hating herself for not having the courage to do what she wanted to do.

Hadasah was the judge for the fancy dress competition, and much to her mother and Aunt Lebana's pleasure, Yael won the first prize.

Nobody saw Yael's reactions as she was still mummified. She was not pleased to have won the first prize.

Hadasah was amused, for she knew the reason Yael was dressed like an Egyptian mummy, as Daniyal had told her the whole story.

That evening, after he had written down Yael's name, Daniyal had returned home confused and asked Salome why the word mummy was written with a capital M.

She asked him to consult a dictionary. So he had gone upstairs to ask Ezra, but not finding him there, had gone up to Hadasah's apartment and told her what had happened.

She told him the meaning of the word, and her heart went out to the mummified little girl.

Not at all pleased that she had won the first prize, Yael sat in the women's gallery on the first floor of the synagogue, removing the bandages. She was thinking that she was removing not bandages but so many skins of her hidden desires. As she rolled the bandages abstractedly, she looked down often at Leon, dancing like one gone crazy, and she felt very alone, sitting upstairs and rolling the bandages.

Had her father been alive, he would have allowed her to wear a Gujarati dress. However much against her mother's wishes, he would have even bought her a chaniya-choli suit.

But, she had some doubts, would he have given her permission to wear a backless choli?

For the simple reason that it was never worn with a brassiere there was a certain element of nudity attached to a backless choli. But if half of Ahmedabad was wearing backless blouses during the Navratri festival, why couldn't one little Yael wear one little backless choli? It was a futile question.

Yael had often discussed with Radha the thousand and one ways of wearing a backless blouse. Radha was an expert on the subject.

Just before Navratri Radha's mother sent her to garba classes. They went to club garbas on the posh Gandhinagar–Sarkhej highway and Radha always won a prize as the best dancer in her age group.

She had about twenty different chaniya-choli suits for the Navratri garbas. Each had a different color, design, and cut, and a matching dupatta. And she had pounds of junk jewelry, bought from the walled city.

Radha was Yael's best friend and even offered her a dress as a gift, but Yael refused, as she was sure that both Mother and Aunt Lebana would never approve of such a generous gesture. They would be suspicious of her intentions. Yael's eyes had grown wide with wonder when Radha had told her in a matter-of-fact tone that the latest craze was hanky tops. The blouse was shaped like a large table napkin and just about covered the breasts. The shoulders had to be exposed and if possible painted with tattoo marks.

In preparation for the possibility that her mother and aunt would allow her to wear a chaniya-choli suit, Yael had asked cautiously, not wanting to look stupid, "How can I wear a backless blouse and still not expose my back?"

"Simple," said Radha reassuringly, "All you have to do is ask a tailor to stitch a small four-inch band at the back, so you eat your cake and have it too! The second method is to cut off the straps and bands of an old brassiere and stitch the cups into the blouse. It looks good, in fact, the breasts look bigger."

Imagining herself in the big-cupped backless blouse, Yael sat enthusiastically rolling up the innumerable bandages she had removed from her body. She would have liked to throw them in the dustbin but Aunt Lebana, always afraid of some imaginary calamity, had wanted them back, "Just in case," she had said.

Yael hated the bandages, they reminded her at first of her father in hospital, bandaged from shoulder to toe, then of his shroud, in which he, also, looked bandaged, and where, worst of all, his eyes were closed. At least in the hospital he would wink at her, and she would hope he would not die. But then she had seen her mother crying and telling Aunt Lebana that he was going to die.

In those days, Aunt Lebana lived in a rented house next to the synagogue. After Father's death she had come to help Mother. But soon she had moved in with them to protect her sister from the evil world, as Mother was still a young woman. In a way, Aunt Lebana had taken upon herself the role of Father.

She handled all finances, paid the bills, and also made all major decisions of the house, for example, to wear or not to wear a backless blouse.

Yael closed her eyes and the tears flowed. She did not want to see another bandage ever again. All she wanted was a flared skirt and a backless blouse; she would then dance with Leon, matching jhatka for jhatka. When her sobs subsided and her tears dried, she opened her eyes, and to her amazement saw the dress of her dreams lying on the bench next to hers. She was sure she had not seen it or had not noticed it when she had entered the women's gallery. Except for a Hanuman's tail and a pair of cheap anklets, she had thought there was nothing in the room upstairs.

Gingerly she picked up the green backless blouse. The skirt was folded and pinned like a dhoti, but when she removed the pins the pleats fell around her. It was a pink ghaghra, full, flared, and embroidered with peacocks, parrots, and lotus flowers. A shimmering peacock-blue sequined dupatta was also part of the ensemble. Perhaps the prophet had heard her prayers.

Holding the dress close to her breasts, Yael went into the furthest corner of the gallery and put on the ghaghra, carefully slipping out of her jeans. She unhooked her brassiere and, slipping out of both the tee shirt and the bra, she put on the blouse. As she tied the strings at the back, she could tell it was the correct fit, although she was embarrassed about the beak-like shape of her breasts and quickly covered them with the dupatta. She pushed the tee shirt and jeans into the bag for her bandages and on impulse put on the anklets lying abandoned on the bench. Now all she needed was a bindi and a mirror. These not being available, she looked at her reflection in the broken glass screen in the women's gallery. Except for the fact that the socks did not match the dress, and that she did not have bangles, bindi, mascara, and lipstick, she looked good. She was glad that she was not wearing her sneakers, which were with her mother downstairs.

With determination and new-found courage she removed her socks, pushed them into the bag, picked up the hem of her skirt, and daintily climbed down the stairs, back to the hall downstairs. Aunt Sipporah was making announcements and suddenly Yael was afraid to face the congregation. She took a deep breath and stood behind the screen, reading the brass plaque which said it was made in 1913 for the old Itzraeli prayer hall in Mirzapur.

She had never noticed it before. It was of wired glass and was fixed in an old wooden frame, like her grandfather's writing table which was handed down to her. She then remembered one particular photograph of her grandfather dressed in a turban, angrakha, and flared pajamas, sitting next to her grandmother who was dressed in a nine-yard sari and wearing a nose-ring, anklets, and bracelets. If they had worn such clothes, she could at least wear something as simple as a chaniya-choli suit.

So she jauntily swirled in the doorway and joined the women's group dancing the fusion hora-garba.

Nobody noticed the difference; in fact, everybody thought it the most natural thing on earth that Yael was dressed in a chaniya-choli suit. In fact, one of the girls even asked her if she had bought it especially for the festival. She nodded her head and said nothing. Yael kept her eyes studiedly averted from Aunt Lebana.

Mother being a widow and Aunt Lebana an old virgin, these two did not join in the garba. They were watching the dancers from the fourth row and talking to Salome, who was perhaps asking why this particular mummy was written with a capital M.

Once in a while, Aunt Lebana looked upwards and wondered why Yael was taking so long to come downstairs.

Yael refused to look at her, but knew exactly when her aunt noticed her, as she started nudging her mother, telling her to look at Yael. They were shocked and could hardly believe their eyes, because they were sure Yael had been wearing jeans and a tee shirt.

They also knew that she did not have a chaniya-choli suit. Both sisters looked at each other, wondering how she had found one. Then they whispered something to each other, Yael was sure what it was: "Keep quiet, smile, don't show anything, what will people say if they realize that we did not know that Yael had a dress like this."

They did not know how to react. Her mother noticed that Yael looked beautiful: she had a fair waist and a tiny belly button. They did not like scenes in public so they kept quiet and looked around to see if anybody else had noticed the change of dress. Nobody had. Anyway, Yael had received the first prize so they had reason to be happy.

When the last prayer had been recited, the Torah caskets were put away and the ark closed, it was time to leave. Yael was terrified of facing both Mother and Aunt Lebana. The next best thing was to rush up to the women's gallery and pull on the jeans and tee shirt. But there was no time, they were moving towards the door, kissing the mezuzah, and going home. Mother and Aunt Lebana looked at her and signaled that she should follow them. They still had to find a rickshaw to go home. At one point, when the three were together on the steps leading to the backdoor of the synagogue, Lebana hissed, "Did you get this dress from Radha?"

"No," she said in a loud clear voice, "I found it upstairs."

"Speak softly. I refuse to believe your story. Till we reach home, behave normally and please wear your shoes," she said, giving her a plastic bag with her footwear.

Aunt Lebana was so annoyed that she did not say a word after this, but just grabbed the bandage bag from her and kept marching towards the rickshaw stand as Yael stopped for a second to slip on her shoes.

It was then that Yael felt watched. It was Leon following her.

Her heart was beating, she could feel his hot breath on her neck and he was saying, "Yael, can I have a word with you?"

Yael took a step backwards, her back curved, the dupatta had shifted and her fair waist and the bird-beak breasts were pointed at him sexily. She was hoping he would say, "You are the most beautiful girl on earth." Instead he said, "You damn well be careful with that dress, it's mine. Will come and get it, don't know how."

She was so shocked she almost fell off the steps. All she could say was a meek, "Yes," and wonder, "Now, how could a skirt like that belong to Leon?" Then on second thought she faced him, hands resting on hips and told him, "I think there is a mistake, Mister, the prophet Elijah gave it to me."

Leon looked at her in disbelief, "What the hell are you talking about? It's mine."

Yael did not answer. She half ran, following her mother, swinging her hips rather provocatively and giving him a look which said, "It can't be yours, it's mine. Anyway, what the hell were you doing with a dress like that? If it is yours, then perhaps you have a girlfriend." Suddenly she was worried about her future.

Life without Leon appeared bleak.

Abigail, Aunt Lebana, Rivka, the local matchmaker, and the gossipmongers of the community had noticed this little interlude. "What are these young people up to?" they asked each other.

Anyway they made a good pair. A pair to watch, they smiled.

They were relieved. It is always good to marry within the community. So what if Yael was older by a year or two; it did not make a difference. At least it kept the community together.

Leon's mother started worrying whether he was interested in the mousy Yael. Perhaps she was a bad influence on her little boy who was two years younger than her. How dare she even think of him?

In the rickshaw, Mother wanted to know, "Why did you stop to speak to Leon?"

"It was nothing," said Yael, maintaining a dignified silence.

It was nobody's business.

For years the residents of Shalom India Housing Society believed that Leon and Yael were in love and the mystery of the chaniya-choli suit remained unsolved forever.

4 Salome

Salome realized that Abigail and Lebana were not listening to her. She was hurt, more so because they did not reply when she asked them why this Mummy character Yael was playing was written with a capital M.

As usual, she started telling them how she had lost a child when she was seventeen. The memory of the only pregnancy of her life made her eyes moist. Salome was embarrassed; perhaps she had told them this story so many times that they knew it word for word and would have liked to tell her, "No, not again, not the same old story." But they were polite and had always listened attentively. But today something was wrong; they were nodding their heads but looking elsewhere. She wiped her eyes with the end of her sari and followed their eyes. They were watching Yael, faces tight with tension, brows furrowed, and their eyes narrowed to pinpoints of fire.

Salome could not understand what was the matter. Dressed in a bright chaniya-choli suit Yael was dancing the hora-garba with the rest of the women. Salome did not understand what was bothering the two women, so she sighed, "How would I know what it means to be a mother?"

But then, Lebana had also never conceived, so why was she glaring at Yael like an angry schoolteacher?

Salome remembered that from the time Abigail had conceived, her sister Lebana had always been there to help her. A nurse by profession, she always knew more than Abigail.

And Yael's father, may his soul rest in peace, was hardly ever around, always busy as he was working in an engineering firm. It was convenient for Abigail to have Lebana for company. Yael had practically grown up in Lebana's lap, so she was almost like a second mother to Yael.

Salome had been surprised that Yael had arrived for the fancy dress competition all tied up in bandages, as if in a shroud.

Now why did they have to dress a young girl in bandages?

They could have easily dressed her up as a Kashmiri girl.

In an embroidered phiran, colorful headscarf, mojdis, and silver jewelry, she would have looked like a daughter of the valley with her milk and roses complexion. It would have been so much easier to hire a readymade Kashmiri dress instead of tying all those messy bandages.

She wondered why they had pinned empty water chestnut shells over the bandages. Salome was convinced that some educated women complicated their lives with crazy ideas, especially as Hadasah said it was an original idea and even gave Yael the first prize.

Salome told herself that she might not be educated like Abigail and Lebana but she did know that at Yael's age girls wanted to look beautiful. She smiled, admiring the beautiful young girl. But why were her mother and aunt upset? Salome sighed and blamed her barrenness for her lack of understanding.

Now, if she had a daughter, how would she dress her for the fancy dress competition?

Salome was dreaming, seeing in her mind's eye the daughter who was not to be, a young girl like Yael, dressed as a Kashmiri girl.

She covered her head with her pallav and felt a sob rising in her chest as she wiped a tear before it rolled down her cheek.

Salome slipped back in time.

During her pregnancy, the doctors had asked her to lose weight as she was short and fat. It had been a difficult delivery. The doctors were afraid that she would not survive, but she did. When she regained consciousness, she held the baby in her arms, looking at the crumpled face and thinking she was the most beautiful child on earth. Salome had even asked her mother to apply a dot of kohl on her cheek to ward off the evil eye. Suddenly, as she was counting the baby's fingers, it gave a hiccup and lay limp in her arms. The doctors tried to revive her, but she passed away and was never returned to her mother's arms. Salome still remembered the softness of the child in the crook of her arms as her breasts ached to feed her. Arranging the pleats of the sari, Salome touched her breasts. Even after all these years, she always felt her breasts were hard, like stones. The shock had frozen the milk into milk-white infertile rocks of crystal.

Salome's eyes were glued to the child dressed as baby Krishna. She was sure her baby would have looked exactly like that. How she ached to have a child of her own. Now it was too late. If the baby had lived, by now she would have had grandchildren as old as the baby Krishna.

That night Daniyal was the highest bidder for the right to pluck the fruit from the succoth hut made with bamboo matting covered with palm fronds for the Feast of the Tabernacles.

It had been stiff competition between him and the eighteen-year-old Yacov, strong, young, and well built. Yacov was learning from him how to play the shofar, so did not really want to compete with his guru. But Daniyal had jumped higher than him to pluck the holy citron before falling on the floor. He must have looked ridiculous slumped there as Yacov helped him up to his feet, "Now what secret wish do you have at your age, Uncle Daniyal?"

Embarrassed, Salome had looked away. She hated it when Daniyal made a fool of himself. It was the third evening after Yom Kippur. He had kept awake all night in the succoth hut. He was tired, yet after a quick nap had got up to do some pull-ups. He had said he wanted to win because he had a secret wish.

The men had built the hut the day after Yom Kippur, erecting a tent on poles in the open space behind the synagogue. It was a square room with an open doorway, decorated with fruit hung from the ceiling. There were pineapples, oranges, apples, bananas, and citrus like the holy etrog. The highest bidder was supposed to pluck the citrus and ask the Lord to fulfill a wish.

In her younger days, Salome was rarely seen at the synagogue. This was because she and Daniyal lived far away in Bapunagar and the only vehicle Daniyal had was an old bicycle. Autorickshaws were expensive and the bus took two hours to reach the synagogue.

If she did feel like going to the synagogue for a wedding or a prayer to Eliyahu Hannabi, she would ask Daniyal to take her with him, saying she would sit on the carrier. And he would invariably poke fun at her, saying, "If you sit on the carrier of my bicycle with your big fat bottom, it will break."

Words like these always hurt her.

But she had accepted Daniyal the way he was. She was habituated to both his taunts and his occasional acts of affection, like buying her a string of flowers. She would find the flowers on the kitchen counter, and as she tied them around her chignon she would ask the prophet Elijah to shower her with happiness.

When Daniyal was in an unusually good mood, he would tell her, "If we had money, we could have adopted a child, nako?"

But he knew that adopting a child would be difficult. Considerations of age were a major hindrance. If something happened to one of them, what would happen to the child? Also their finances were always low, as they lived on charity, and would be unable to provide a proper future for the child.

Often, when Daniyal and Salome considered adoption, the discussion veered to caste and community and they knew that they could not possibly find a Jewish orphan. Daniyal was uncomfortable with the idea of adopting a non-Jewish child.

Although, he argued with himself, religion was given to children by their parents. Then he would start thinking about profound matters like purity of blood in the Jewish race and wondered why Indian Jews looked like Indians, Russian Jews looked like Russians, and Chinese Jews looked like Chinese people.

But race, caste, and religion were matters of dispute between the couple and he did not have the courage to adopt a child from an orphanage and call it his own. So he spent a lifetime wanting to adopt a child, any child at that, but never had the courage to adopt one.

Daniyal knew Salome was lonely and had strong maternal instincts, which she would shower on him as if he were her baby. But she hesitated to show affection to other people's children, in case they thought she would cast the barren woman's evil eye upon them.

Daniyal felt guilty that he was not man enough to give her a child, for she would have made an excellent mother.

The night he won the bidding he slept badly. Salome woke up at the sound of his sobs, asking if he had asked the prophet for a child.

Daniyal turned to her, hid his face in her breast and cried, "It is too late isn't it?"

"No," she smiled, holding his head closer and murmuring in his ears, "Didn't the matriarch Sarah conceive when she was ninety, and I am just around sixty, so I still have a chance, don't I, even if I have reached my menopause? Because miracles do happen."

Daniyal felt comforted as he suckled her enormous breasts, his hand slipped under her petticoat and caressed the softness of her hips, "You are beautiful," he murmured. She lay in his arms, panting with desire, her hands probing around his loose pajama strings, arousing his sex, and whispered in his ear, "But I am fat." They were both crying as he entered her, whispering, "You are my mother."

5 Sippora

Sippora was different.

From the day she had come to Ahmedabad from Bombay and married Opher, everybody knew that his life would never be the same again.

Sippora was always at the helm of all cultural activities at the synagogue. At the fancy dress competition, as she stood on the first step below the holy Teva, she knew that she was the cynosure of all eyes.

She liked to be different and shock people. Abiding by the rule that Jews should be covered properly from head to toe, she had worn a slinky black figure-hugging dress. She had thrown a shimmering scarf over her head, which trailed behind her like a veil. The dress had a slit and exposed a beautiful leg above her stiletto. So in principle she was fully dressed and the slit was where it should be, at the correct length had she been wearing a skirt. She made many women at the synagogue envious as she was comfortable in heels and could carry off anything from gunny cloth to chiffons. Faces turned green with envy when she entered a room and she was a favorite topic of conversation, but one had to accept that she was popular in the community and that everybody liked her. She was affectionate and was comfortable in Marathi, Hindi, Gujarati, and English. So she put everybody at ease from simple Salome to fancy Ruby.

Sippora had set up a beauty parlor in Shalom India Housing Society, so everybody relied on her for threading, waxing, manicures, pedicures, hairstyling, henna, mehendi, bridal makeup, and the occasional facial. Sippora had warm hands, strong slim fingers beautifully manicured, and soft palms, so when she gave a facial, women fell into a trance, half asleep, half awake, and their tongues loosened as they became pulp in her hands.

They told her everything about domestic problems, husbands, lovers, children, maids, health matters, the in-growth of a nail, hormonal changes, dry skin, a difficult menstrual cycle, and a stubborn hair on the nose which often appeared unannounced.

Like a psychiatrist, Sippora had her work ethic and never gossiped about one to the other. No wonder Opher worshipped the ground she walked upon, yet they fought so much that they brought down the entire housing society with their shouting and screaming. Nobody interfered, as in a few hours they would again be seen walking hand in hand on the lawns of Shalom India.

It was a mystery what they fought about and why.

As a rule, whenever Sippora was busy, she had the habit of leaving her bag with Salome. The two women were as different as an apple from an onion, but were deeply attached to each other.

For Sippora, Salome was her pillar of strength. She relied on her for everything, from leaving her daughters at her apartment to buying bread or asking her to cook a meal when she had too many clients.

Salome was always there for Sippora. The main reason being that Salome never asked her why she and Opher fought so much.

And if Sippora came down with a headache or was very tired, she slept in the lap of Salome, who gave her a good massage till she was able to relax. Sippora knew that her secrets were safe with Salome.

They had bonded like sisters ever since Sippora had come to Ahmedabad.

Everybody loved Sippora, as she was always organizing community dinners, picnics, competitions, games, and their favorite activity, the fancy dress competition.

For this particular competition, Sippora's eldest was wearing a Bengal sari and her two younger daughters were dressed as fairies. They looked cute, fully made up, wearing wings on their sequined white dresses and holding wands with stars. There was no chance that they would win prizes, but it was important that they were happy, playing hide and seek with Hanuman and Krishna.

Sippora made the announcements with style and made everybody laugh. The only person who disapproved of her act was her husband, Opher. He was uncomfortable with her showing her leg.

Even after eight years of marriage, there were times when he could not accept her flamboyance, and they often fought because Opher wanted her to wear a sari at public functions, especially at the synagogue.

Later that night, Salome woke up with a start, sure that she had heard Sippora scream. She sat up in bed and reached for a glass of water from the side table as the clock struck the hour. It was three. "Now what?" she asked herself. It was too late to go up to Sippora's apartment to see what was happening; anyway she was not sure whether Opher would appreciate her interfering.

The next morning, Daniyal left early as there was some errand to complete at the new graveyard on the Ahmedabad–Baroda expressway. Salome was sitting at the dining table with her second cup of tea, reading the Gujarati newspaper, when she heard a short ring at her door. It was Sippora.

She opened the door and saw her standing at the door looking ragged in a blue dressing gown with enormous red flowers. Her hair was a mess, and overnight she had acquired dark circles under her eyes. Salome invited her in, offered her their only horsehair armchair and went to the kitchen to make her a cup of coffee.

Salome was telling her that she had overslept, as Daniyal had left early. He had left the door open and the cat had almost toppled the saucepan of milk.

Sippora was not listening, and cut her off mid-sentence, saying, "Aunty, I think I am pregnant."

"Mazal tov, that is what they say in Hebrew, isn't it?" Salome looked pleased.

"No, Aunty, I don't want another child."

Salome's jaw dropped, "Why? It is a gift from the Lord."

"No, Aunty, it is going to be very hard. What about my parlor and Opher is always away, so who do you think will look after the girls?"

"I will look after your girls." The words slipped out of Salome's mouth as Sippora watched her surprised, "No, no, Aunty, I don't want any more children," she said. "You have to come with me to the gynecologist."

"Why?"

"For an abortion."

"But that is a sin."

"Nothing is a sin, living like this is a sin."

"Like what?"

"My oldest is eleven, my middle one eight, the youngest is six. I cannot possibly go around with a big stomach like that," she said, mimicking a pregnant woman.

"You have done it thrice before; you can do it once more."

Sippora was not listening, "Tell me, Aunty, will you come with me?"

"I will come with you," Salome said, feeling both angry and concerned for Sippora.

"Then be dressed and ready at four in the afternoon, I don't want to go through this all alone."

Salome nodded, but she was indignant that Sippora was making her a partner in sin.

Salome chose to wear a black sari that afternoon and Sippora started laughing, "Aunty, you look very arty, but why are you wearing black?"

"I am in mourning," answered Salome seriously.

"Why, who is dead?"

"Nobody, but your decision about having an abortion is such that I feel I am in mourning."

"Oh come on Aunty, don't be so sentimental."

"When someone like me does not even have one child, what else can I do?"

Sippora was sad, and did not know what to say, so all she did was hug Salome as they walked towards her car hand in hand.

Sitting in the waiting room, they did not know what to say to each other and Salome was praying to the prophet to knock some sense into Sippora's head.

The clinic was spacious and airy with women in different stages of pregnancy sitting in the waiting room, the walls of which had pictures of babies. A baby Krishna caught Salome's eye. She gazed at his chubby cheeks and the peacock feather stuck in the crown on his head.

Had she had a baby boy, she would have dressed him like Krishna for the fancy dress competition.

She was wondering what Sippora's baby looked like, as all her daughters were beautiful.

Would it be a boy or a girl?

When her name was called out, Sippora felt a chill run down her spine. Salome gave her a big warm hug, wiped her eyes, and started to flip through the film magazines, her lips moving in a silent prayer to Eliyahu Hannabi to show Sippora the right path.

An hour later, when Sippora emerged from the examination room, Salome was relieved to see her smiling. Sippora kissed her and whispered, "Aunty, I am going to have the baby."

Driving home in the car, Sippora had an incredible story to tell Salome. When she was lying on the examination table, back flat, legs strapped and spread out, with the lady doctor's gloved fingers probing her, she was looking backwards, her eyes glued to the poster of baby Krishna on the wall. She felt giddy, the room swirled around her and she felt she was sliding backwards, falling into space and being swept away by a turbulent river. To steady herself, she held onto the table and kept her eyes on the poster and felt she was half awake, half asleep, watching a scene from *The Ten Commandments*.

She felt she was standing in knee-deep water, hidden behind the papyrus bushes, and watching the baby Moses floating down the river Nile in a basket. Suddenly, she saw an Egyptian princess pick up the baby and hold it close to her breast.

When the princess looked up, she saw that it was Salome, looking radiant and beautiful in the royal robes.

Suddenly, the world stopped spinning and Sippora had a sudden revelation that she wanted the baby. Perhaps the vision she had just seen was divine intervention, it seemed to tell her something.

So, when her gynecologist, Priti Parikh, was through with the examination, she asked Sippora, "Are you sure you want to go through with the termination of the pregnancy?"

Sippora clasped her hands and replied, "No, Doctor, it was a mistake, I want the baby. Because it belongs to someone else."

As Sippora paid her fees and prepared to leave, from under lowered eyes the doctor was looking at her in disbelief, wondering if she was losing her mind. But she looked fine and the doctor let it pass as a misinterpretation.

Outside, Salome was imagining the worst, and she closed her eyes and prayed to the prophet Elijah. She could not bear the thought of the child in Sippora's womb being reduced to a pool of blood in the kidney tray.

But when Sippora emerged from the examining room earlier than expected, Salome was relieved to see the smile on her face, and understood that Sippora was keeping the baby.

The prophet had heard her prayers.

Salome was thinking, perhaps the prophet had made a mistake and the child had gone to Sippora's womb instead of her own.

After all, she would always be there for Sippora through the pregnancy and delivery. And after the baby's birth she would look after it as her own.

Salome wondered if it was a girl or a boy.

Sippora already had three girls and Salome was sure the prophet would bless her with a boy, because Sippora had seen a vision of the child Moses at the clinic. She made a mental note to speak to Ruby and ask her the meaning of Sippora's vision. Ruby spent a large part of her time interpreting dreams, her own and those of others. Salome knew that she was very particular about time, as she had fixed hours for meditation and music. One could never ring her doorbell and walk into her apartment, because she only met people by prior appointment.

When the two women returned to Salome's apartment, Sippora sat in the ancient sofa chair as Salome fussed around her with coffee and biscuits. When Sippora left, Salome locked the door, had a bath, changed her sari, and powdered her face. Then she wiped the frame of the prophet's picture with a clean cloth, lit a candle, and placed it on a tripod, and covering her head with her pallav, folded her hands, bent her head, and thanked him for giving her the gift of a child. So what if the womb was not hers?

6 Ruby

Ruby had not gone to the fancy dress competition at the synagogue. It was her wedding anniversary and Gershom her husband had died a few months back in a road accident.

Alone in her apartment she studied the two photographs on the mantelpiece.

In both she was dressed as a bride. The one on the left was her wedding photograph and the other had been taken when she was seven and had dressed as a bride for the fancy dress competition at the synagogue in Bombay and won the first prize.

Her gaze returned to her wedding photograph. She was wearing a white wedding gown with lace trimmings, silver stilettos, held a bouquet of satin roses in gloved hands, and her gossamer veil was carried by bridesmaids dressed exactly like her but in different colors.

And Gershom, who had just returned from London, was dressed in a grey three-piece suit, all trim and proper.

Their wedding photograph had appeared in the *Illustrated Weekly of India*, and a faded clipping from the magazine was inserted in the right-hand side of the photograph.

Gershom had died on the day of their silver wedding.

She remembered every detail of that fateful morning.

She was half asleep, half awake when she heard the alarm.

She went to the front door, collected the milk, and, as she was about to close the door, noticed that the Hebrew letters of the *Shema Yisroel* in the casement of the mezuzah seemed to be turning in circles like a lighthouse.

Ruby panicked, her grandmother had always told her that when the Shema started turning in circles it spelled doom.

Ruby closed the door and looked at the time. It was too early to phone Saul Ezekiel and ask him the meaning of the rotating *Shema*.

She made a mental note that though it was going to be a hectic day, at some time she would call Saul Ezekiel and confirm her doubts. If necessary, even ask him to change the parchment of the tube inside the mezuzah. She knew that would be difficult as it was not easy to find original parchments with Hebrew letters. She would have to write to her daughter to send one from Canada.

Ruby was also disturbed because she had had a dream that she was floating on a raft of diamonds.

Leaving the milk in the kitchen, she returned to bed and carefully laid her palm on Gershom's chest so as not to disturb his sleep, still wondering what the dream meant.

He turned towards her in his sleep and held her in his arms.

She was sure that as usual he would have forgotten the date of their wedding anniversary.

When the alarm in his cell phone rang, Gershom jumped out of bed and went to the bathroom. He hated being late for the office and prided himself on having never been late in his entire life.

His schoolteacher mother Sybil had seen to it that he never wasted a minute. Even if he went somewhere, he was supposed to go early and wait outside till the doors opened. And while waiting he was supposed to work on his favorite quiz book, so that he was always doing something useful.

Gershom had a flourishing legal practice and a plush office on the tenth floor of Gayatri Towers on the upmarket C.G. Road.

Ruby lay in bed, feeling upset that for Gershom each day was no different from the other. The only liberty he allowed himself was of getting up late on Sunday mornings. He would then sit at the table reading the newspapers, waiting for his tea. Even if she wanted to laze in bed, she had to rush around and prepare his tea. Sometimes she felt like telling him to make his own tea, but never dared to.

Her mother had taught her that a woman was the queen of her kitchen. Her shining black counter was spotless and all kitchenware was kept in the assigned place, not a thing here or there. Though she often felt like telling Gershom to make his own tea, she knew it was useless telling him anything, as he could not even boil an egg. There had always been someone to serve him. First it was his mother Sybil and now wife Ruby.

Both women had looked after all his needs. And when Mama had lived with them before she departed to the other world, she had made sure that their lives revolved around Gershom.

From the bathroom, Gershom went towards the door as Ruby stretched lazily to catch his eye. She was wearing a black satin dressing gown. She knew that normally he never noticed what she wore, so it was of no use to be provocative, it would only leave her frustrated. But this morning was different as it was their anniversary. Hoping that he would kiss her, she drawled, "Gershom . . . "

He turned around distractedly, looking at her but not really looking at her.

She smiled, "Darling, do you know the date?"

"Twelfth," he said, rather irritable. All he wanted was a cup of tea and the newspaper.

"Remember," she whispered, raising a hand over her head and exposing her breasts.

"What?"

"Do you know what happened today?"

"I don't," he answered brusquely.

"Okay, so as usual you have forgotten, it is our wedding anniversary." She sat up adjusting the gown over her breasts. His eyes were glued to her breasts. "When did you buy that?"

"Yesterday, for our silver wedding. Like it?"

"It is sort of nice. I hope you will wear something over it when you go to the kitchen, you know these servants, they should not see you like this."

"I know," she answered, and again repeated in measured tones as though telling him the tap was not working, "It is our wedding anniversary. I have given the cook and the maid leave."

He smiled, hand on handle and halfway out of the room. Ruby felt like telling him that he should smile more often, he looked so good that her heart missed a beat. He closed the door, returned, took her in his arms and kissed her, smelling of toothpaste and after-shave lotion, mumbling, "Happy anniversary."

She held him in her arms, dragged him back to bed and kissed him passionately. He responded, then releasing himself, whispered in her ear, ". . . must go."

As he stood up, she wanted to scream at him. Instead she said rather feebly, "It is our silver wedding, let's make love, come," and opened her arms to him.

He stood shocked.

"Silver?" he asked, "You mean we have spent so many years together?"

"Yes," she smiled, amused, and followed him out of the bedroom.

All her plans to seduce him failed. They spent a normal sort of morning. He sat with his newspaper; she gave him his tea with a plate of toast and packed his lunch box.

Ruby dressed and sat at the dining table, staring blankly at the newspaper and wondering how to celebrate their wedding anniversary. She could have invited friends for dinner or organized a malida at the synagogue. Her gaze was glued to the picture of the prophet over the mantelpiece and she asked Eliyahu Hannabi to inspire Gershom to give her a gift of diamond earrings.

She had always been a great admirer of the queen of England and for her silver wedding had asked Sippora to give her a similar haircut. She hoped some day she could wear diamond earrings and get herself photographed looking exactly like the queen in a mauve dress. Friends often said that she resembled Queen Elizabeth. So she dressed like her.

She came from an anglicized family and often wore dresses and trousers, much to her mother-in-law Sybil's horror. Ruby had continued wearing dresses even after marriage and although Sybil was fond of her, she never got used to her dress sense. Even though once in a while Ruby wore a sari to please Sybil.

But for her wedding Ruby had refused to wear a sari. All her life she had imagined herself in a gown, similar to the one worn by Queen Elizabeth on her wedding day. Grudgingly, Sybil had agreed; after all it had been so hard to find a bride for Gershom. After Gwen-Li, Ruby was the first girl in whom he had shown some interest.

That morning, realizing that he was being insensitive to his wife's feelings, Gershom stopped at the door and asked, "What are we doing today?"

She smiled, "We could order a pizza and have a candlelight dinner, because I don't feel like inviting friends, too much work. Instead, why not buy me the diamond earrings, the ones we saw at the jewelers' near your office? Didn't you say they would suit me?"

He agreed, gave her his habitual peck on the cheek and said they would buy the earrings and have lunch together.

Ruby threw him a flying kiss, closed the door and told herself that this was unlike him, but she was happy.

She removed her clothes and studied herself in the mirror. She still had a good body, though the breasts were beginning to sag and there was a little curve around her stomach after the birth of her second child. Fortunately the half-light did not expose all those little areas of flab and wrinkles. She massaged her face with cream, trying to wipe out the little lines which had started appearing around her eyes. Lovingly, she massaged her breasts and gave them an upward lift. She was uncomfortable when her nipples tightened. Her hands then moved downwards towards her stomach and she massaged it in circular movements. Her hands then stopped above her pubic region. Did it matter, she asked herself.

Gershom had not really seen her in the nude since the children were born, a son and a daughter. And from day one, whenever they had sex Ruby always felt it was too hurried and she was not satisfied. Perhaps tonight they would celebrate by making up for lost time, she told herself.

Ruby chose a black pantsuit, laid it on the bed, and had a leisurely shower. She washed her hair, wore her dressing gown, dried her hair, painted her nails, and dressed slowly. Then she sat at her dressing table studying her face and applying foundation, eyeliner, and a bright red lipstick. She then touched a little perfume behind her ears and between her breasts, hoping it would excite Gershom— that is, if he noticed it.

She was sure later that night her daughter would call from Canada and her son from Delhi. Gershom would then open a bottle of champagne saved for this occasion. They would have a candlelight dinner with Mozart for background music.

No, she would not order pizza, it would not go well with the mood. Gershom liked Chinese food, it really turned him on. Perhaps he should have married Gwen-Li. Sybil had often joked about the fact that in their Naranpura house, where Gershom had grown up, they had had Chinese neighbors with a daughter named Gwen-Li. Her father was a dentist, a Buddhist, and her mother, a devout Catholic, had a beauty parlor in the same building.

Gershom never spoke about Gwen-Li, but Sybil had told Ruby that she made him laugh. Whenever Gwen-Li spoke in Gujarati, Gershom thought it was funny, just because she had a typical Chinese face with almond eyes. So when he was expecting her to speak in Chinese, she would end up saying something very colloquial in Gujarati.

Ruby sighed; perhaps he had been in love with Gwen-Li, but had not told her because good Bene Israel boys are brought up to marry girls from their own community so that the tribe increases.

Ruby could not deny that he was the perfect Bene Israel husband, even if passion and romance were not a feature of their daily life. As she put on her sandals, she decided not to think of gloomy matters. Before leaving, she saw her reflection in the mirror once more and thought she needed something to cheer herself up, so on impulse pulled out a bright turquoise scarf and threw it around her shoulders. She checked if she had everything in her handbag, locked the apartment, and took an autorickshaw to meet her husband at his office.

He had a surprise for her; as she opened the glass doors, she found an air of festivity in the office. Her heart missed a beat when she saw a heart-shaped cake on his table, which said, "Happy Anniversary Gershom Sir and Madam." The staff had collected around the table, laughing, talking, shaking hands, and the office manager raised a toast to many more years of marital bliss.

Ruby smiled and Gershom stood next to her, hands folded behind his back and formal. Sometimes she wished he were not so reserved. But this was exactly the quality she had liked the first time she had seen him. She wanted a husband who was a leader, always in charge of the situation, well dressed, well mannered, and who could waltz with ease. She also wanted him to understand western music and she was very pleased when he bought a video player on their tenth wedding anniversary. They spent many an evening watching operas and concerts. He ordered the video especially from Singapore. Sometimes he also taped concerts of western classical music from television programs. They would sit still, tapping the tune on their knees, sometimes nodding in appreciation. And when not watching the video, she would play the piano while he sat listening, eyes closed. These were moments when they were in total harmony with each other and made the perfect picture of a happily married couple.

They cut the cake and fed each other as the staff clapped. There were also ordered two huge pizzas with soft drinks. There was an atmosphere of well-being as they left to buy the diamonds.

He offered his arm to her and she slipped her hand in happily. He was unusually chirpy, remembering their wedding day.

At the jewelers' he sat on a chair and waited for her to choose the earrings. He was surprised that she did not take long and knew exactly what she wanted: a pair of star-shaped earrings.

For a moment, Ruby sat holding the diamonds in her palm. Her mother had often advised her that one must wear a diamond for a trial period to see if it is lucky or unlucky. She wondered if she could ask the shopkeeper to let her keep it on trial for two days, but hesitated. Had she been alone, she would have asked, but one look at Gershom's face and she knew that he would have dismissed her fears, saying diamonds were just stones. He paid by credit card and she thanked him with eyes brimming with love. She would have liked to kiss him, but knew that he did not like public displays of affection. She squeezed his hand and said, "Thanks darling, I will just find an auto and go back home to make preparations for the evening."

She still had to buy him a gift.

He smiled, "I will drop you home and go back to the office . . . will be back early."

He left her at the gate of Shalom India Housing Society and drove away. Ruby clutched her bag with the diamonds and rang for the elevator, entered her apartment, locked it, again saw the revolving mezuzah, and called Saul Ezekiel at the synagogue. He said it was a serious matter and that he would have to look into it right away. She refused, saying she was in a hurry and would meet him in the late afternoon.

Ruby opened her bag and sat at the dressing table to put on the diamonds. As she finished screwing the prized diamond earring into her left ear, Gershom was dead.

After he dropped her back home, Gershom did not take his usual route to C.G. Road. From Satellite, to avoid the traffic, he turned towards Vejalpur Ring Road, where he saw a crowd of people. He did not look properly, or he would have noticed that it was not a crowd, but a mob. He had not bothered to look, because after December 2002 there had been hardly any riots. So he drove on and as he neared the two warring groups, he knew he had made a mistake when he saw the swords and saffron bandannas. They were chasing a group of Muslims; perhaps there had been a stabbing in the area. When he had driven Ruby home, there had been nothing. But Ahmedabad was like that, violence erupted suddenly. So he turned left towards Gupta Nagar, hoping he could drive straight to Paldi and turn towards C.G. Road. He still had important meetings before he could wind up for the day. With a sinking heart, he cursed the riots. He decided to call Ruby right away and tell her not to leave the apartment. He did not want to spoil her pleasure by telling her what he had seen. He would tell her later in the evening. As he turned towards Gupta Nagar, the scene was worse. He saw houses burning. He realized he should have turned around and gone back home. At least Ruby would have been happy to spend the afternoon with him. Sweating profusely he drove towards Gupta Nagar, as it was impossible to turn back. Suddenly, he felt something hit the car and saw from the rear window that it was on fire. Quickly, he called his office and told the manager, Kantibhai, where he was and that he needed help. By the time Kantibhai had managed to get police help, call an ambulance, and reach Gupta Nagar, Gershom's car was burning and he had rolled some distance away. When they reached the hospital, it was already too late. Gershom had died of cardiac arrest.

When Kantibhai called Ruby, her hand was still at her earlobe and she knew it was the evil influence of the diamond.

Quickly Ruby unscrewed the earrings and put them away in her jewelry box. She never wore them again. The meaning of the dream was clear to her. The rotating *Shema* and the diamonds were responsible for Gershom's death and the terrible loneliness she would have to suffer for the rest of her life. As she had seen in her dream, she would float endlessly on the raft of life, alone and unhappy. Since then, she had started divining dreams and, more or less, she was always right.

That was how she first met Franco Fernandes.

Franco lived in Block B of Shalom India in the apartment exactly opposite hers. He often saw her sitting on her balcony reading, or heard her playing the piano.

Then there was the shadow he saw on one of her curtains.

It was the shadow of a nude woman who had forgotten to switch off the lights inside the room so that no one could see her silhouette on the thick curtains. She might have aged, yet she had a well-proportioned body and a nice drop of hair, which reminded him of Suzanne.

Since Gershom had died, Ruby had made a habit of drawing all the curtains and walking about nude in the apartment. Sometimes she even played the piano without a stitch on her body.

This woman, her shadow play and her music, obsessed Franco.

He lived alone. A bachelor. It was not that there had been no women in his life.

To start with there was Suzanne who had lived next door to him. They went everywhere together and were in great demand at dance parties.

Suzanne and Franco had seen all the Elvis Presley films and had practiced the rock-and-roll dances so well that everywhere they went people asked for more. Suzanne wore umbrella skirts, high-heeled shoes, and tight tops. She had a mop of hair like Ruby's, which she purposely swung around as she danced.

As often happens in the movies, Suzanne and Franco were in love and engaged to be married. He still remembered their passionate embraces. But somehow he could never remember what had gone wrong.

After four years, she had suddenly broken off the engagement a month before the wedding.

That afternoon, Suzanne had asked him to meet her at the Havmor restaurant on Relief Road, where they usually met for samosas and espresso. It was a cramped little place with ten tables, each wall a different color, like the ice creams they served there.

Suzanne was wearing dark glasses, and instead of the usual samosas and coffee she asked for tea.

Suddenly feeling dry in the throat, Franco asked for a glass of water. Suzanne's face was swollen and she kept removing her glasses to wipe her eyes.

He held her hands in his and waited for her to speak.

She watched him, then removed the engagement ring from her finger and returned it to him, sobbing, "I cannot marry you Franco, forgive me," she said.

He was angry, "Is this a joke? We are getting married next month. We love each other. How can you do this to me? . . . Suzy, please, wear your ring. I am sure you are just jittery, like most brides . . . "

Suzanne shook her head and kept staring into her teacup.

Suddenly, he was suspicious. With eyes bloodshot, lips clamped, Franco asked, "Is there somebody else . . . ?"

"Yes," she whispered.

He banged his fist on the table as she wept, eyes lowered; then, embarrassed that everybody was watching them, she ran out of the café with Franco chasing her.

He caught her near the Bata Shoe Shop next to Advance Cinema where they had watched many an Elvis film together. Franco grabbed her arm and demanded, "Who is it?"

"Franco, let go, please."

Franco watched her, feeling lost and cheated.

Then, silently, they walked towards Bhadra Fort and Teen Darwaza. When Suzanne saw that he had cooled down, she spoke to him in a small voice, "Franco, you have to listen and face facts. I could have disappeared from your life and you would have never known what had hit you. Perhaps my parents would have told you the details. This morning I married Vinod Bhardwaj. You know him, my guide for the doctorate."

"That old . . . "

"He is not that old. I meant to tell you, but could not, because it meant telling both families. I just came to tell you, because I felt it was my duty. I left home this morning forever and I am not returning."

Franco could barely speak, "How, why . . . ?"

"Please, do not misunderstand me Franco. I really enjoyed dancing with you, but I cannot spend a lifetime dancing and baking cakes. I want to do other things, like a doctorate in clinical psychology, become a professor and . . . "

Franco was trembling, " . . . are you telling me that you are leaving me just because I am not educated like your Bhardwaj sir?"

"I never said that," she said. Raising herself on her heels, Suzanne kissed him, stopped a rickshaw, and disappeared from his life.

Franco had stood under the arches of Teen Darwaza, feeling stupid in his white dancing shoes, skintight jeans, standard black tee shirt, and lock of hair falling over his forehead, just like Elvis. After that he had gone from one woman to another, till the family gave up on him. He became a music teacher in a missionary school and lived there as a housemaster. When he retired he bought himself the apartment in Shalom India Housing Society.

It was hard in the beginning. He could not get through the day, so he asked his old school to allow him to work as a volunteer. They had known him to be a good teacher and gave him one of their classrooms to start a music school. He played the violin, but also taught the guitar and drums to his young students, mostly boys, who also learned singing from him.

Franco felt better, making a living out of what he knew best.

Early mornings, Franco went jogging with his dog, Caesar, an Alsatian. With the leash tied to his wrist, they went round the block and returned to the apartment. He gave the dog a good brushing and started elaborate preparations for a big breakfast. At lunchtime, Shanker, who kept house for him, came in to clean the apartment and make chapatis for Caesar and Franco. He also made a subzi for Franco, served him the frugal lunch and took Caesar down for a romp. Then it was time for Franco to leave for his music class, while Caesar slept on his quilt on the balcony.

Franco returned exhausted and happy, to eat dinner in front of the television, mostly leftovers from lunch or some junk food he bought on his way home.

Next it was time to take Caesar for a walk. He would return to lounge on the balcony, lights switched off, and all his senses focused on the shadow which fell on the curtain of A-104.

Later, when the lights were switched off in the apartment across the way, it was again time to leave on his scooter. Nobody knew where he went, but a general rumor was that he went looking for women of loose morals. They left him alone, except Daniyal who liked talking to him and often dropped in to listen to music. Sometimes Franco played him a tune from *Fiddler on the Roof* on his violin.

Lately Franco had been having nightmares. He saw himself running in an alley.

When the dream recurred for the tenth night, he was so exhausted that he cancelled his classes, did not leave the apartment, and stayed in bed. He needed to speak to somebody, so he phoned Daniyal and asked him to spend some time with him. Salome felt sorry for him and sent some food over with Daniyal.

He confided in Daniyal, who suggested he meet Ruby, the lady who lived in A-104, and who divined dreams.

For a second, Franco closed his eyes and refused. He felt awkward about the fact that he had made it a habit of watching her shadow when she was perhaps nude or maybe wearing a body stocking, he was not sure. He did not know that Ruby also enjoyed watching him. When he went jogging with Caesar in the early morning, Ruby stood on her balcony, watching the ebony-black muscular man dressed in a tracksuit, with a lock of white hair falling over his forehead just like Elvis Presley.

Man and dog made a fine pair, Caesar and Franco. Both had sinuous muscles and strong legs. They had a certain sensuous energy that she found attractive. It was good to wake up in the morning and see the man running his dog. She had also noticed that he was a musician and had seen him playing the violin standing on his balcony.

Daniyal spoke to Ruby about Franco's nightmares and arranged a meeting, informing her that Franco was a music teacher. She was excited at the prospect of meeting him, but without expression agreed to meet him with the message that she was an amateur interpreter of dreams and sometimes her interpretations were incorrect.

On the day of the appointment, Franco spent the whole day ironing his clothes and polishing his shoes. He was looking forward to meeting Ruby and was trembling with anticipation. Ruby had invited him at five, her fixed tea-time when she met people who came to see her about their dreams.

Franco rang the bell and when the door opened, he saw the beautiful Ruby dressed in a white pantsuit. He could not help but notice her feet, as she was wearing sandals. Her toes were fleshy and the toenails, painted a bright red, were pressed together and had a certain sensuous quality.

They shook hands, and Franco bowed and kissed her hand, "Madam, I am honored to meet you," he said.

She led him into the apartment and gestured for him to sit on the sofa.

She sat on a high-backed chair.

Behind her he saw the piano.

The tea things were laid out on the table between them and she bent to make him a cup of tea, "Sugar?" she asked.

"Three," he said, and she smiled, "That may be the reason you have bad dreams." Closer, he looked better, like an older and blacker version of Elvis Presley, her teenage hero.

As they sipped tea, she asked him about his dream.

He sat back in his chair feeling relaxed and told her about his dreams.

She listened with eyes closed and sat still for five minutes, inhaling the fragrance of his aftershave lotion, as he looked around the apartment.

It was neat, clean, and orderly. The piano stood off-center, and the walls were covered with family photographs. Franco remembered her husband and that they had made a handsome pair.

Ruby opened her eyes, "It appears to be something about your dog."

He sat up in his chair, " . . . Caesar?"

"I am not an expert."

"But, in my dreams, I see somebody chasing me."

"You say you see yourself running in an alley. Do you see the dog running with you? Normally you run together, don't you?"

"Every day I give him a run, but I do not see him in this particular dream. What can I do?"

"Take good care of him."

Awkwardly he asked, "Your fees, madam?"

"Nothing."

The idea of losing Caesar frightened Franco. And he wanted to change the subject, so he looked at the piano and asked, "Do you play the piano?"

"Sometimes."

"Why sometimes?" he asked, "Did you lose the desire to play the piano after your husband died?"

"Almost. It was different when he was alive."

"But, I suppose, one plays music for oneself."

"I do play sometimes, but not regularly."

"Can I play the piano? I would like to play a tune to thank you."

"Do you play the piano?"

"Yes, I am a music teacher. I play the piano, the violin, drums, and the trumpet."

Ruby was impressed, and gestured towards the piano and said, "Yes, do play if you want to."

She watched his straight back as he walked towards the piano, thinking, "He walks like a dancer."

He sat at the piano and played the Elvis number, "Love Me Tender."

Ruby started to enjoy herself, then suddenly felt nervous and sat up worried. What if one of the neighbors saw them together? They would immediately suspect her of having a love affair with Franco.

So, as soon as he finished a number and looked at her with a smile, she stood up with a wry smile and he understood it was time to leave.

As he bowed and thanked Ruby, his eyes met Gershom's in the photograph.

A table lamp was placed behind his laminated photograph, glowing like a candle in his heart. And as the door closed, he felt there had been a look of warning in Gershom's eyes.

Franco left feeling a little sad. He would have liked to spend more time with her, but it seemed impossible. He knew he had overstayed his welcome and she had been uncomfortable. She did not want him to stay longer, just in case somebody misunderstood; after all she was a widow and had to be careful. After this initial meeting, they often met in the parking lot, at the gate, or at the bakery and exchanged greetings. Ruby was relieved that Caesar was still with him and almost regretted saying what she had said about his dog, which fortunately was in good health.

That year, it so happened that Hanukah and Christmas fell on the same day. So the society's entertainment committee decided to celebrate both festivals together with a Hanukah tree and a Christmas tree.

Shalom India Housing Society was decorated with bunting, strings of colored lights, streamers, torans of mango leaves, and flowers. A huge paper star was common to both trees. A stage had been erected between Blocks A and B, and microphones, halogen lights, and chairs had been rented for the big day. Both blocks had shared the expenses. It was voted unanimously that fat D'Souza would play Father Christmas as he had the perfect beard for the role and he looked grand in the dress.

Franco was at the forefront of organizing the party. He had been holding practice sessions with the children, who were putting up two plays, about Hanukah and Christmas, with Israeli folk dances and carols.

Salome was in charge of the food and was asked to make cakes, samosas, chips, mini-pizzas, biscuits, and a big vegetable pulao for all. She set up a mini-bar in her home with aerated drinks, bottles of rum, whisky, and gin. Such occasions helped Salome to earn extra cash, which she kept in the bank for a rainy day.

Ruby stood on her balcony watching the preparations in the gardens of Shalom India Housing Society. Had Gershom been alive, she would have taught Hebrew songs to the children.

Franco was dressed in his trademark black tee shirt and she ached for him. She had seen the same look in his eyes. She decided to keep away from him; perhaps she would go down for dinner, sit around with the women for a while and return to her apartment as soon as possible.

Times had changed; it was no longer necessary for Ruby to wear widows' weeds. But she did not want to give the impression that she was a merry widow. She had worn a deep blue silk sari with a string of pearls and a dash of pale pink lipstick.

Dressed and ready, she was not sure whether she really wanted to go down and join the crowd. She almost decided to stay back, change into a nightgown and play a tune on the piano, but that would be too jarring with the music downstairs. She decided to wear her earplugs and snuggle into bed with a hot teenage romance. In fact she blamed these books for casting a spell on her, otherwise why should Franco start resembling the tall, dark, and handsome heroes from the romances she read before she fell asleep? With a sigh, she sat on her piano stool; it often helped her make decisions. She sat there pirouetting on the stool and watching Gershom's photograph with the light shining in his heart, when the doorbell rang.

Yael was at the door, looking pretty in a rather old-fashioned red kurta. Ruby was sure that the young girl would have liked to wear a short skirt with a spaghetti-strap top, but she knew Abigail would never allow her to wear a dress which revealed her flesh.

Yael brought her a message from Ezra, asking if she would please come downstairs. They needed her help with the music. Ruby agreed; it was almost as if she had been waiting for a formal invitation. Yael sat on the piano stool and Ruby went to her bedroom to get her party purse. On impulse she called out to Yael, asking her if she would like to wear some perfume. Yael shook her head, confused, and said, "Mummy . . . "

Ruby smiled knowingly, "Try," she said and sprayed a little perfume on her. "Good, isn't it?"

Yael closed her eyes and breathed deeply of the fragrance and Ruby was reminded of her own daughter, so far away in Canada. She missed her and on impulse kissed Yael, who smiled and felt honored to have been kissed by such a stylish lady.

Ruby made a mental note to give a bottle of perfume to Yael as a Hanukah gift. She would have to leave it on the Hanukah tree in a cloth bag with Yael's name pinned to it. Ruby slipped the bottle into her black-sequined party purse, locked the door, and hand in hand with Yael, went downstairs looking for Ezra.

Yael told Ruby that she was supposed to play the piano as part of the celebration. Ruby said it was impossible to get the piano downstairs, but Yael smiled knowingly and said, "You don't have to, a piano is already there."

The piano was there on the stage, in the right-hand corner. Ezra was standing leaning against it. When he saw her, they shook hands wishing each other a happy Hanukah, and he asked if she would please be kind enough to play the piano for them. He was looking at her, certain that she would refuse; instead she surprised him by lifting the piano cover, touching its keys tenderly and asking, "Now how did you get this?"

"Franco brought a truckload of musical instruments from his school. By the way, Ruby sister, do you mind if Franco plays the violin? With you on the piano, it will be quite a concert."

Ruby's face stiffened and Ezra was afraid that she was offended, while she was thinking, "How romantic! I always wanted to play the piano for an audience."

At last Eliyahu Hannabi had heard her prayers. She only hoped he would not mess up like last time, when he had granted the diamonds and taken away Gershom.

Ruby shrugged her shoulders, sat regally on the piano stool and asked grandly, "Okay, so where is your violinist, we have to be in tune before the show starts." She sounded casual, but was very happy.

It was romantic, sitting under the canopy of stars.

Had Gershom been alive, he would have disapproved of her playing the piano in public with a total stranger.

"Music," he had said, "is for personal pleasure."

Gershom never knew that all her life she had wanted to play for an audience. Perhaps one thing would lead to another. As she sat playing a tune to warm up, she was already dreaming of playing at the Town Hall. She had just to close her eyes to hear the thundering applause of the audience.

When she opened her eyes, Franco was standing in front of her, wishing her a happy Hanukah. She wished him a merry Christmas and asked him about the various tunes they were to play together.

Ruby was surprised that Franco was a good musician and they were in perfect harmony as they played together.

The music cast a spell on them that would end as soon as the party was over. As a finale to the party, they played a waltz together and there was applause, the likes of which she had heard only in her dreams. And then everybody wanted to shake hands with her and congratulate her, calling her "a great musician."

With a heady feeling, Ruby shook hands with everybody, while the children clamored for her autograph.

Yael offered Ruby a plate of food and she sat with a group of musically inclined youngsters, who suggested that she start piano classes. They would join her class and even find her more students, or she could start a music class with Uncle Franco at the tiny community hall of Shalom India Housing Society.

Ezra approved of the idea and offered to organize everything if Ruby agreed. Ruby noticed that Franco was watching her intently, hands resting on the piano. She liked his shoulder blades, so she smiled, but did not accept the offer, saying she needed time to think about it.

Then after checking that Yael was at the door deep in conversation with Leon, Ruby hung her gift on the Hanukah tree and almost ran up the steps to her apartment.

She did not want to break the spell.

Franco's eyes were following her, but she was past caring.

"Yes," she told herself, "I am in love with Franco. But what can I do? Nothing. Just go to bed and dream about him."

She entered her apartment and saw Gershom staring at her accusingly from his photograph.

Annoyed, Ruby switched off the table lamp and changed into a sexy lacy see-through nightgown she had never worn before, switched on the night-light and opened her cupboard singing her favorite Marilyn Monroe number, "Diamonds Are a Girl's Best Friend," as she opened her box of diamonds, held them against her ears and saw them shining in the mirror. She smiled and put them back in the box, then went to bed, read all the hot parts from the new romance she had bought the day before, and imagined she was in Franco's arms. She could feel her body throbbing with desire and did not know when she fell asleep. At three that morning, Ruby woke up with a start. She felt Franco was calling her. She opened the balcony door facing Franco's apartment and saw that his lights were switched on and his silhouette was etched in the doorway.

It was like a scene from a film as they stood watching each other in the flickering neon light. She saw him raise his hand and move towards her as he threw her a flying kiss. For a moment she stood transfixed, then stretched out her hand, touched it to her lips and allowed her kiss to fly towards him.

Once the kiss had flown out of her hand, she was ashamed and rushed back into her bedroom and closed the door.

The door remained closed for a month.

Ruby was thinking if they ever made a commitment, perhaps Franco would convert to Judaism as they did nowadays and then they could perhaps get married. But to take such a big step, she would have to take someone into her confidence, perhaps Ezra?

That was a difficult month for Franco, as Caesar died of a sudden stomach infection. Daniyal informed Ruby, just in passing, that Franco was inconsolable. That was when Ruby almost made up her mind to marry Franco, but did not have the courage to make the first move to meet him. This was also because soon after Hanukah her daughter Sofy had arrived from Canada for a fortnight. So Ruby decided to leave the matter for later. Sofy's presence in the apartment comforted her. She had brought a new parchment for the mezuzah. Mother and daughter spent hours talking, shopping, going to the cinema, eating out at restaurants, and meeting old friends. They even had a small ceremony to change the parchment in the casement of the mezuzah. That was when Ezra sent her the Hanukah photographs and Sofy noticed a man playing the violin with her mother and asked, "Mama, who is this man?"

"Nobody," she said, "Just a neighbor."

She knew convincing the children about their mother's marriage to a goy was not going to be easy, so she left it for later.

A day before Sofy's departure, she insisted that they have dinner at Waterfall. Whenever they were together in Ahmedabad they would have dinner there. That evening, when they were dressing, Ruby had shown Sofy the diamonds and told her that they were unlucky as her father had died soon after buying them. Sofy had laughed and convinced Ruby that a person could not possibly die because of a pair of earrings and insisted that she wear them for dinner.

Like her father, Sofy did not like her mother to be superstitious. Ruby wore a wine-red salwar-kameez suit and brushed back her hair so that the diamonds glowed like stars. When they reached Waterfall, they passed through the glass doors, entered the foyer, and walked into the restaurant to the sound of music. Three musicians dressed like Mexicans were playing boleros to entertain the guests.

Ruby would not have glanced at the men, had it not been for a familiar fragrance which hit her when she passed. She looked up and her eyes met Franco's.

He was grinning sheepishly.

She went white in the face and could not eat anything.

Sofy was worried and asked if she was sick. Ruby choked, "No, nothing," she said, "It's the earrings . . . "

7 Rachel

Rachel was in tears.

Not yet fifteen, she wanted to take part in the fancy dress competition, but both her parents refused to have unnecessary expenditures on such trivial events.

They did not mind if she participated, but it had to be free of cost.

Her mother opened all the cupboards in the apartment and said, "Look, why don't you wear a sari and dress like Indira Gandhi? There is this white Calcutta sari with a red border; you can wear it with one of my old blouses. I can alter it to your size."

Rachel just shook her head and said, "No, Mummy, I don't like saris."

"Why," said Sheba, "you will look perfect with specs and a handbag. You can even wear my new sandals."

Rachel took one look at the familiar saris, sighed and closed the cupboard as her mother shouted, "You are just being stubborn."

Rachel burst into tears, "No, Mummy, I am not being stubborn. I want to wear something different."

"Like what?"

"I don't know," she said and her eyes met those of the prophet Elijah in the poster in the dining room and begged him to make her mother understand her.

Rachel sat down at the dining table to finish her geography home-work but could not concentrate. Her mind wandered and she started doodling in the margins. She scribbled, "What do I want to wear?"

As an answer to her question, she started drawing a young girl in tight jeans and a tee shirt. Suddenly she smiled and called out to her mother, "Mummy, I want to dress like an Israeli girl."

Her mother asked from the kitchen, "How? You don't even have a pair of jeans."

Rachel's heart sank as her mother suggested, "Why don't you alter Daddy's old jeans on the sewing machine?"

She brushed aside the suggestion, saying, "He won't like it."

That afternoon, in the elevator, she met Aunt Sippora who want-ed to know if Rachel was taking part in the fancy dress competition. "You would look beautiful as a gypsy girl," Sippora suggested kind-ly, studying her full figure and long black hair.

Rachel shrugged her shoulders. "No, that's old-fashioned, Aunty. I want to dress as an Israeli girl."

"Israeli girl? But that would be ordinary."

"Why ordinary?" asked Rachel defiantly, "They are different from us. They are cool."

"Really now, how is that? We are all Jews."

"Look at all those books on Israel we have at the synagogue. Do Israelis look like us?"

Sippora tried to recollect, "Okay tell me, how are they different?"

"Well, they wear these short shorts and small-small tee shirts, or figure-hugging jeans with strappy sandals, dark glasses, and a cap. Look at us, with our salwar-kameez suits, saris, and all these dupat-tas and yards of saris. They bore me."

"It is not so bad, because we also wear shorts and jeans."

"Look closely, Aunty, there is something different in the attitude."

"Well, to me, any girl in jeans, in India or Israel or New York looks the same."

"No, no, Aunty, there is a difference."

"Dress as you like, I will announce you are dressed as an Israeli girl and it's up to the judges to decide whether you look like an Israeli or an Indian."

"Thank you, Aunty." Rachel was smiling.

But Sippora was not convinced. "Are you planning to dress in shorts or something? I don't mind; I used to wear shorts before my marriage or when I played tennis. The problem is, do you think your parents will allow you to wear shorts? Do you have a pair?"

"No, but I can always borrow my friend Prity's jeans. I could also ask for her shorts, and about Papa and Mama all I have to do is just convince them." Despite her words, Rachel looked worried.

Sippora patted her reassuringly, "Ask your parents. I am afraid it's not going to be that easy, and then if they do agree, come to me and I will find you a pair. But even if they agree, and if you do wear shorts, you would have to wax your legs. I am sure you don't want to go on stage with hairy legs. Will Sheba allow you to wax your legs?"

"No," Rachel said, looking sad, but then she brightened up, "But I could convince Mama to allow me to wax my legs. I am fifteen going on sixteen and all my friends in school wax their legs and underarms. I feel ashamed, so I never wear skirts, always these long salwar-kameez suits. I wish I could come to you and polish myself up. Actually, Aunty, I really want to go to Israel."

Sippora smiled reassuringly and watched Rachel and marveled at her confidence. She thought that it would be impossible to convince her parents.

As they parted, Sippora knew she would not see Rachel till the evening of the fancy dress competition.

Rachel was desperate. She asked Prity if she could borrow a pair of jeans. Prity laughed, "Look at your hips and look at mine. I am like a stick insect and look at you, four times bigger than me."

When Prity saw the sad look on Rachel's face, she held her hands and said, "Oh Rachel, don't look so sad. Now let me think . . . last year my cousin was here from the States and left behind her old pair of jeans. I suppose they would fit you. She was your size. But they are old. You can take them, if you don't mind?"

Rachel felt elated, "Can I come to your place and pick them up today? Tomorrow is the competition, and I still have to think about what to wear with them."

"Yes, come, only it may take time to find them."

Prity found the jeans and with them a black tee shirt. The clothes fitted Rachel when she tried them on in Prity's home. Rachel studied her reflection in the mirror happily; she liked what she saw. She had never worn jeans before.

Rachel showed the jeans to her mother and saw the disapproval in her eyes. "They are rather too tight around the buttocks," said Sheba. Rachel convinced her that her backside would be covered with the tee shirt.

By the end of the evening, Rachel had convinced her mother that it was a decent outfit, besides having come free of cost. Rachel was sure that Sheba would tell Hyams what a conscientious daughter they had.

That night, as her parents sat watching their favorite show on television, Rachel closed her bedroom door, put on the jeans and struck poses in front of the mirror to see what she looked like and came to the conclusion that she did not look like an Israeli girl.

Then she sat on her bed, thinking, "How does one look like an Israeli?"

Rachel changed into her pajamas, went to the drawing room, and carried the family albums back to her room and studied the photographs of her Israeli cousins.

Then with her mother's permission Rachel went to Ilana's apartment and borrowed some fluorescent watercolors.

Late that night, she sat painting on the tee shirt the words "Somebody is waiting for me in Israel."

Even then she was not satisfied, so she took a pair of scissors and cut the bottom half of the tee shirt off, wore it and saw that she was closer to her image of an Israeli girl.

Rachel slept badly, thinking about Israel and wondering how different her life would be if she migrated. She wanted to leave for Israel as soon as possible. Every year youth groups went to Israel but she knew her father would never agree to send her unless she was married and for that she was still too young.

When she tried on the tee shirt again the next day, she felt she was already in Israel, working on a kibbutz, plucking oranges, and dancing to her favorite Hebrew song, Hava Nagila, on a full moon night in the desert air.

When Sippora announced Rachel's entry on the day of the fancy dress competition, she was relieved to see her swing into the room dressed in tight-fitting jeans, obviously borrowed from one of her classmates. Rachel's hair was tied in a ponytail and pushed under a cap. She was wearing strap sandals and a short black tee shirt with fluorescent letters scrawled across her busty bosom, "Somebody is waiting for me in Israel." For effect, Rachael had asked Ilana to play a cassette of Hebrew folk songs when she made her entry dancing. She received hearty applause from the audience, much to the embarrassment of her parents. But they could not complain, as she had obeyed all their rules about covering her body, not wearing anything that showed her flesh and not spending a naya paisa on the outfit. She had followed the law, yet her movements were provocative and sexy.

When Sheba had seen Rachel in the short tee shirt fifteen minutes before they left for the fancy dress competition, it was too late. She looked at her daughter, wondering how Hyams would react, and told her to cover herself with a dupatta or her father would surely refuse to take them to the synagogue. Quickly Rachel grabbed a dupatta and when she went down to the parking lot, he was waiting for them on his scooter with the side-car. The engine was already humming and he did not even notice what she was wearing.

Actually, it had been easy for Rachel to convince her parents, because all the photographs from Israel showed her cousins in jeans and often in short dresses.

For more reasons than one, the fancy dress competition became a turning point in Rachel's life. Gone were the old salwar-kameez suits she had been forced to wear; she only wore jeans and tee shirts, and almost lived in the black tee.

Hyams had even given her permission to buy two pairs of jeans, though he had insisted that they should not be skintight. She had agreed, but had bought body-hugging stretch jeans. Fortunately, her father had not noticed. Sometimes Rachel thought he hardly ever noticed her.

Both mother and daughter were like the furniture; they assured a good square meal, a comfortable home, clean clothes, and a warm bed. The only time he appeared to look at his wife was when he asked her for the list of vegetables, which as a rule he bought on his way back from the railway station. He had a set timetable. He took his first cup of tea while reading the newspaper, watched the news while having his breakfast, then went for his bath as Sheba prepared his lunch box, packing it in the insulated carrier. He emerged from the bathroom with a towel tied round his waist, went into the bedroom, dressed, and left for the office.

On his return he gave Sheba the bag of vegetables, had a cup of tea, changed, read the newspaper, and often had dinner in front of the television, as Sheba and Hyams did not like to miss their favorite shows.

Rachel was tired of their lifestyle and often escaped to Ilana's home. Her father Noah ran an English school where they all studied. Illana had a computer at home and that attracted Rachel, who often spent the whole evening playing computer games till Sheba came looking for her, either to tell her to finish her homework or asking her to help in the kitchen.

Rachel was a good cook and it was decided that she would go to a catering college in Bombay. Rachel liked the idea, but was not willing to spend the whole day in the kitchen. In contrast, in Ilana's home even if the television was off, somebody would be watching a DVD on the computer or listening to the radio, or one of the boys would be playing basketball in the drawing room. The only discordant note in this home was Yacov, Ilana's eldest brother.

He annoyed Rachel as he chose to lock himself in one of the bedrooms to practice the shofar. This year he wanted to play the shofar with Daniyal and so he was always practicing whenever he was at home. It is hard to blow air into a ram's horn. And although he locked the door, the whole apartment, in fact the whole society resounded with the sound of the shofar, because he was still at the first long note of the Tekhiya.

Everybody found the shofar noisy, but nobody complained since after all it was for a religious cause. Uncle Daniyal was getting old and playing the shofar tired him out. So there had to be a line of youngsters learning to blow the shofar.

Ilana and Rachel often browsed the net and giggled when they found all those love-dot-com websites. One night, Rachel stayed longer than usual and her mother came up to see what was happening. When Ilana opened the door, Sheba saw that the lights were dim, loud music was playing on the cassette player, the girls were on the computer, and nobody else was at home. Sheba marched Rachel back home and wanted to know what they were doing on the computer.

Rachel convinced her that they were searching for some information for a class project.

Rachel changed, brushed her teeth, and asked her mother if she could please join computer classes. It was always good to learn computers as they were important for any profession, even catering.

Sheba switched off the lights and said they would have to think about it. Rachel lay in bed, praying to Eliyahu Hannabi to convince her father that she wanted to explore the world of computers.

The next day, at breakfast, her mother told her that Hyams had agreed to have her learn computers but she would have to take the cheapest course. The next day she registered for classes, but to her disappointment, the instructor told her that they could do everything but access the Internet. Rachel was disheartened.

Not one to be defeated, after the computer class Rachel would go to a cyber café. She was addicted to browsing. In a month, she had explored all the sites she had wanted to see. Then one evening she wanted to do something different and started looking for Jewish sites and suddenly came upon a dating site.

Once she understood what had to be done, she typed in her e-mail address and sent it off, praying to the prophet that he open new horizons for her.

There was no answer for a month, then there was an unknown name in her inbox. It said, "Moshe, Israel, answer to your mail."

Her heart racing, Rachel read:

Shalom, I am Moshe Levi from Kiryat Gam. I am sixteen years old and am interested in knowing you. I am in the last year of school and like to swim and play tennis. I plan to study medicine. I am fascinated with India and imagine you are a beautiful Indian girl. I would like to make friends with you. Tell me about yourself.

Immediately Rachel answered:

Hi, you already know my name, yet I will repeat I am Rachel. I am fifteen and am studying in class nine. I am not into sports, but I plan to become a chef or go into the hotel industry. I like cooking. And I dream of settling down in Israel, after all it is the Promised Land, no?

Every evening there was an e-mail waiting for her and every night she made it a point to answer Moshe's mail. Even if she had to rush to get back home on time, she wrote a line or two to him. And if she could not make it to the cyber café but had to go to the synagogue or attend some other social obligation, she fretted, worried, and felt angry.

Communicating with Moshe had become a passion. She longed for his letters and felt close to him. When she could not write to him or open his mail, she came down with a fever and a headache. And if at that point she heard Yacov practicing the shofar on the fifth floor, she felt like killing him. Her head throbbed; she stuffed cotton in her ears, pressed the pillow to her ears, and slept.

Lately, he was getting on her nerves by giving her long sheepish looks whenever she went to meet Ilana. He was older than her by four years, and was in college. Once, when they had met downstairs in the foyer of Shalom India, he had been bold enough to ask if she would like to be his partner for the badminton doubles they were playing on the lawns.

She refused—didn't he know that she was in love with Moshe? —but then how was he to know? After all, it was cyber love, a secret between her and Moshe. Anyway, she did not have a divided skirt and could not wax her legs till she had her mother's permission, which meant she could not play badminton. Then she started thinking wistfully about Moshe, wondering whether she would ever meet him. Rachel decided that she had to meet Aunt Sippora as soon as possible and find a solution for waxing her legs and shaping her eyebrows. It was the done thing.

In six months, Moshe and Rachel had exchanged so many e-mails that they had become the best of friends. Moshe had even asked her to get her photo scanned and send it to him. He wanted to see what she looked like. He had said, "I feel so close to you, I want to see you."

Rachel panicked, she was not sure if it was correct to send her photograph to a stranger. She had seen so many Hindi films about blackmail that she could not trust Moshe. So, after a lot of contemplation, she replied, "I feel the same. But I also want to see you. Why don't you send me your photograph before I send you mine?"

Much to Rachel's surprise, it was there when she opened her mail.

She kept staring at it, disappointed. He had a pink baby face, blue eyes, and a small butterfly mouth. He said his mother was an American, so he spoke English, and his father was a Russian Jew.

Her first instinct was to delete everything and forget about Moshe. Then she saw that he looked innocent and was not the cheat she had thought he might be. Anyway, he was her passport to Israel; they would fall in love, he would propose, and they would get married. Perhaps he would come for the wedding with a plane full of Israelis and on the wedding night they would all dance to the Hava Nagila.

Rachel got her photograph scanned and sent it to Moshe. The message came almost immediately. "You are beautiful," he said, "Much more than what I had imagined you to be. Do you wear saris?"

Not knowing how to answer such an endearing statement of affection, she logged out, ran back home feeling happy and almost bumped into Yacov, standing at the gate and smoking. "Hello," he said, "Care for a walk?"

"No," she said, "How dare you?" and ran up the stairs, avoiding the elevator. She needed time to compose herself before she entered the apartment. She did not want her mother to see her flushed face.

The next day she wrote to Moshe saying how nice it was to see each other's photographs, and no, she did not wear saris.

The cyber romance continued for six more months, and Rachel was sure that the prophet would fulfill her dreams and at last she would fly to Israel. In one of his e-mails, Moshe had also asked her if she could find an Internet café with a web camera. If she did, they could see each other and even have a conversation.

Rachel tried looking for a cyber café with a web camera and found it was expensive. She would have to use all her savings for just one conversation, but it would be worth it. She sent Moshe an e-mail saying that she had found one and would wait for him on such and such a day at such and such hour. She had also decided to wear the black tee shirt she had painted, so that he could read that somebody was waiting for her in Israel. Moshe never answered that e-mail. Day after day she checked her e-mail, but there was no news from Moshe. Crestfallen, she waited a month for an answer, but there was none. Rachel felt stupid at their having never asked for each other's phone numbers, or she could have called him.

Then suddenly after two desolate months, there was a message from Israel in her inbox. It was Moshe's mother, Monika. Her two-line mail shattered Rachel's world. It was a block message to Moshe's friends:

Moshe died during the suicide bomber attack on Dizengoff
Square. His ashes will be laid to rest at the Mount of Olives
cemetery in Jerusalem, on Sunday morning, 10 a.m. In grief,
Monika and Dov.

Rachel was sitting frozen in front of the computer in the shabby
cyber café, feeling lost and frightened, not knowing what to do. She
knew she could not cry in public.

Then, zombie-like, she stood up, collected her bag, and walked
back home like one in a trance.

Rachel was far too young to suffer such a personal tragedy all
alone.

She wanted to tell somebody. She wanted to cry and for that she
needed a shoulder. There was nobody she could trust.

Rachel also knew that nobody would understand. Her parents
would be furious if they ever came to know about the cyber romance.
Perhaps she could confide in Ilana or Prity, but they would be
shocked. Imagine having a cyber romance, when they were just
learning how to wear a brassiere and to wax their legs!

Thankfully, the foyer of Shalom India was deserted.

The buildings looked dark and distant and Rachel felt lost and
lonely.

The sobs were rising in her chest and tears were filling her eyes,
so she rang for the elevator and went up to the terrace, where there
was normally nobody. It was dark. Rachel slumped in a corner, sobbing, crying, and calling out to Moshe.

Cutting through her sobs, Rachel heard the familiar sound of the
shofar. The sound soothed her and she felt better.

She looked up and saw Yacov standing on the western side of the
terrace, blowing the shofar.

Quickly, she stopped sobbing and wiped her tears with the
dupatta. She did not want him to see her crying.

Rachel bent to pick up her bag and felt a hand at her elbow. It
was Yacov, the shofar tucked under his arm; he was helping her
stand up.

His closeness was comforting and the next thing Rachel knew, she was clinging to Yacov, crying on his shoulder, and trying to tell him all that had happened.

Then she looked up at him, sobbing, and said, "I want to go to Israel."

Yacov held her face in his hands, looked deep into her eyes and said, "We could, you know . . . "

8 Juliet

Juliet and Rahul were childhood sweethearts and even as toddlers had decided to get married. They did not know then that they belonged to different religions.

It was a closely guarded secret till the night of the fancy dress competition at the synagogue. Rahul was often in and out of Juliet's home, exchanging notes, books, or music, since he was a close friend of Juliet's brother Gideon and they went to the gym together. Juliet's parents were convinced that she was safe with Rahul. It was the same in Rahul's home; Juliet was always there with his sister Megha. They were even allowed to go out together in a group to the cinema or for pizza.

Their families were so close that they often ate together and even watched cricket matches together, in one home or the other, cheerful and happy like one big family. Both families were fond of Hindi film songs and Juliet, who had a good voice, often treated them to old songs. As Rahul's family name was Abhiram and Juliet's father's name was Abraham, people sometimes went to the wrong building and rang the wrong doorbell.

The two families were so close that when Juliet received a marriage proposal from a Bene Israel suitor from Bombay and he invited her for dinner, her parents hesitated, discussed the matter in hushed tones in the kitchen, and came to the conclusion that she would be safe in the company of Gideon, Rahul, and Megha.

At Sheba, the restaurant on C.G. Road, the three conspired and the nice young suitor paid a hefty bill.

Juliet had openly flirted with Rahul, assuming that it would frighten away the suitor. She was in for a shock, though, for the young man's father sent a message saying that the boy liked the girl. Juliet's mother Rebecca was pleased and even confided in Rahul's mother Sudha that it was a good match. The boy was good-looking, and had a steady job as a chartered accountant with a big firm in Bombay. What more did a girl want?

Juliet panicked and tried to convince her parents that she did not like the suitor because he was too thin. "Look at me," she said. "I am big and fat, do you think we will look good together?"

Halfheartedly her parents let the proposal slip from their hands, unaware that the prophet had other plans.

Juliet was a fun-loving girl, who won prizes for everything from sports to public speaking to fancy dress contests. Whenever Juliet took part in a competition, both homes fell into the project whole-heartedly. Like, for the Hanukah fancy dress party, when it was decided that Juliet would dress as an Indian bride, Sudha lent her wedding dress to Juliet: a brocade ghaghra, silk bandhni odhni, an embroidered backless blouse, and matching jewelry complete with gold bangles.

That evening, dressed in the finery, Juliet looked so beautiful that everybody was sure that she would win the first prize.

Rahul even offered to drive them to the synagogue, so they all packed into his father's Fiat. But even before the car reached the gate, Juliet came down with a stomachache and said she could not possibly make it to the synagogue, but begged her parents and brother to go ahead for the Feast of the Tabernacles.

Reluctantly they agreed, advising her to change, put away the jewelry in the cupboard, and rest. Rebecca even offered to stay back, but Juliet refused, saying she would lock herself in the apartment and sleep. At the synagogue, try as she might, Rebecca could not focus on the prayers or fancy dress competition. She was upset and annoyed when Yael won first prize. She was also uncomfortable with the fact that Juliet was alone at home.

From the women's gallery, Rebecca signaled to her husband Abraham that she was going back home and left hurriedly. She found a rickshaw, reached home, and saw that Juliet had switched off all the lights; perhaps she was sleeping.

Rebecca opened the door of the apartment with her key and entered the apartment quietly, not wanting to disturb Juliet. She saw that the television was switched on but the sound had been turned down, so she switched off the television and turned on the light, went to the kitchen to get herself a glass of water, and saw that there was a box of pizza on the counter. She was surprised; if Juliet had a stomachache, why had she eaten pizza? She was rather annoyed that the kitchen was in a mess, so she folded the box and pushed it into the garbage bin. Then she went to her room, changed into a nightgown, folded her sari, put it away, unscrewed her gold earrings, removed her gold bangles, left them on the dressing table, and went to the bathroom. On her way back, she saw that Juliet's door was ajar, so she peeped in to see if she was awake.

Horrified, she stood staring at Juliet's bed.

In the dim light, she thought she had seen two bodies move. To make sure, she switched on the light and screamed when she saw Juliet and Rahul in bed together.

Dazed, they sat up, staring at her in disbelief, their eyes full of dreams.

Juliet was still dressed as a bride, her makeup smudged, her ghaghra pulled up to her knees, while her odhni and blouse lay scattered on the floor with Rahul's kurta.

Eyes lowered, Rahul stood up, pulled on his kurta, slowly tied the drawstrings of his pajamas, and left without a word.

Frightened and disheveled, Juliet stood and reached for the blouse and the odhni, but before that Rebecca fell on her in a mad fury, beating her and crying simultaneously.

Juliet took the blows with tears streaming down her face, but when she could not bear it any longer, she held Rebecca's wrists firmly and shouted back at her, "I love Rahul and don't you dare touch me."

Rebecca seemed to have gone deaf; she was staring at Juliet, fascinated that her little girl had such big breasts, with nipples as big as strawberries.

Standing in the doorway and watching Juliet dress, she made an instant decision that Juliet had to be married right away to a good Bene Israel boy. Because if Juliet eloped with Rahul, as she probably would, how would Rebecca ever face the Jewish community? She was always showing off, saying that Juliet was a born winner, and an act like this would immediately make her a loser. All along they had maintained a reputation of being good, God-fearing Jews. She felt ashamed that a daughter of her house had gone astray even though she had been brought up with the best values of Jewish womanhood.

Rebecca was in a state of shock at Juliet having the guts to offer her breasts to a young man who was not yet her husband, and at seeing that her breasts were big and round when she had always bought brassieres a size smaller than Juliet's actual size.

Obviously Juliet had burst out of all restrictions imposed by brassiere, family, community.

Rebecca could not understand why Juliet had chosen Rahul when she had the choice of the best suitors in the community.

Rebecca told her day after day that she was a Jewish girl and had to follow the law by getting married to a Jewish groom and increasing the tribe?

Rebecca was disturbed that her daughter was a liar, because Juliet religiously followed all Jewish rituals. She even observed the Day of Atonement like a well-brought-up Jewish girl, then why was she secretly sleeping with Rahul?

Rebecca was worried. Was this just lust, a temporary infatuation, or a serious affair? She wanted to believe that her daughter was a good Jewish child and it was Rahul who was evil and had led her astray. But then if Juliet was a well-raised girl, why was she not wearing a blouse when Rebecca had caught them in bed? Had they planned to meet that night and had Juliet lied about the stomach ache?

Obviously their meeting was preplanned.

Perhaps she was no longer a virgin, and Rebecca started counting the days to see when Juliet had had her last period. Rebecca blamed herself; she should have been careful from the very beginning and not have allowed so much familiarity between the two families. Nobody had guessed that they might fall in love, because they behaved as though they were brother and sister.

The next morning Juliet's father took her to Bombay, and in a week sent her to Israel on a tourist visa. He did not leave her alone even once and made sure that Juliet did not get an opportunity to contact Rahul.

In a day, relations between the Abhirams and Abrahams had soured; they stopped speaking to each other and behaved like strangers. The children were ordered not to speak to each other. In the presence of their parents they behaved as though they did not know each other, but kept in touch through their secret code of communication. Rahul received all information about Juliet and her whereabouts. He knew she was staying in Israel at her aunt's house. He even had her phone number, address, and knew when she was alone at home.

Rahul bought a pre-paid card and called her from STD phone booths. It was expensive and they had to speak to each other quickly, telling each other how much they loved each other. After a month, all they were asking each other was, "What shall we do?" "How can we meet?" "Why don't you come to Israel?" "Can't you return to India?"

But they knew there was no solution.

During one such conversation, Rahul's world fell apart when Juliet told him that the family was trying to get her married to a distant cousin as soon as possible. They asked each other, "Now what shall we do?"

Things came to a dead end when Rahul told her rather abruptly, "I am jealous." Juliet started crying and while waiting for her to stop his phone bill came to a fortune.

So the next week he did not call her, and she assumed he did not love her anymore. When he called again, she asked, "What is the matter, why are you so cold?"

"I am not cold," he said.

"Is there somebody else in your life?" she asked.

"No," he answered brusquely. Then she heard a click at the other end and spent the whole night crying.

The next morning, she woke up early, feeling rotten. She went looking for a phone booth, counted her shekels, and called Rahul.

Juliet recognized his mother Sudha's voice at the other end and hung up, saying nothing. Then she called again, hoping he would pick up the phone. Fortunately it was Megha, who was excited to hear her voice. Quickly Juliet told her that she needed to speak to Rahul.

When Rahul came on the line, all she could say was, "Do you love me?"

"Yes," he said, his voice hoarse. Juliet felt better, at least his voice was soft and affectionate.

That afternoon, Juliet continued her vigil at the phone between exactly two and three, but the phone never rang. It was as if it had gone dead and Juliet often picked up the receiver to see if there was a dial tone. She was biting her nails, worrying, and waiting for his call.

It was three and she knew in fifteen minutes her aunt would be back. At the dot of three the phone rang. It was Rahul.

Feeling breathless, Juliet asked if he loved her. Yes, he said, but he was confused with the problems of countries and religion. While he was speaking, Juliet heard the key turn in the lock and knew it was her aunt and, not knowing what to do, put the receiver back.

Aunt Hannah walked in asking if it was a call from India.

All Juliet could say was, "It was a friend from India." She tried to distract her, asking, "Would you like a cup of tea?"

Aunt Hannah shook her head and smiled. Juliet was surprised that she did not appear particularly angry, though she had caught her speaking to Rahul.

Juliet went to the kitchen and returned with a plate of samosas she had made in the morning. She had taken to cooking, realizing it was all she could do while she was in Israel.

Aunt Hannah thanked her, took a samosa, complimented her, and asked, "Was that Rahul? You don't have to hide from me." For the first time, Juliet saw that her aunt was kind and understanding. It was also the first time since her mother had caught her in bed with Rahul that someone was speaking to her with sympathy. Juliet saw that she could trust her aunt.

So she sat down, poured a cup of tea for herself and said in a matter-of-fact voice, "Aunty, I am in love with Rahul."

"I know. Your parents have told me everything."

Juliet looked at her aunt rather suspiciously, not sure whether she was making inquiries because Hyams had asked her to, or because she was really interested in Juliet's life.

But she sensed that Aunt Hannah was honest, not cunning, and was not trying to get a story out of her. Instead, Hannah hugged her and said, "This is the curse of belonging to a minority community."

Juliet was surprised. "Why do you say that?"

Aunt Hannah wiped her eyes. "I also had a Rahul in my life. But I was forced to marry your uncle. Fortunately, he is a good man. I had to come to terms with my fate and I lead the life of a good Jewish woman, a loving wife, and devoted mother."

"Who was your Rahul?"

"It does not matter anymore. But why do you want to suffer? If you love him, why don't you make your life with him?"

Not sure how to phrase her sentence, she asked, "Aunt Hannah, will you help us?"

"Yes," said Aunt Hannah quietly, "But let me warn you, once you take the final step, neither community will accept you or your children."

"So, what shall I do?"

"Convert."

"How?"

"I suggest you convince Rahul to convert to Judaism. That will be the easiest. Actually, it will take longer in Israel as he would have to study the Torah and even undergo circumcision. I am told it is faster in India. There is a special short-cut to conversion. I have read that many American Jews prefer to convert in India rather than Israel. Nothing to worry, the circumcision could be done by a urologist in Bombay."

Juliet was sitting huddled on the sofa next to her aunt, biting her nails and asking, "What if Rahul does not agree?"

"Then you could become a Hindu. But I suggest you ask him to convert and settle in Israel. You told me he wants to start a restaurant. Indian restaurants work very well here, look at that tandoori place in Tel Aviv."

Juliet was not sure how Rahul would react to such a suggestion; after all, he had obligations to his family. A Hindu family would never agree to have their son convert to a strange religion called Judaism.

Six more months passed and Rahul became desperate for Juliet. He had become a member of Friends of Israel, and then he bought himself a ticket to Israel. He found himself on the kibbutz Yavne as a trainee chef. On arrival, the first thing he did was to call Juliet and tell her that he was calling from Israel. She could not believe her ears and was so excited that she wanted to take a bus to Yavne right away. But there were other problems: Aunt Hannah would have allowed her to meet Rahul, but not Uncle Rahmim. He was very conscious of keeping the family honor intact and had already decided that his nephew Ralphi was the perfect groom for Juliet. Her parents were more than happy, and just to spite Rahul's family they distributed sweets, telling everybody including the Abhirams that Juliet was soon to be married and that they would be flying to Israel for the wedding.

That night, Juliet confided in Aunt Hannah that Rahul was in Israel and she wanted to meet him and could not possibly marry Ralphi.

Aunt Hannah advised her to act immediately as her parents had okayed the alliance with Ralphi. His family had been looking for a good Bene Israel bride for their son, and she was the perfect choice. The only problem he had with her was that he wanted her to dress in shorts and smarter western clothes.

Juliet held Aunt Hannah and wept, "I love Rahul, not Ralphi." Aunt Hannah looked deep into her eyes and whispered, "Go, find him."

Hannah and Juliet had to plan carefully so that Uncle Rahmim was not suspicious about their occasional outings.

When Juliet met Rahul at the Tel Aviv bus terminal after almost a year, Aunt Hannah accompanied her. They hugged, kissed, and did not want to part.

In the next month Rahul and Juliet met often, but always with Aunt Hannah.

Rahul liked Israel and was enjoying his stay at the kibbutz. In fact Juliet joked that he was putting on weight.

And whenever they met, Aunt Hannah tried to convince him about conversion. If Rahul converted, it would be easier for them in both countries, but they knew Rahul's parents would protest. He did not know how to convince them about taking such a big step, which also involved circumcision. But Rahul was adamant, he wanted to marry his childhood sweetheart and he would at all costs.

The Israeli atmosphere went to his head and he felt fearless and bold; he would brave all odds for Juliet.

A month later, Aunt Hannah bought an airline ticket for Juliet, and made all arrangements for them. On arrival in Bombay, an old friend of hers was to receive them and arrange for an Arya Samaj marriage. After that Rahul would have a meeting with the cantor of the Thane Synagogue and start the process of conversion. It would take three months. On departure Aunt Hannah gave them a check which would help them pull through the initial difficult days.

As they kissed her goodbye, Aunt Hannah blessed them, praying to Eliyahu Hannabi to ward off all difficulties from their path.

In Bombay, it was easier than expected. They married according to Arya Samaj rites and informed their parents. Both families fumed and fretted at first and then they came together and made plans to receive the young couple at the Ahmedabad railway station.

Aunt Hannah's plan had worked; both families welcomed them back into the fold with open arms. If Rahul's parents were disturbed about his decision to convert, they did not say anything, but seemed to have accepted it halfheartedly. Both families had their misgivings, yet they welcomed bride and groom.

Once the conversion was completed, Rahul and Juliet had another wedding at the synagogue in Ahmedabad. Juliet insisted that Aunt Hannah be present. When she arrived from Israel, she was moved to see Juliet in a gossamer silk wedding gown and Rahul dressed like the perfect Jewish groom in a three-piece suit with a prayer shawl and wearing a skullcap his kibutznik friends had sent as a gift from Israel. After the conversion in Thane, Rahul had the right to take part in a minyan, the group of the ten Jewish men necessary to hold a prayer service.

The Abrahams and Abhirams were happy to be together once again like the good old days. After the wedding, both families organized a grand reception inviting relatives and friends from both communities, where they gave new names to the couple. They began the journey of wedded life as Romiel-Rahul and Juliet-Priya. Standing on the flower-bedecked dais, the young couple greeted their Hindu relatives by touching their feet and shook hands with their Jewish guests, often hugging and kissing each other. And, if there was discomfort about the unique cross-cultural ritual, nobody commented. That evening, at the reception, between the welcome arti for the bride and groom, the wedding march, the cake-cutting ceremony, and a toast over glasses of wine, both Abraham and Abhiram announced that they had bought an apartment for the couple at Shalom India Housing Society.

The residents of Block A of Shalom India Housing Society loved the young couple and made Rahul feel that he was one of them. Not once did the Abhirams feel that they were different. Nothing mattered as long as they had a mezuzah on the door and they said the Sabbath prayers. They loved to tease the young couple, often referring to them as the Romeo and Juliet of Shalom India Housing Society, or saying Abhiram sounded exactly like Abraham, so what did it matter that Romiel was Rahul. They also invited Rahul's family for malida ceremonies and other festivities, at times even asking Rahul's mother Sudha to make Gujarati snacks for the congregation. Rahul's parents did not enter the synagogue, but they felt welcome in the courtyard where the festivities took place.

Eventually, when Rahul and Juliet emigrated to Israel, Rahul's parents were invited for an offering to Eliyahu Hannabi. Rahul's father wore a kippa and his mother pinned a handkerchief on her head just like a Bene Israel woman.

On the eve of their departure, Rahul-Romiel and Juliet-Priya left the keys of their apartment with Ezra.

It was soon afterwards that Prophet Elijah visited their apartment and flew over to Israel to see them. He had heard Juliet's prayers calling out to him and asking him to help her decide about her future.

Was it to be in Israel or India?

She needed the prophet's advice, but he thought it was too early to decide. Only time could tell what lay ahead for them.

When Ezra had built Shalom India Housing Society, it was decided that Block A would be reserved for Jews. But it would be difficult to find a nice Jewish couple like the Abhirams for A-107.

9 Ben Hur

The sound annoyed him when people called him Ben Hoor instead of Ben Hur, and he would correct them, "It is Hur to be said like "her," not Hoor, like Noor."

At the rebellious age of thirteen he was almost rusticated from school just because he had objected when the class teacher had pronounced his name the wrong way.

The teacher had complained to the principal that Ben Hur had threatened her with fists clenched and a menacing look in his eyes. His father Ezra was summoned to the principal's office and was told that Ben Hur was rude to his teachers. Without asking for details, Ezra had slapped him. When his wife Sigaut told him the truth, Ezra regretted that he had slapped him.

Ben Hur hated his name and wished they had given him an ordinary name like Moses or Samson.

Much to Sigaut's embarrassment, Ezra often joked that Ben Hur was conceived on the night they had seen the film *Ben Hur*, so his father loved him more than his other children. Ben Hur smirked that his parents must have had a real wild night after they had returned home from the cinema. Because every time they spoke about it, their eyes softened and his mother blushed.

For the fancy dress competition at the synagogue, it was decided that he should dress like the character from the film *Ben Hur*. After all, he had just turned eighteen, was muscular and would look perfect dressed as a Roman charioteer. But then, he had been Ben Hur the year before and also the year before that, so he objected and said:

"I will dress as Joseph and wear a coat of twelve colors."

Even as a child, he had liked the illustrations in his children's Bible. The cover had a pop-up picture of Noah's ark and although frayed, it was still in good condition and he kept it next to his pillow. It had stories about Adam, Noah, Abraham, Moses, Joseph, and Samson, with the drawings done in an old-fashioned realistic style. The drapery had a heavy rendering which he liked, and the characters looked as though they had walked out of the Bible.

There were two pictures of Joseph, one as a child, the other as a teenager in his coat of many colors.

The story, titled "Joseph and his Brothers," read like this:

Jacob, who lived in Canaan, had twelve sons, but it was Joseph, next to the youngest, whom he loved best. So, the ten older brothers were very jealous of Joseph, especially since he could think faster than them. And, when Jacob gave him a fine new coat of many colors, the brothers were very angry.

Joseph loved to dream and divine his dreams. One day while they were tending their flock, he said to his brothers, I dreamed we were binding sheaves of grain and my sheaf stood up straight, but all yours bowed down to it.

The brothers were angry, tore off his coat and threw him into a pit. They dipped the coat in goat's blood and showed it to Jacob saying a wolf had killed Joseph. Joseph was rescued by some tradesmen who sold him as a slave. A few months later, his master was annoyed with him and put him in prison. And it was only when he deciphered the Pharaoh's dreams that Joseph was released and became an important courtier in the Pharaoh's court and later his brothers did bow down to him. This is how his dream came true and Joseph was known in the land of Egypt as a learned man.

Joseph's coat had cast a spell on Ben Hur. He dreamt of becoming a fashion designer and wondered if he could design biblical clothes like Joseph's coat in a contemporary style.

When Ben Hur informed him that he was planning to join design school, Ezra had thrown a fit. How could a son of his ever want to become a designer, when he had been brought up to be a patriarch? He had expected him to study law, engineering, or medicine.

Ben Hur was his favorite child. How could he ever go against his father? But, like his ideal Joseph, Ben Hur dreamt of things which were beyond his reach in many ways, like Lolo.

He had met Lolo at the drawing class, which prepared students for admission tests to design schools. As soon as Lolo had entered the class he had fallen head over heels in love with her. She was unlike the girls he knew. She had spent her childhood in London, had traveled to Europe, the States, and had spent a year in Switzerland.

Her first day in class had been spectacular and had given Ben Hur goose pimples. She was wearing tight hipster jeans, a tiny tee shirt, and boots; had blonde-streaked spiked hair, wore pale pink lipstick on her bee-stung lips, and was always chewing gum. Lolo was aware that boys ogled her and girls turned green with jealousy.

Lolo was friendly and went out of her way to speak to everybody in class, often making them feel stupid as they had names like Satish, Mina, Priti, Priya, Seema, or Paul, while she had a name which matched her personality. Yet she did look up in surprise when she heard Ben Hur's name, "Nice name," she said.

That evening, when the drawing professor Malti Sahani took attendance, there was pin-drop silence when the name Lata Patel was called out and nobody answered.

Professor Sahani took one look at the faces in the class and her gaze stopped on Lolo's face. She looked sternly into her eyes and said, "When I call out your name, please answer."

Lolo or Lata Patel shook her head obediently and looked almost meek as she lowered her eyes. She had forgotten she was registered as Lata according to her birth certificate, not as Lolo.

Ben Hur's heart went out to her; he was sure she felt stupid after her dramatic entry.

As often happens at this particular age, it was love at first sight for Ben Hur and he did not care about the Lata bit, after all, what is in a name?

That evening when class ended at eight, he waited for her, taking longer than usual to start his scooter. He had noticed she had looked rather crestfallen and wanted to befriend her.

When she walked past him, giving him a sunny smile, he asked, "Hi, want a lift? Where do you stay?"

"Bodakdev," she said.

"Come on," he said tapping the back seat, "I'll drop you, that's real far. How come you live there?"

"My father just got transferred to Ahmedabad; it is a company apartment, nice place."

As she sat behind him, he liked the softness of her breasts and thighs brushing against him as they chatted about the problems of having names like Ben Hur and Lata.

"What a pain . . . " she was saying, when he asked if she would care for a cup of coffee. She whooped a happy "Yeah," and they raced towards the Barista on the classy C.G. Road.

This became a habit. Every evening after class they headed for their favorite coffee shop, and Ben Hur could not remember when exactly they started kissing, petting, and then found themselves in her bedroom, naked and groping. After which Ben Hur could think of nothing but sex.

That was when he was supposed to participate in the fancy dress competition. He felt stupid. After all he was a grown-up man who had sex with a real woman, how could he behave like a child?

But he could not argue with Ezra and was supposed just to follow his instructions. Ben Hur was also afraid of Ezra's reactions, if he came to know about Lolo.

But since Juliet and Rahul had married, Ben Hur was confident that one day he would also have a runaway marriage. "Real love," he kept telling himself, "can break all barriers," because Ezra had been one of the first from Shalom India Housing Society to congratulate Juliet and Rahul. Yet when he presided over the dining table he often said, "Such marriages never work. I warn you, do not marry outside the community. You need life partners with the same habits in food, clothes, community matters, and everything else."

After a lecture like this, Ben Hur would bite his nails and start worrying. From the photographs in Lolo's apartment and the little that she had told him, he knew that she was an only child and a spoiled one at that.

Often when they were together in Lolo's apartment, Ben Hur was puzzled that there was nobody else at home. But the fridge was always stocked with food, which Lolo heated in the microwave and they ate from the same plate, sometimes feeding each other, listening to trance music.

It was a happy existence.

Ben Hur discovered that he liked to be sprawled out naked on Lolo's bed with her head resting on his chocolate-bar stomach as she played with his sex. She once asked, "Why are you circumcised?"

He was never sure why. All he knew was that all Jewish males had to be circumcised. He hesitated to ask his father, in case he became suspicious, so he decided to read up on it in the synagogue library, but between early-morning and late-night classes, Lolo, and his own home, he never had any time for himself.

In fact, every evening he was so tired that he could barely keep his eyes open and fell asleep as soon as his head touched the pillow. And however well he may have eaten at Lolo's, he had to keep up pretenses at home and make a show of eating. Sigaut was worried about his lack of appetite and took him to the family doctor, who diagnosed fatigue and prescribed some vitamins.

On one idyllic afternoon, he was telling Lolo about his desire to make a garment similar to Joseph's coat and told her the story from the Bible.

Lolo liked the idea so much that she decided to make him the coat. That would be her gift to him for giving her so much happiness.

They went to the walled city on Ben Hur's scooter and bought all the fabrics that Lolo wanted, especially the traditional striped mashru, woven with silk and cotton threads. It was similar to the illustration in the children's Bible.

Back in Lolo's apartment, Ben Hur watched in amazement as she pulled out a small sewing machine and, like an expert seamstress, cut the material and sewed an overcoat.

He tried it on, standing in front of the mirror, posing like Joseph. She laughed till she was rolling on the ground because he was naked and wearing just the coat.

Soon after, Ben Hur wore the coat to the synagogue and all heads turned to look at the handsome young man. He had worn a black tracksuit under the coat and walked around the Teva like a professional model. But he did not win the prize as the judges said the coat was more beautiful than the character he represented.

That night, Ezra appeared to be angry with him. As soon as his act was over, his father took him aside and hissed, "How did you get this coat? Have you started buying clothes from your favorite designer shops?" Ben Hur smiled. Without flickering an eyelid he assured his father that his friends from the design class had made it for him.

When his father was pacified, he preened in the coat, fully aware that all eyes were upon him. But he was rather stung that busty Diana ignored him.

Since they were kids, the two families had an unspoken agreement that Diana and Ben Hur would get married. Even if it bothered him that Diana was hurt for reasons he did not know, he knew that somehow he had to put an end to her hopes and to all the matchmaking efforts of both families, his and hers.

With Lolo in the picture, he worried as to how he would introduce her into the miniscule Jewish community.

He made a secret prayer to Eliyahu Hannabi that he wanted Lolo as his wife, even if she was going to put everybody off with her spiked hair.

But he was not quite sure after he met Lolo's father.

One afternoon, when they were together in Lolo's apartment, listening to her favorite trance music, they heard a key turn in the front door.

He saw the look of panic in Lolo's eyes as she whispered, "My father."

Ben Hur felt suddenly awkward. Lolo had made their afternoon meetings so casual that Ben Hur had never imagined that someone could ever intrude on their perfumed garden.

In the beginning he used to panic at the slightest sound at the door, but since nobody ever entered the apartment, he had stopped worrying about being found out. In fact, he often felt that he was in his own apartment, until he heard the key turn in the lock and the real owner walked in, a dapper, middle-aged man.

Ben Hur saw the look of suspicion pass over the older man's face as he shook hands and introduced himself, "Sir, I am Ben Hur, Lolo's classmate."

Lolo suddenly became quiet and was not her usual self. She went into the kitchen to get her father a glass of water as Ben Hur beat a hasty retreat.

When Ben Hur returned home, he would have liked to phone Lolo and ask if she was all right, but he did not have the courage, and instead went down to play basketball with the boys.

He saw busty Diana standing at her window and watching him, but he avoided looking in her direction. He was thinking about Lolo.

The next day, Lolo was not in class, so during the tea break he called her on her cell phone, but she had switched it off.

Ben Hur did not see Lolo for two days and he missed her.

On the third day, he went to her apartment and rang the bell, she opened the door, left the safety catch on and said, "Ben Hur, go away, I cannot see you." She looked haggard and he was sure that she had been crying.

After a lot of persuasion she opened the door.

Ben Hur was surprised to find her distant. Dressed in an old tee shirt and shorts, she slumped on the sofa in the drawing room. Ben Hur sat next to her, held her hands and said in one breath, "I love you Lolo I cannot live without you."

"It is useless," she said, "My life is in a mess." Tears were running down her face and she made no effort to wipe them. Ben Hur held her in his arms as she whispered, "Ben, I like you, because you never ask me awkward questions about me or my family, must be because you love me so much. You know, sometimes I tire of acting, because I am just simple Lata, not the Lolo you see in me. You want to know about my life? You must have often wondered about my parents, my mother especially. Do you see any family photographs in this apartment? No, because we live in a home without memories or family. Yet our fridge is always full. Well, Latabehn looks after everything, the kitchen, the apartment. There is a cook who comes in the morning and I make sure that there is enough food in the apartment, as Mr. Patel eats well and if it is not enough, I might get a beating. You will wonder why Mr. Patel is not 'daddy' or 'papa.' It is because he is not my father. Don't look shocked, yes, he is supposed to be my father, but he is not. My mother was a widow when she married Mr. Patel; we were in London when my original father, another Mr. Patel whom I have never seen, died in a car crash. My mother had a boutique of Indian clothes, she was an expert seamstress, that is why I have a hand for tailoring. Remember how quickly I made your coat? For a while, we were happy, but our peaceful existence ended when my mother met this Mr. Patel when I was eleven. He is a banker, and was kind to us in the beginning, but I never liked him and even told my mother so. She assured me that he was a good man and I would take a liking to him once we lived together in the same house. I knew she was lonely and was finding it hard to go through life all alone.

"I loved my mother and wanted to see her happy, so I pretended that I was happy.

"Then, when I was sixteen, she died of breast cancer. She had ignored it. It was sudden. I shudder at the memory of the year of her death. She took a promise from Mr. Patel that he would look after me, but I knew I would have been happier in an orphanage. We did not have any relatives, except for an aunt in Kheda, who did not want to take responsibility for me. So, Mr. Patel gave my mother a promise that he would look after me, just like in a Hindi film. Last year, suddenly he sold off Mother's boutique in London and got himself transferred to India.

"Actually, when Mother died and I found myself alone with Mr. Patel, it was the hardest day of my life. That day I cried so much that since then I have never cried, till this very moment, when I was sure that I had lost you. I feel so close to you. I want to live with you forever.

"The day before, when Mr. Patel almost caught me with you, he beat me up and made me promise that I would never see you. And, although I have received a letter of admission from the fashion institute, he does not want me to continue my studies. You know, he wants me to stay home, almost like his wife . . . "

Lolo was sitting with legs locked and hands knotted together.

Tenderly, Ben Hur took her in his arms and asked, "Does he . . . ?"

She shook her head, her eyes wide and frightened like a child as she clung to him.

Ben Hur took a deep breath and asked, "Will you marry me?"

"How?"

"I know this sounds ridiculous, we are still in our teens and I don't even have a job, but I can speak to my father."

Ben Hur

"Can you?"

Ben Hur looked worried. "It is not going to be easy. You know we are Jewish and normally our families do not accept brides from outside the community but if you do not mind you could convert to Judaism and we would not have any problems," he said all this in one breath, not knowing how she would react. He knew that his father would not accept even a convert, but he would try to convince him.

Ben Hur saw that Lolo was staring at him with her mouth open, looking innocent and vulnerable, as she did not understand the implications of what he was saying. Of course, she had had Jewish friends in London, but she knew nothing about Indian Jews. She was even more taken aback when he asked her if she followed any religion in particular.

She thought aloud, "Not really, but if you offer me a new life, I am willing to accept your god."

"My god is faceless and does not even have a body like Krishna. Is it okay with you?"

Lolo just shrugged her shoulders.

They were confused as they sat hand in hand, wondering about religion. They had never thought about it when they first kissed. Then they had just been man and woman, like Adam and Eve, mused Ben Hur. Lolo laughed when he compared himself to Adam and she picked up an apple from the table and offered it to him.

When Ben Hur returned back to Shalom India Housing Society, he saw that there was a letter waiting for him saying that he had been admitted to the fashion institute. There was an air of festivity as the whole family gathered, kissing him, thumping his back, and congratulating him. Sigaut sent Daniyal to buy a box of pedas and then lit a lamp thanking the prophet Elijah for the letter of admission.

Sigaut spent the evening distributing pedas to the residents of Shalom India Housing Society, telling them that Ben Hur had been admitted to the most prestigious fashion institute of India.

But their pleasure was short-lived.

As soon as Ezra entered the home, the scene of festivity changed to mourning, as he tore up the letter and threw it back at Ben Hur saying, "No son of mine is going to do a woman's job."

Ben Hur tried to explain that fashion design was no longer a woman's field. Ezra looked at him scornfully and said they were all eunuchs and ordered his wife to serve dinner.

Ben Hur lost his appetite and felt very small and helpless in the face of patriarchal authority. He wanted to become a man as soon as possible.

When he was thirteen, at his bar mitzvah, hadn't they declared that he was a man?

Soon after dinner, the family sat around the television watching their favorite show, but Ben Hur went to bed, feigning a headache.

His mother threw a pleading look at her husband, hoping he would allow Ben Hur to join fashion school, but Ezra was concentrating on the show and his wife knew that it was useless to speak to him when he was in such a mood.

Ben Hur changed, put on his Walkman and lay in bed listening to music till he fell asleep and dreamt that he saw the prophet Elijah in his chariot of gold.

Half asleep, half awake, he asked the prophet to help him.

The prophet seemed to smile as he disappeared into a blue cloud. Ben Hur woke up in a sweat, determined to speak to his father, come what may.

He pulled off the Walkman and saw the lights had been switched off and everybody had gone to bed. But from Block B he could hear Franco Fernandes playing the violin. The music soothed him and he went to his father's room. As usual the door was open and the curtain was fluttering. He called out to his father.

Ezra heard him and sat up frazzled. When he came to the door, Ben Hur whispered that he needed to speak to him.

Ezra closed the bedroom door and they sat at the dining table. Ezra made himself a drink and asked Ben Hur if he would like some whiskey. He needed one, and his father made him a chota peg with soda and ice. He then lit a cigarette and offered one to Ben Hur, saying, "I know you smoke behind my back, from now on you better smoke in my presence. So, tell me young man, what is bothering you? Have you fallen in love or something like that?"

Ben Hur weighed the question in his mind and decided that it was a godsent opportunity, so he said, "Yes," looking straight into his father's eyes.

For a moment, he was terrified, as he did not know how his

father would react, but relaxed when the older man spread his hands on the table and asked, "Diana?"

"No."

"Then, who is it?"

"Lata Patel."

"How long have you known her?"

"Six months."

"And you are already in love. What do you plan next?"

"A career in design, then marriage."

"Not design, you are going to engineering college."

"No, I am not."

"Why?"

"Because I am going to study fashion design."

"No, you are not."

"Papa, I want to. What is the point of going through life doing something I don't want to do? I'd rather do something I enjoy doing."

"How do you know you will not like being an engineer?"

"Because the thought of it bores me."

"What future do you have in fashion?"

"Plenty, Papa. Look, there are so many men in the fashion industry and all doing well. And I know I have the talent. You didn't even see the letter properly before you tore it. It said I have topped the list."

Ezra looked almost stupid as his mouth fell open and he said, "That indeed is a great honor, my son, then you must go in for this fashion design course, but just one request, please do not dress like a woman." Ben Hur saw that his father's eyes were wet and his voice choked.

Ben Hur was elated that his father had given him permission.

Ezra poured another drink and asked, "What about the love angle? Who is this young lady?"

"Lata," said Ben Hur, watching his father guardedly.

"You said you met her at the design class."

"Yes."

"How old is she?"

"My age."

"What about her family?"

"No idea."

"Does she know that you are a Jew?"

"Yes."

"How does she react to that?"

"No reactions."

"Would she convert?"

"Yes."

"How do you know?"

"I asked her."

"Does she know what it means?"

"Yes."

"If you have discussed so much with her, how come you do not know about her family?"

"I think she has a father, but he is not her real father."

"Doesn't make sense, but before you make a commitment, I must tell you some hard truths about Jewish life. Do you know, if you marry this Hindu girl, there will be many problems in the Jewish community, and later on in life your children could have problems."

"There were no problems when Juliet married Rahul."

"Some."

"But then it ended well, didn't it?"

"Yes, but there are other considerations, like food habits. She is a vegetarian, no? Sometimes, after marriage, small problems like food get enlarged into big problems. So, it is better to get married to someone of our own kind, like Diana. We have the same habits, the same upbringing, the same values, the same religion."

Ben Hur smiled, "Papa, look how our food habits are changing. We eat pizzas and hamburgers."

Ezra smiled too, "What about Mama's kheema patties?"

"Women learn," said Ben Hur, folding his arms and resting them on the table.

Ezra tried to change the topic. "Why don't you like the girls of our community? There is Diana, she is beautiful and you like her, don't you?"

"Diana is like a sister, I cannot love her the way I love Lolo."

The name just slipped out of his mouth and he stared at his father rather frightened, not sure how he would react.

"Lolo?" asked Ezra, "Who is that?"

"Lata," said Ben Hur lamely, "her pet name is Lolo."

"So, you are already on pet-name terms. What does she call you?"

"Nothing special, just Ben. Actually Papa, she is very talented, you will like her. You know, when I took part in the fancy dress competition, the coat you asked me about was made by Lata."

He made a mental note, if Lolo was ever invited to his home, he would have to remember to introduce her as Lata, not Lolo.

Ezra was undaunted, "I am not saying anything at this moment, but where your mother is concerned, it is quite another matter. If you think it will be easy to convince your mother about Lolo, you are mistaken. Young man, remember, when it comes to your bride, she has decided that it has to be Diana and has already bought saris and gold jewelry. And, if she ordered pedas when you received the letter of admission, she can also bring down the house when she hears about your Lolo fixation. For nothing on this earth will she accept a Hindu girl as her daughter-in-law."

"Even if she converts?"

"Try and see."

"So, what shall I do now?"

"Just go to sleep, get up early, and go pay your fees," Ezra then stood up, kissed his son, and went to bed. Ben Hur stood there, watching his father's back, and knowing very well that he was trapped.

Ezra had cleverly agreed to let Ben Hur join fashion school and not said anything about Lolo. He had left the matter hanging in the air, leaving his fate in the hands of his mother.

Yet Ben Hur felt he had won half the battle. He had to make plans to introduce Lolo to his family. He was sure if he played his cards well and Lolo started visiting the apartment, his mother would take a liking to her and eventually accept her as his bride.

When he told Lolo about the conversation he had had with Ezra, she was furious with him for having given her false hopes. She said she knew that he was much too young to liberate her from her stepfather's tortures. Ben Hur tried to explain, "This is not true, I told my father about you at the cost of being thrown out of the house. Last night, we sat down at the dining table and talked about you and the design course, man to man, and as we spoke, I realized that getting married to you right away would be difficult. I still have to convince my mother. She does not know a thing about us. I have to find the right moment to broach the subject. It is extremely important that my father has agreed that I join fashion school, which means we can be together during a major part of the day. About the future, we have time."

Lolo seemed to understand, but she felt crushed. With Ben Hur's help, she had hoped to run away from home. Now it appeared a distant dream.

After a year together at fashion design school, Lolo felt happier as she was often away from home. Lolo, Ben Hur, and a small group of their friends made a habit of working together at Ben Hur's apartment when there were assignments to be completed.

In this way, he hoped to involve her in the family.

Ben Hur was nervous when he first introduced Lolo to his mother along with the others, Vijay, Malav, and Tanya.

Ezra had not told his wife that the sexy young lady with blonde streaks in her hair was her future daughter-in-law. He was playing for time, hoping that his wife would take a liking to Lolo.

His heart went out to the girl, so young and vulnerable. But sometimes he grew nervous about accepting Lolo as a daughter-in-law and hoped she would disappear from Ben Hur's life, so that he could pressure him to marry Diana.

Yet Ezra wanted to give Ben Hur liberty to choose his own bride.

He was amused that his son, who had been brought up in the best Bene Israel traditions, had chosen a spunky girl named Lolo.

As the group became regular visitors at Ben Hur's home, Diana watched them from her balcony. Her heart sank and her childhood dreams were shattered. Ben Hur had changed since he started studying fashion design; he did not even bother to acknowledge her presence when they passed each other. He also avoided going to the synagogue, so she never saw him. Instinctively, she knew that he was closer to the blonde. Diana was surprised that every evening Aunt Sigaut came for a chat with her mother and continued to treat her like the daughter-in-law to be.

Diana had become edgy, because Lolo gave her a complex.

She felt inadequate and not fashionable enough for Ben Hur.

And if, by chance, Diana's mother teased her about Ben Hur like before, she would snap back, much to her mother's surprise.

Blind to Diana's agony, Ben Hur was happy with Lolo, his friends, and fashion school. Often, he took the key to Juliet's apartment, which was kept with his father's office papers, and sneaked into the apartment with Lolo. They made love on the floor, oblivious to the prophet Elijah watching them from the poster on the wall.

Every evening, their idyllic existence came to an end and they parted in silence as they realized that their problems remained unsolved.

After four semesters, design students had to undertake six months of office work. Not willing to be separated, Ben Hur and his friends decided to work together in Bombay, which also meant living together in an apartment.

When the plans were finalized, Ben Hur felt he was on top of the world; at last he was reaching closer to his goal of becoming independent.

The night before they were to leave for Bombay, Lolo sprang a surprise on Ben Hur. He was playing basketball with the boys when his mother called him, saying there was a phone call from Lolo.

She sounded breathless, saying she wanted to see him as soon as possible.

Ben Hur rushed to her home and saw Lolo waiting for him at the door. She looked tense and troubled and told him abruptly that she was leaving for London.

He stood there staring at her in disbelief, as she stepped out of the door and asked rather wistfully, "Do you want to come with me to the airport? My taxi is waiting downstairs. I want to leave before Mr. Patel returns. My flight is at two in the morning, so I will hang around at the airport."

He just nodded and followed her zombie-like, not knowing what was happening. He helped her with the bags and while going down in the elevator, he asked, "I thought we were all leaving for Bombay tomorrow night. Yesterday, when I gave you your train ticket, you never said anything. What is happening?"

Lolo tried to soothe him by holding his hands, but they remained clenched into tight fists as he demanded, "Where do you think you are going?"

"London," she said as they got into a taxi.

"Why?"

"I did not tell you, but I had asked for office work at my mother's friend, Aunt Minal's fashion studio in London. I did not receive an answer from her for a long time as she was on tour, so I did not tell you, as I was sure I would never receive an answer. But she called this morning and I am leaving, right away. This is my great opportunity to escape and I am not losing it."

"Why were you so secretive?"

"Listen Ben," she said, sitting huddled in the corner of her seat, "if I had told you, you would have stopped me from leaving for London. Let us face facts. You know the situation with my stepfather and how hard my life has been so far. When we fell in love and you spoke about marriage, I thought it would work like a magic wand. Like the story of the princess locked in the demon's dungeon, you were like my Prince Charming and I was waiting for you to whisk me away and we would live happily ever after. But nothing like that happened, although I must give you credit for finding me temporary respite from my nightmares, as your parents made me feel welcome. At the end, I even felt your mother would have accepted me as her daughter-in-law. I know you were waiting to finish your studies and find a job, so that we could get married, but I have no more patience. Do you think we could have had a live-in relationship?"

Ben Hur stopped her. "That is exactly what we were going to do in Bombay."

Lolo looked at him quizzically, asking, "Do you really think so? Every single moment in the last two years I have wanted to move in with you, as it has been impossible with my stepfather. But, I knew that your parents would have never agreed to such an arrangement and you . . . " She stopped mid-sentence.

Ben Hur was furious, "What about me? I have been most supportive. I was always there for you. I even convinced my father and he gave me permission to see you. He could have created hell for me, but he did not, he understood. If you remember, he did not even want me to do fashion design and was pushing me into engineering.

No doubt, I have not spoken to my mother, as she is an old-fashioned woman and it would have taken some time to explain everything to her."

"Why?" she asked sarcastically, "When I had already agreed to convert to your religion, about which I know hardly anything. Why did your father say that we had to wait till you had a job? Would he have said that if I had been Jewish?"

"Yes, because earlier it was a normal practice to marry our cousins even while we were teenagers, but now they insist that we get a job before we get married. Isn't it the same in any family?"

Lolo was angry and shot back, "Okay, so did you have the guts to tell your parents about my stepfather?"

"I did," said Ben Hur defiantly.

"What? That he sleeps with me?"

Ben Hur watched her aghast. All he could do was throw a nervous glance at the taxi driver and say, "How can you speak like that?"

"I can, you do not even know how I have suffered every time I went back home."

Ben Hur looked away embarrassed. "I did not know . . . "

Lolo looked at her wristwatch, they still had half an hour to go. She sighed and said, "Do you know what it means to sleep with two men in twenty-four hours, one you love and one you don't? Although I told you about my helplessness, did you ever ask me how I felt living such a dual life? You behaved normally, in some stupid dream where there was only you and me, while you knew very well that once in a while I had to succumb to the demon's demand. There were times when I wanted you to be jealous, there were times I wanted you to ask questions, there were times I wanted you to kill the demon. But you did nothing like that.

"You know Ben, what I think of you; I think you are very selfish. You were only thinking of the fun you were having, but it was at my cost.

"Do you know how many times I hoped you would be man enough and fight and liberate me? But you did not. So, I lost faith in you and when I spoke to Aunt Minal, I told her everything. I am going to live with her and she is going to look after me. If my stepfather tries to claim me, she is going to start a police case against him. Actually I need someone like Aunt Minal to look after me.

"Ben, you are a coward, but I don't blame you. After all, when we met you were just a boy, just out of school, what could you do? And I became a woman at thirteen, so there is a whole generation gap between us. Because you look up to your family, their assurance, their backing, their security, their comfort and let us face facts, without them you cannot survive.

"And, do you know, if you had told your parents about my real problems, they would have branded me a prostitute, not good enough for their son. Believe me, they would have never allowed me to enter your home. Isn't it true, Ben? Am I right? And, what do you mean by saying, 'I did not know?'"

The taxi made a turn and they were at Sardar Patel International Airport. Awkwardly, Ben got out, opened the door for her, got her a trolley, helped with her bags, and knew that it was time to bid farewell, there was no way of stopping her.

All he could do was hold her hands, kiss her cheek, and say, "Listen, Lolo, I love you. And I know you love me. It is just that . . . "

Lolo shook her head, "I pity you Ben. You are still a child."

Then suddenly she smiled, gave him a kiss full on the lips, and pulled out a packet from her bag. "This is for you, a small gift."

Quickly she walked past the gates and disappeared from his life.

Ben Hur returned home, opened the packet, and saw that it was the coat of many colors.

Ben Hur folded the coat into a small bundle and hid it in the storeroom on the topmost shelf.

Soon after, he left the fashion institute and took a break from studies.

The year after, he joined the college of engineering.

When he finished studies, his family sent a marriage proposal for Diana.

She refused and Ben Hur chose to remain a bachelor for life.

When he was thirty-seven, he changed his name from Ben Hur to Joseph and made an announcement in the local newspapers.

The older he got the more religious he became, and he was invited to lead all Hebrew prayers. So he spent a major part of life reading the Holy Scriptures.

10 Diana

Dear Ben Hur,

I am sure you will be surprised to receive this letter from me.

I suppose inviting you to my wedding reception is the ideal moment to write to you. I feel free and liberated and can say all that I have wanted to tell you for a long time. Because I have been bound to you since I was a baby.

Almost like a Chinese girl whose feet are tied from birth, so that they are tiny and seductive for her husband. All their life, Chinese women hobble and live in pain, just for the love of one man.

That is exactly what happened to me. From the day our parents decided that we would make the ideal Jewish couple, my growing-up years revolved around you.

I have happy memories of our childhood. Remember, how you taught me basketball, got me interested in cricket, and insisted on plaiting my hair? But once we grew up I felt you loathed me. Per-haps, you were looking for somebody who was smart and beautiful. I had become too familiar for you.

Now that my life has changed, I can say that you detested me because I was not beautiful like your Lolo from London.

When Uncle Ezra and Aunt Sigaut allowed your crazy group of five from fashion school to work in your room, everybody in Block

A and B of Shalom India knew that you were in love with Lolo, although your mother insisted that her name was Lata Patel and that she was just a good friend. But nobody believed her. It was obvious and I knew by instinct that there was more to your Lolo than what met the eye.

I could tell, because I have known you since we were kids.

I had some doubts, but when I saw you sneaking hand in hand with Lolo into Juliet's empty apartment for obvious reasons, I tore up the drawings of my wedding dress.

I had grown up dreaming of our wedding day.

After making innumerable sketches of wedding dresses, I had decided that I would wear a satin gown with lace trimmings embellished with sequins and pearls.

In those days, I was not bold like your Lolo, so although I would have liked to show my cleavage, I was shy about my big bust and did not have the courage to wear a dress with a low neckline, so all my drawings had high necklines.

I knew you were fond of smart clothes and I had even bought myself a magazine of western wedding dresses. I learned drawing from my best friend Anju, who was an art student.

When everybody went to bed, I would sit at the dining table and draw my wedding dress. Mother thought I was studying. I must have made about a hundred drawings, trying out different lengths, sleeves, collars, low necks, and high necks, but never satisfied, till I tore up all the sketches and decided I would wear a white sari with a veil, gloves, bangles, and heels. I came to the conclusion that I would be most comfortable in a sari.

I remember, when we were in our teens, often your eyes were glued to my breasts. I was embarrassed and covered myself with baggy tops and heavy dupattas; I knew you boys had nicknamed me busty Diana.

In those days, I hated my body, but not anymore.

I am now married to Manav and he makes me feel beautiful.

Of course I was simple, not glamorous like your Lolo. But, I had one advantage: if she was petite with a flat chest, I was taller and had an Indian goddess figure, long of limb, slim at waist, but top heavy.

I think first of all you guys never knew how to appreciate me, nor could you ever find the right word to tease me, so you all ganged together and labeled me as busty Diana.

Manav tells me that when we met for the first time he was struck by my looks, but hated the type of clothes I wore. He helped me change my style.

I saw it in your eyes when you broke up with Lolo. For a while you tried to cover up and gave the impression that you were still with Lolo.

Soon, everybody knew. As she had disappeared and you left fashion school and joined engineering college, we knew something had gone wrong in your relationship with Lolo.

From the way you started looking at me with new eyes, I could see that you had lost Lolo.

When your family at last sent the much-awaited proposal of marriage, your parents and mine were in a state of shock when I refused.

Nobody knew that I was already seeing Manav and we had decided to get married.

I was the most unlikely girl in Shalom India Housing Society to fall in love with a man from another community.

Everybody wants to know how I fell in love with Manav. I do not want to tell them the real story, but I want to tell you, just because you rejected me for Lolo.

Although we were childhood friends, when you were going steady with Lolo, you were rude and behaved as though you had conquered the moon. You made me feel I was nothing to you, not even your friend.

When I tore my wedding-dress sketches, it was the beginning of the end. I realized you did not really like me anymore.

Perhaps, you were being forced to marry me, just because we were both Jewish and our parents were not only friends, they were also related to each other. So if we had married, we would have been like our parents, bored with each other and leading a dull life. We would have had the tag of being happily married, but it would have been just another marriage of convenience.

I knew we were not made for each other.

There was also the matter of color. When we were kids I never felt I was dark, but after we grew up, there were moments when you, your family, and the entire community made me feel I was ugly just because I was dark.

While Manav tells me that he was attracted to me entirely because of my color, he thinks my skin is like black velvet.

Your mother was very fond of me, yet she often commented on my skin and gave remedies so that I would be fair of skin by the time we married. She had even spoken to Aunt Sippora to give me a fair makeup for the wedding, but she had suggested a gold makeup, which goes very well with dark skin. I smiled and made no efforts to become fair.

Your mother had this irritating habit of asking if I had tried this cream or that lotion for my skin, sometimes even suggesting that you liked fair girls like Lolo. That really hurt and I started hating my skin. These were delicate moments, when I really felt like an outsider.

Later, when it was clear that you and Lolo were lovers, you did not even speak to me. It was obvious that our unsaid engagement was broken, after which there were many offers for marriage. I went through the torture of being seen by various Bene Israel suitors from Ahmedabad, Bombay, and Israel.

They came, they made polite conversation, and left, and instinctively I knew I was like a rejected piece of surplus merchandise. Some found me too dark, others thought I was too tall, some thought I was too heavy, and someone even asked Mother if I had a squint. Then there was this nice young man studying my ankles who refused to marry me on the grounds that I had fat legs.

Of course you must remember Reuben, because he was crazy about me. But he had kept away because it was a known fact in the community that I was Uncle Ezra's daughter-in-law to be, so from a distance he kept giving me these sick looks. But when it was common knowledge that you were with Lolo, he continued to give me those sick looks but never asked me, because his mother thought I was too dark and would breed dark, fat, ugly children. So he listened to his mother, that stupid mummy's boy. Actually, you know we were always together on youth activity programs at the synagogue and I really thought he was intelligent and witty. So what if I was dark and fat, we could have been reasonably happy. We had similar likes and dislikes, including our choice of ice cream. But that was the end of the Reuben story and he continued to give me sick looks till he married Rubina.

Even now, although he is a married man, sometimes I catch him giving me those stupid, abandoned-dog looks.

But, on his own, he never moved a finger to get me.

Then, there was Uncle Ashton, Allon's father. He had sent a proposal for marriage for his son through a relative.

One evening, he came to the apartment when nobody was at home. They had all gone to the cinema and I had stayed back to finish an assignment when the doorbell rang.

It was Uncle Ashton; I always marveled at his resemblance to Hitler, only he was taller and thinner. I knew negotiations were under way between their family and ours.

I opened the door and told him that Father was not at home.

I had no intention of inviting him in, but he stood there smiling sheepishly and asking for a glass of cold water.

He came in, closed the door, and I went into the kitchen. When I returned he was sitting on the sofa watching television.

I was annoyed and sat on a chair, wondering how to get rid of him, when suddenly he was on his knees, holding my hand and asking, "Diana will you . . . "

I thought he was asking if I would marry Allon, so I reminded him that Allon did not particularly like me, and he said, "It is not about Allon. You know when I came to see you for Allon, I was struck by your beauty, you are a beautiful girl, could we . . . " His lips were almost on mine and he was caressing my breasts. I pushed him away and stood up, quickly walked to the entrance, opened the door, and asked him to leave or else I would have to call for help.

Uncle Ashton stood up, gave me a disdainful look, and the next day we received a refusal from their family.

I was relieved, but hated you for putting me in such a mess. Life had been idyllic as long as it was common knowledge that we would marry each other. So every night I said a special prayer to Eliyahu Hannabi, asking the prophet to send me a man who would love me and appreciate me.

Mother was worried about my marriage and kept talking about the refusals, especially when we were washing dishes, chopping vegetables, or stirring curry. The moment she started talking, I left the kitchen and she did not even notice that I had left the room. I felt sorry for her when I heard her talking to herself. I guessed she was worried about my future. But I did not want to encourage her as she only depressed me.

Her condition also made me realize the seriousness of the situation and I told my father that I did not want to see Jewish suitors.

I rejected every proposal my parents brought for me from India and Israel. Especially the Israeli ones. I told Father not to bother me with them, since I had been seeing how girls there have to work like slaves, both inside and outside the home.

Do you remember my cousin Thelma?

She was really ugly, shapeless, tall, big, but she had a heart of gold. She did not receive a marriage proposal till she was forty. I must tell you that she was a romantic at heart. She imagined she would have a fairy-tale wedding with her Prince Charming, make a dream house, and live happily ever after. So when Aunt Irene sent her nephew Jethro to India with the sole idea of getting them married, Thelma was happy. She came rushing to tell me about the possibility of an early marriage at forty, not bad, she laughed. She was an architect and a good one at that; she had her own office and was known to have done some very artistic interiors. I had just been disillusioned with you, so I advised her that she did not need a husband. Because she had told me that Jethro was an elderly twice-married electrician. Nobody knew anything about him except that he belonged to a Bene Israel family.

I was worried, but she was so happy with the idea of marriage that it was difficult to talk to her.

At the wedding they looked odd, she ugly, but stylish, and he an uncouth blue-collar type, making stupid jokes at the mehendi ceremony. He had all the qualities I dislike in men.

Thelma's dreams were shattered in a year. She wrote that all she did was clean the house, wash clothes, cook, and shop. It was a backbreaking job and to add to that Jethro did not trust her to work in an architect's office. He was the lord and master and she could not possibly earn more than him, nor have a higher status. She had to be the doormat. Thelma was stuck in a situation she could not handle and her photographs showed that she had lost weight and looked unhappy.

After a year, Thelma returned to India with the incredible story that Jethro was a wife beater and, according to the law of Israel, she had lodged a complaint with the police. Once he was behind bars she had returned to India and filed the divorce papers and now had to start again from scratch.

Then, there was the bride who was sent to Israel to marry her cousin and did not know that he was half blind. Once there, she could not cancel the wedding, and worked as a maid in other houses to look after her husband and two children.

Not all such marriages have gone wrong, because there are happier stories of couples of our community, who are settled in Israel and doing well.

I did not want a fairy-tale marriage, and chose to make my own life and informed my parents that I wanted to concentrate on a career.

I enrolled for post-graduate studies in psychology, hoping I would eventually work with the mentally challenged. But the classes were in the morning and I was free in the afternoons and did not know what to do with myself.

It was around this time that I saw an advertisement in the newspaper which said that a modeling agency was looking for an English-speaking part-time telephone operator. The only qualifications were for the candidate to be presentable, a graduate, and to speak English.

I got the job and that is where I met Manav.

Manav came from Bombay every alternate week as a trainer.

He was different from any man I had known before. I had just learned to speak normally to men, without blushing and feeling funny in my stomach.

He was dashing and so comfortable with himself that I felt inadequate in his presence. He was taller than me and always wore loose blue jeans sliding down over his hips with skin-tight black tee shirts. He is good looking in a strange way; he has a sharp, beak-like nose, big black eyes, sunken cheeks, and big broad lips. Actually he is funny, but he rarely smiles. And, ah yes! He is very fair and has a crew cut, which makes him look bald. The first time my parents met him, they were in a state of shock, but he put them at ease and now they like him so much that they have forgotten all about you and their dreams of a Jewish wedding for me.

So what if all my dreams of that beautiful Jewish wedding are shattered? My love story moved so fast that I am sure you will think it more fiction than fact. I am sure you never thought I would fall in love so quickly with someone like Manav.

But that is exactly what happened.

Perhaps Eliyahu Hannabi was up to mischief on that particular day.

Whenever Manav was in Ahmedabad, he made it a habit to sit at my table and hold his class right there with the students sitting in front of him on the floor. He said it was his favorite room as there was an open window on the left, framing a champa tree. He said he did not like closed classrooms; he likes his surroundings to be open, full of light, joy, and fun, like himself.

So as he sat there teaching I had a grand view of his shapely backside and shoulders. I was so embarrassed and nervous when the phone rang that I just grabbed it, never allowing it to ring longer lest it disturb him, but he was so cool that slowly I started relaxing and listening to all that he was saying about the body, self-esteem, and self-confidence.

I enjoyed his lessons.

A new world was opening up for me.

During one such session, during the lunch break, Rima, a tiny girl with a round face, could not get her walk right and was practicing right next to my table, asking my advice as I sat there eating jamuns.

So I wiped my hands and started walking with her, up and down the room, showing her how models walked, as I had watched Manav day after day. When Rima got her walk right, I felt happy and danced my way to my chair. That was when I heard someone clap. It was Manav.

He thought I was good and asked me if I would model for his next show in Bombay. He felt I was a natural. Then, much to my embarrassment, he walked up to me, came very close to me, touched my lips with his finger, and said the color suited me, they were tinged a deep purple, the color of fruit.

I rushed to the washroom and studied my reflection in the mirror: my face looked different with nature's very own lipstick. I washed my face and returned back to my chair, my face flushed and heart racing.

Yes, I wanted to become a model, but refused, just because my parents would never approve. Somehow Manav convinced my parents.

I loved modeling and wearing beautiful clothes. I was flattered, as Manav and his team felt I was lithe, graceful, and carried off Indian wear to perfection. The money was good and I learned the ropes quickly.

My parents were unhappy, but I told them I was deeply hurt with all the insults I had received from my reluctant Bene Israel grooms. I even told them about the incident with Uncle Ashton and they gave me permission to go to Bombay. Manav convinced them that I would be safe when we traveled to other cities. I was excited, as I had never traveled anywhere but to Bombay. So, I modeled for shows in Bombay, Bangalore, Calcutta, Chennai and there were more offers for shows in London, Milan, and New York.

One show led to the other and I went everywhere. Each show gave me the confidence I had lacked all my life. I was popular and always in demand.

Manav helped me change. My waist-length hair was crimped, curled, and highlighted with copper streaks. I wore jeans with short tops and was no longer ashamed of my bust. The makeup was subtle and Manav insisted I wear dark shades of lipstick, so that my face resembled an African mask.

Life was like a roller-coaster ride, and sometimes I stopped and wondered at the way my life had moved from Shalom India Housing Society to the fashion ramps of the world.

My parents were happy that I earned my own living and was doing well. And with the money I sent home they bought new furniture and painted the apartment; it looked good.

The only sorrow which tinged their otherwise happy existence was that we did not see each other as often as we would have liked to.

Sometimes when I was back home at Shalom India, I saw you and waved breezily, making it a point never to stop. I had no feelings for you, not even pity. You looked bent, old, depressed, and boring in your synthetic suits.

The tables had been turned on you. In fact, you were supposed to be the bright star of the fashion world, but I had beaten you to it.

By this time, Manav and I had fallen in love and decided to get married.

It was at a fashion show of bridal wear in Agra, on a full moon night with the Taj Mahal as a backdrop. The music was soft and romantic.

I was wearing a white strapless ankle-length gown with a gold bodice and a sari-like gossamer veil attached, high heels, and had flowers strung in my hair. It was similar to the dresses I had dreamt about. I was eventually to wear one not as your bride, but as Manav's.

One of the assistants whispered that I had only two entries, one in the beginning, the other at the end, when normally I had seven to eight entries. So, I took it easy and waited. The last entry was to be on Manav's arm. He was wearing a long white overcoat, double lapelled and quilted at the collar, a purple silk shirt underneath, and white linen trousers.

Manav was watching me; there was something intense in his eyes as we held hands. Halfway through on the ramp, he leaned over and asked me if I would marry him.

I just smiled, flushed with excitement.

I did not remember anything, my parents, religion, family, community, or Shalom India Housing Society.

It was a magical moment.

There were just the two of us in the entire universe, standing against the Taj Mahal, under a full moon. Manav led me to the car and the chauffeur drove us to a small Arya Samaj temple, where we were married in a simple ceremony.

Everything took place in silence; we did not feel the need for words.

We returned to a boisterous party, where Manav announced our wedding. As the champagne flowed, I was elated with happiness. Manav called my parents and gave me the cell phone; I told them I had married Manav. With voices quivering with emotion, they blessed us.

I was not sure how our community would react to the wedding, but they are a kind and large-hearted people.

When we returned to Ahmedabad for the reception, the Jewish community came with gifts and flowers. They were so nice that they even accepted the fact that like a Hindu bride I had sindoor in the center parting of my hair. And, they were pleased that I was wearing a chain with a Star of David pendant and a mangalsutra with the hexagonal bead worn by Jewish brides.

Now, as I fly between the fashion capitals of the world, memories of you sometimes come to me as a flash and I feel sorry for you. Thank you for having abandoned me for Lolo.

Now I am my own person, with my own life. This would not have been possible had I married you. I would have been your obedient wife like my mother or yours. I must thank you for having ignored me, because till I was sixteen or seventeen my world began and ended with you.

When you were in love with Lolo I was hurt, but from then onwards I stopped living in daydreams, made a career for myself, and found a man who really loves me.

Once in a while, when I feel guilty about forgetting that I am Jewish, I make it a point to visit synagogues in whichever country I may be. I always fast on Yom Kippur, so that God forgives me for what he considers wrong.

And on full moon nights, I thank Eliyahu Hannabi for giving me Manav and his love.

That's all for now. For years, I wanted to write to you; after all, we grew up together, didn't we?

Best wishes, from Diana.

P.S. By the way, I forgot to mention that I met Lolo at a fashion show in London. She did not recognize me, but she is doing very well. She has a boutique in London, where she caters to Asian brides and has a good reputation as a designer.

I am sure you want to know about her personal life, but I do not know anything. Next time, perhaps, I can find out about her; that is, if you want to know. D.

Ben Hur never answered Diana and never asked for news about Lolo.

When she was visiting her parents at Shalom India, Diana was surprised when one afternoon the doorbell rang and she opened the door and saw Ben Hur. He stood at the door, looking haggard and ridiculous with his thinning hennaed hair, and refused her invitation for a cup of tea, saying he had to prepare for the next day's lecture. He gave her a brown paper bag, saying it was a wedding gift for her.

He moved a step backward when impulsively she thanked him and tried to kiss him on the cheek.

When she made a gesture to open the packet, he stopped her and asked her to open it when she was alone.

Then, he turned round and went to the elevator and disappeared, his hand raised in adieu.

With a heavy heart Diana closed the door, sat down on the sofa, and opened the packet. It was the coat of many colors.

11 Ezra

Ezra had given up on Ben Hur.

He had made innumerable pleas to Eliyahu Hannabi to find Ben Hur a Jewish bride. The prophet never answered; he seemed to have gone deaf where Ben Hur was concerned.

Ezra cursed the day Lolo had entered their lives, and the day they lost Diana to Manav.

Ben Hur was not the only problem of his life; he had five housing schemes in different areas of Ahmedabad, which meant he spent hours going from one site to another. Then there were small problems to be solved at Shalom India Housing Society, like water shortage, leaks, and clogged gutters. To add to his troubles, he had received an e-mail from Juliet. She wanted to sell her apartment.

> Dear Uncle Ezra,
>   Shalom.
>   You will be surprised to receive a letter from me after such a long time. But ever since we came to Israel it has been difficult as we could not find work immediately and we also had to learn Hebrew at the Ulpan. So, we were staying with Aunt Hannah. We have at last found a small apartment in Dimona in south Israel and have settled down. We are both working

in the kitchen of King David Hotel. It is a hard life, as Romiel has night duty and I work during the day, so we see each other at odd hours. We also have financial difficulties, and to make ends meet, I take catering orders from Indian homes for snacks and sweets. Sometimes I also supply Indian food for small parties. Last week, I did something bigger, catering for an Indian wedding. We both enjoy cooking and God willing, Uncle, I hope one day we will have our own restaurant in Israel. Because it looks as though we are going to live in Israel. After days of discussion, both Romiel and I have come to the conclusion that we can only survive in Israel if we sell our apartment in Shalom India Housing Society.

We feel a little sad about this, as it was a gift to us from both our parents. And, it also means we may never return to India. Yes of course we will come to see everybody, once in two years if possible. Soon after our marriage, we were not sure whether we wanted to make a home in India or Israel, so as a beginning it was good to stay in our own home at Shalom India Housing Society.

When we first came to Israel, I was not very sure whether Romiel would settle down. But he is doing well and is better adjusted than me. He is fluent in Hebrew and has made many friends at the hotel. He is taking their advice about loans and other legal matters we should know if we want to start an Indian restaurant in Israel. We have not made up our mind about the location and are undecided between Tel Aviv, Jerusalem, Haifa, or we may even go to a smaller place.

The cost of living is very high in Israel, so we would need to invest all our money in this venture. The financial implications are immense. And so we need to sell our apartment in India. I know I am asking too much of you, because it means a lot of work, but I assure you my father will help you. I have written to him and also to my father-in-law. They have promised to help. The papers of our apartment and other details are with my father. Please keep us informed as to what is being done in the matter.

I know you are a very discerning person, dear Uncle, and we want you to make the final decision about the sale of the

apartment. In case you need the power of attorney, do let me know.
Thank you very much Uncle Ezra, for being there for us.
With best wishes to everybody at home,
Yours affectionately,
Juliet

After consultations with Abraham and Abhiram, Ezra put an advertisement in the local newspapers for the sale of A-107 in Shalom India Housing Society. But there were few takers, because most people assumed that only non-vegetarians lived in Shalom India.

Yet most prospective buyers came to see the apartment on Sundays, much to Ezra's annoyance. He hated wasting his Sunday mornings, but that was the only day Abraham and Abhiram and the buyers were free.

Some families saw the apartment, liked it, and then refused to buy it. They saw religious artifacts on the doors, like mezuzahs and stars, and did not know whether "Jew" was a caste or a religion. To add to their confusion, they saw Bene Israel women cooking elaborate lunches. The unusual smells of meat and fish dishes wafted down the stairs. In turn, the Jewish women resented it that strangers peeped into their apartments and felt the strangers were encroaching upon their privacy.

Every week, Ezra sat on the packing case in A-107, sacrificing his precious Sunday morning to show the finer points of the apartment to prospective buyers, as the prophet smiled knowingly from the poster on the wall.

It appeared the prophet had his own plans for the apartment; perhaps he wanted to make it his permanent abode.

Ezra screened all the offers and finally decided upon Raghubir Chopra, who was willing to pay the full sum. Chopra lived in New Jersey in the United States and had not yet seen the apartment, but his nephew had sent him all the details.

Before finalizing the deal, Ezra called a meeting of the Jewish residents of Block A to discuss whether he should start negotiations to sell Juliet's apartment to a non-Jew.

He invited one elder from each family to his apartment. As Sigaut passed around glasses of rose sherbet, Ezra read aloud Juliet's

letter and said he had put the apartment up for sale and had received
an offer from a Raghubir Chopra of New Jersey, who was planning
to return to India. Ezra said the offer was good, but he did not want
to make the final decision alone, because it meant Chopra would be
the only non-Jewish resident of Block A, and he wanted their
approval before the final deal was made. For Juliet, the money was
more important than the person who lived there, and anyway the
constitution of Shalom India was secular and there was no rule that
the apartment could not be sold to non-Jews.

No doubt, after the riots of 2002, they had decided to live
together. But the community was so small that it had been difficult
to get enough Jewish families to fill Block A. Ezra had eventually
decided to accept other communities for Block B, like Christians
and Parsis who were looking for a mixed society.

It was for all these reasons that the offer from Chopra needed
discussion. Ezra expressed his doubts, which were confirmed by
reactions like, "Since we came here, we have been living like a family, wonder how we will feel with a Punjabi amidst us?" "We should
have Jewish residents in Block A and other communities in Block
B," and "Is there an empty apartment in Block B?"

"No."

"It would have been perfect to give Chopra an apartment in
Block B, and we could look for a Jewish tenant for Juliet's apartment."

"There is hardly anybody left, there are three families who live
near the synagogue, four live in apartments they bought in the sixties, seven have bungalows, we are here and the rest have left for
Israel. This Punjabi gentleman is willing to pay the entire amount,
no loans, nothing. We could find a Jewish tenant who could pay in
small installments, but Juliet needs the money immediately, so we
cannot rent the apartment out to a Jewish family."

"In that case, Chopra's offer is ideal."

"Perhaps we could ask Chopra to give her the amount in Israel,
in dollars, so that we don't have to go through the hassle of money
transfers. That would be a great help to dear Juliet."

"So, we all agree to sell the apartment to Chopra . . . ?"

"I suppose yes, but, er . . . I was just wondering if he has children?"

"Maybe."

"Do you know what age?"

"No. I never thought of asking."

"I was just worried, what if Chopra has young sons and daughters?"

"Why do you ask?"

"Because, just in case . . . "

"Nothing to worry, see how well our Juliet managed the whole problem or for that matter even Diana . . . "

"I don't think we need to worry about such matters. He may be a bachelor or a widower. Instead, shall we start worrying about our single women? If we do not make a decision right now, we may never find such a good buyer later. If we agree, I will call a meeting of the executive committee right away and finalize the matter. What do you say?"

"Sounds good."

12 Ezel

On Passover night, the prophet had felt worried about Ezel, sitting all alone on the balcony and calling out to him.

The year before he had not been alone. His wife Tamar had been in the apartment with the two children, Amy, aged six, and four-year-old Benny. The seder table had been overflowing with food and drink.

Later that year, during the Hanukah fancy dress competition, Amy and Benny had dressed as Radha and Krishna, and Ezel had shot the whole ceremony with his handycam.

Soon after, Tamar had left Ezel.

When Ezel received an invitation for Hannukah, he decided to brave it out. But as soon as he stepped into the synagogue, he saw Samuel's twins dressed as Radha and Krishna, and was reminded of Benny and Amy. And all he wanted to do was rush back home, make himself a stiff drink, and forget them.

Instead, he kept smiling and did not show that he was missing his family.

At Shalom India Housing Society, everybody knew Tamar had left Ezel. But they were sympathetic and did not want to hurt him by asking obvious questions. Ezra did not particularly like him, but he had gone out of his way and invited him to be one of the judges for the fancy dress competition.

Ezel agreed, but when the competition started, his eyes brimmed with tears watching the children and he left on the pretext of a smoke.

Months later, after that lonely Passover evening, he beat a similar retreat during the Rosh Hashanah or New Year's Eve prayers.

In the six o'clock traffic, he was driving his scooter like a madman, not sure where he was going. Then suddenly he was enveloped in a cloud of black smoke from the exhaust of a truck speeding by, and had to veer to the right and stop. He pulled out his handkerchief and wiped his face.

Ezel had stopped at Chalte Pir ki Dargah near Delhi Gate Char Rasta. He did not know how he had landed at the shrine of the Walking Saint. Through the heavy evening traffic, he could see Rani Rupmati's mosque, the sandstone domes shining in the halogen lights.

The small box-like Shrine of the Walking Saint had an ornate blue grill and stood at an oblique angle next to the pavement, almost in the middle of the road. Innumerable rags and strings were tied to the grill. The grave was covered with a green cloth and bright red roses. He had heard from friends that wishes made on Thursday evenings at this shrine were often answered by speed mail.

Standing there in the traffic, Ezel felt lost, lonely, and desperate, so he tore up his handkerchief and tied a strip to the grill, asking the saint for the return of his wife and children.

Then, feeling stupid, he returned to his scooter, made a quick turn and rode towards Mirzapur, past the cycle-repair shops, helmet shops, St. Xavier's School with its church, the grotto with the Madonna of Lourdes, and Famous Samosa Shop, where he brought his scooter to a screeching halt. He ordered a plate of non-kosher mutton samosas. Did it matter to anyone whether he ate kosher meat or nothing at all?

It was 8:30, perhaps snacks were being served at the synagogue, but he had no stomach to meet the Jewish community. The samosa shop was sooty, gloomy, and smoky as the piping hot samosas were drained in a huge colander and packed, or served on tin plates on grubby sky-blue Formica tables.

Ezel was of two minds. Tamar would have never approved of his eating in such a dirty place. So he almost asked the man at the counter to pack the samosas, then changed his mind, not liking the idea that Tamar still ruled over him. Ezel shared the bench with two workers and ordered a plate of samosas with two warm maska buns.

He ate slowly, relishing the samosas and thinking about Benny and Amy, who were perhaps already in bed. Tamar was very strict about their bedtime.

Ezel looked at the clock above the counter. It was almost 8:45 and he could see the children in their grandfather's apartment in Bandra with the heavy silk drapes, pearl-pink walls, fresh flowers, the menorah on the wall, and the Sabbath lamps on a side table. He wondered whether Benny and Amy were allowed to play and make a mess with their toys and books in the neat and orderly home where everything went like clockwork. Perhaps not, as every evening Tamar took them down to the public garden to play.

Their dinnertime was at seven thirty and Ezel was sure Benny and Amy sometimes protested, or perhaps they would just behave themselves, afraid of their grandfather. Feeding the children had always been a matter of disagreement between Ezel and Tamar, which often led to quarrels.

After a long day, when he reached home at eight, the children were washed, powdered, and dressed in their nightgowns, waiting to kiss him goodnight. They would giggle, laugh, and climb all over him, with Tamar calling out to them irritably.

Ezel ached for the children and could not eat any more.

He returned home, taking the longest route, from Gandhi Bridge to Ellis Bridge to Gujarat College, Mithakali Circle, Law College, Manekbaug Hall, from where he turned into the lane leading to Shalom India Housing Society.

He regretted returning to the apartment. It was dark and lonely since everybody was at the synagogue and he felt weighed down with grief as he unlocked the door.

The weather was warm, but Ezel was cold when he entered the apartment. He left the packet of leftover samosas on the table and started looking for a sweater.

Ezel had depended on Tamar to hand him everything from socks

Ezel

to keys. He looked everywhere, but could not find his sweater and started pulling out the clothes from the cupboard.

In the process, he found a bottle of rum. He smiled, retrieved the samosas, sat on the bed, pulled on his socks, wore a monkey-cap, covered himself with a quilt, drank straight from the bottle of rum, and sat there eating the samosas.

Feeling better and still wearing the quilt like the prophet Elijah's cloak, Ezel opened the door to the balcony and slumped down in the colonial chair he had inherited from his grandfather. He sat there drinking and nibbling at a samosa. Between ten thirty and eleven he heard his neighbors returning from the synagogue and was jealous at the sound of their easy laughter.

Around midnight, he saw the lights in Block B of Shalom India Housing Society being switched off one after another, all except that of Franco Fernandes. At midnight, Ezel saw him standing on the balcony and playing his violin.

It was like a ritual and Ezel related to him. They were two of a kind.

In the silence of the night, Franco's violin could be heard loud and clear. There was something sad about his music and Ezel started feeling hot, as though he were running a fever, and then ran to the bathroom and was violently sick. Half an hour later, he sat in his underwear in the dark bedroom, head throbbing, watching a Hindi film with tears running down his cheeks. He tried to find a handkerchief and in the flickering light he suddenly saw the poster of the prophet Elijah looking down at him.

Ezel lay on the bed watching the prophet, wondering why the chariot appeared to be moving, till he fell asleep rolled in the bedclothes.

He slept fitfully for two hours, when suddenly a shrill sound seemed to knife through his troubled dreams. At first it sounded like an electric drill, then like a distant banging, then like a fax machine, and eventually like a doorbell, when he suddenly sat up with the realization that the telephone was ringing.

Ezel reached for the phone hidden somewhere in the bedclothes. He was in a panic, as it sounded like a long-distance call and he was sure it was bad news about the children. So he started throwing the clothes on the floor till he found the phone. He picked it up, repeating his hellos like one who had lost his senses, and suddenly became alert when he heard his father-in-law at the other end sounding cool and collected. "Hello Ezel, this is Moses, how are you, sorry to disturb you at this hour. Tamar is leaving for Israel. But she is not taking the children. We have been talking about it all night and feel that you, as their father, could keep Benny and Amy till Tamar makes arrangements for them to join her in Israel. Will you . . . ?"

"Of course," said Ezel smiling, "I am leaving right now. By the way, Happy New Year."

Ezel checked his wallet, his cash, his credit card and his cell phone, pulled on his jeans and a tee shirt, slipped on his shoes, and rushed to the station to catch the early morning train to Bombay.

Ezel bought the newspaper at the station, ordered a hot cup of coffee, jumped on the train and sat down feeling elated at the thought of seeing his children. Then he dozed, half asleep, half awake, thinking about Tamar.

He had first seen Tamar at the Tifereth Synagogue in Bombay at his cousin Shirley's wedding. She was one of two bridesmaids.

She was wearing an aqua-blue shot-silk figure-hugging gown, was short, plump, had straight long hair which reached her waist, and was wearing gold stilettos to match the gold choker round her neck.

At that very moment, Ezel decided that if he ever married, it would be to Tamar. Looking at her intently, he realized he was dreaming about the impossible. Tamar appeared to have a lot of class, while he was just a simpleton from Alibaug who had made it big in the competitive world of software.

Ezel was then commuting between Alibaug and Bombay. Life was hectic: his day started early and he returned home late, exhausted. Often he stayed back in Bombay at a friend's house. His days were a big roller-coaster ride, until he was allotted a company apartment and decided to leave Alibaug and start a new life in Bombay. His mother, Malkha, refused to leave Alibaug, saying she would not know what to do with herself, since his office hours were long.

Life would be easier, but it was not an easy decision to leave his mother, because his father had died of a heart attack when Ezel was not yet eighteen. Together, mother and son had gone through thick and thin. Malkha had discovered on the day of her husband Samson's funeral that he had left behind an enormous debt that he had kept hidden from her. She had to sell part of their property to pay the debts and kept the remaining money in fixed deposits for Ezel's education.

When Ezel moved into his Bombay apartment, Malkha did not stop him, nor did she show regret. She kissed him and reassured him that she had been looking forward to the day when he would become independent. She was still working as a schoolteacher and she promised they would see each other often.

Malkha kept her promise. Often, when he least expected it, she would be there in the apartment. As he turned the key in the lock, from the sound of the radio he knew that she was in the apartment. It warmed his heart.

The apartment would be cleaned, the mess cleared without complaint, and the table laid with clean plates and hot food.

They would spend a quiet evening eating, exchanging notes about daily matters, and watching television.

Once in a while, she irritated him by picking up the topic of marriage, insisting that a man with a good job needed a wife. When he refused to answer, she stopped her matchmaking games, changed the subject, and amused him with Alibaug gossip.

Ezel missed his mother, but did not show it, because he knew they were both learning to live alone and did not want to make things difficult for each other. He made it a point to spend alternate weekends with her. This decision was comforting for both and whenever he returned to Bombay she packed boxes of food and snacks to last him a week.

On one such visit, Malkha casually mentioned that she had met a Jewish girl at a friend's house, who had a masters in computers, was beautiful, and perhaps he would like her.

She was expecting him to flare up when he surprised her by saying, "What if I show you a better girl for your son?"

Malkha was all smiles, "So, you have chosen your bride?"

"Yes, do you remember Shirley's wedding and her bridesmaid, the one in a tight dress?"

The smile disappeared from Malkha's face. "Are you sure?"

"Absolutely."

"That was Tamar. If she is the girl of your choice, it worries me."

"Why?"

"For a simple reason, that she does not belong to our world."

"What do you mean? We are all Jews."

"I know Tamar, because she is Shirley's friend. I never expected you to be attracted to someone like her."

"What do you mean, someone like her?" he asked, annoyed.

Since Ezel had shifted to Bombay, Malkha had been badgering him about prospective brides. And the moment he chose one for himself, she had problems with his choice.

Malkha seemed to read his thoughts. "Of course I like Tamar. But we are simple people. And you know how we have scraped through life. But Tamar has been born with a golden spoon. She has lived a protected and luxurious life, she is very smart and fashionable, so I wonder if she will like a family like ours. Let us send a proposal according to tradition, and see if her father agrees to meet us. Her mother died last year."

"Aai, why have you suddenly become so conscious about class? What if I had agreed to marry that super-stylish female from Israel?"

"Because she was like one of us, fashionable but working class. While Tamar belongs to a rich family. Their lifestyle is different from ours, so . . . "

"Why don't you speak to Shirley and at least send the proposal, then we will see."

"I am so worried; we do not have the finances for a grand wedding."

"Aai, stop it, these are minor matters. If a man and woman like each other, nothing matters, everything else falls into place."

"Since when did you become a philosopher?"

"Since I fell in love."

"Okay, tomorrow I will go to Bombay and speak to Shirley."

Shirley gave them the green light and said that Tamar was a sweet person. She worked as an art teacher in a Bombay school. When her mother had taken ill, Tamar was on her way to Israel to study art, but had decided against it when her mother died.

Malkha sent a proposal through Shirley's parents and waited for a reply. Ezel was on pins till Shirley called, saying that Tamar's father Moses had approved of the match. Since his wife had died recently, he wanted his daughter to be closer to him. But Tamar wanted to meet Ezel before the final decision was made.

The train had reached Surat, and Ezel woke from his reverie, aching for Tamar and feeling edgy. So he stood up, stretched and went to the bathroom. The reflection in the mirror showed a lean old man with a bald pate.

He smiled, because he looked like a traveling salesman.

Seven years back, he had looked different. He had a mop of thick black hair, broad shoulders and wore tee shirts over jeans. His face was strong-jawed, had a determined look and sometimes people mistook him for a wrestler. In an otherwise good-looking face, he knew, his receding chin made him look ordinary.

As prescribed in romances, after the first meeting in a restaurant in Bombay, followed by long walks, candle-lit dinners, and the hasty first kiss at her door, Ezel asked Tamar if she would marry him. Tamar accepted the proposal. Moses had convinced her that Ezel was the perfect match for her. It would be hard to find somebody like him in the Bene Israel community.

Moses wanted to celebrate the wedding with a grand reception at the Taj Mahal Hotel, but respected Malkha's wishes and the couple was married at the Tifereth Synagogue where Ezel had seen Tamar the first time. The wedding was followed by a small reception, the expenses of which were shared by bride and groom.

But Tamar's father did have a small party at the Turf Club, for which the groom learned the waltz. Close friends still remembered that Ezel had danced very well as he led his wife to the dance floor.

Ezel and Tamar started their married life in the company apartment in Navi Mumbai and Malkha went back to her cottage in Alibaug.

From the very beginning, it was clear that mother-in-law and daughter-in-law did not like each other. They did not agree about anything—what to cook, what to wear, whom to meet, and how to set the table. Tamar detested the fact that all Ezel's sentences started with "You know, Aai likes this or that . . . Aai makes it this way or that way," etc.

Sensing trouble, Malkha stopped visiting Ezel.

Instead, Ezel went to see his mother in Alibaug on Saturday mornings and would return by evening. Sometimes Tamar accompanied him or spent time with her father and Ezel picked her up on the way back in the evening. Whenever Tamar visited Malkha, she was cordial but never warm.

On Sundays, Tamar would invite her friends or close relatives for an elaborate lunch and after they left, the couple either went to the cinema or a restaurant, or just stayed home and watched television.

Tamar never invited Malkha to her Sunday luncheons, almost as though she were ashamed of her simple mother-in-law.

Ezel noticed the cold relationship between the two women and did not know how to bring them closer.

But he continued to call his mother every night at nine, just before the news, it warmed Malkha's heart but annoyed Tamar.

Malkha kept away for six months, then decided to mend fences with Tamar. It was one of those days when she was lonely and did not particularly like the idea of spending the Sabbath all alone, so she took a bus from the expressway and arrived at Ezel's apartment at four in the afternoon. She still had the extra key.

When Tamar returned from school, she heard the radio and instinctively knew that her mother-in-law was in the apartment. She rang the bell and Malkha opened the door and stood there smiling, her sari hitched up, the pallav tucked in at her waist, and her hair flying about her face.

Tamar was annoyed, not amused that Malkha had taken the liberty of entering her apartment.

Without looking at her, she threw her bag on the sofa and went to the bathroom. She noticed that the apartment was swept clean, the clutter put away, old newspapers had been tied up and put away for the pastiwallah, the shoes were arranged in a corner, the bed sheets and towels changed, the clothes ironed, folded, and put away. And from the aroma emanating from the kitchen, Tamar knew she had already cooked their dinner, fish curry and rice.

Tamar's favorite tablecloth had been spread over the dining table; a loaf of fresh bread was kept covered for the prayers along with a glass of wine and a plate of salt. Tamar saw that her best glassware, silver, and china had been arranged on the table with the Sabbath candle-stands.

Tamar did not say a word, but locked herself in the bathroom and stood there with clenched fists, trying to control her temper.

She hated this uncouth village woman, her mother-in-law.

How dare she touch her precious linen and tableware?

Tamar emerged from the bathroom and saw Malkha had made tea for her and was asking if she would like some fried bombils with tea. That was the beginning of a fight, as Tamar taunted, "Since when did we start eating bombils with tea? I like ordinary things like biscuits and cakes."

That evening, when Ezel reached home, he saw his wife screaming at his mother. Malkha was sitting on the sofa, her face covered with her sari and sobbing. A cup of tea and a plate of bombils were lying untouched on the dining table. The sentence which hit Ezel was Tamar calling his mother a village bumpkin.

Ezel threw his bag on the floor and shook Tamar angrily. "You don't speak to my mother like that. If she is a village bumpkin, what am I?"

"The same," said Tamar and stomped out of the apartment.

As Ezel held his mother in his arms and allowed her to cry, their entire life together passed before his eyes.

Malkha was still sobbing and asked him, "Please stop Tamar. It was my fault. I did not feel like spending the Sabbath all alone and I wanted to see you."

Malkha was shaken by the incident and wanted to return to Alibaug. She washed her face, wiped it, shook her head, and said, "This is no longer my home."

Ezel tried to explain, "Aai don't be upset, forget her tantrums, why don't you stay with us? You don't have to live alone in Alibaug."

Malkha moved away from Ezel. "Live here, as your wife's maidservant? No thank you, I have my own life in Alibaug. I go to school, I teach, and have a social life with Jewish families and my students' parents. Sometimes I go to the synagogue if there is a service. Before you were married, I often came here. While I waited for you, I cleaned the apartment and cooked for you. Today, I assumed that the apartment would be neat and clean, as you have a wife. But as soon as I entered I saw there was chaos everywhere. So I thought I would surprise Tamar by putting some order to the mess. But then my good intentions just boomeranged . . . " Malkha combed her hair, arranged her sari, and prepared to leave.

Ezel was sitting at the dining table eating bombils with the cold tea. Malkha could not help but smile, "You are the original village bumpkin, eating bombils with tea!"

He smiled, "Come Aai, light the Sabbath candles and let us eat your fish curry and rice."

Stubbornly Malkha shook her head and said, "No, son, not in your wife's home."

As she reached the door, Ezel followed her, saying, "I am coming with you."

Malkha hesitated, "Don't you think you should stay home and wait for Tamar?"

Decisively, he led her out of the apartment, saying, "We are going home together."

The house in Alibaug was small and comfortable with a rose garden in front and a single toddy tree, and a vegetable patch in the backyard amongst tall coconut and areca nut trees. The returns from these were good and Malkha led a simple but comfortable life.

In the past whenever she felt lonely she would rush to Bombay. After the showdown with Tamar, she knew that she could not possibly enter her son's home unannounced.

Malkha prepared the Sabbath table, lit the candle, Ezel said the Kiddush hurriedly and went to the television to watch a cricket match as she returned to the kitchen to make dinner. She looked into the fridge and saw that she still had some bombils, tomatoes, and a loaf of bread. As she fried the bombils, she heard the doorbell and called out to Ezel to open the door. All she could hear were the cheering crowds at the match. Curious to see who was at the door, she came and saw Tamar standing there with her father Moses. Ezel had barred the door with his hands, he was telling them to return to Bombay.

Malkha rushed to the door, asked Ezel to move away, and respectfully invited Tamar and Moses into the house. She saw Tamar's eyes were swollen and still wet with tears and Moses appeared to be angry with his daughter.

As they sat at the dining table, Moses apologized on his daughter's behalf and shamefacedly Tamar looked up at Malkha and apologized, "Sorry Aai, for being so rude."

Malkha held her in her arms and kissed her, as Tamar sobbed, "Really Aai, I am very sorry. It is just that I had had a hard day and was not expecting you. Also, I must admit that I was ashamed that the apartment was in a mess and you put things away, so I felt you were trying to taunt me and I exploded."

"That is not true," growled Ezel without looking up and Malkha tried to cover up by saying, "Come on Ezel, I would feel the same if I was in Tamar's place."

"And what about the village bumpkin stuff? Just because you guys left Alibaug long back and became smart Bombayites, does it make my mother a low-caste Jew? Why did you call her names?"

That was when Moses intervened, "I apologize on behalf of my daughter. She should not have spoken like that to her mother-in-law. I am really sorry, please forgive her, Ezel. She is still young and does not know the ways of the world."

Tamar was in tears. "Ezel, I am really sorry, I will not hurt your mother ever again, believe me, promise . . . "

Malkha felt she needed to change the subject, so she spoke softly to Ezel, "Come on son, be a good host and offer your father-in-law a drink, after all he has driven down all the way from Bombay. Brother Moses, have you had dinner?"

"No, but we have brought food. On our way to Alibaug, we went back to the apartment and Tamar packed the food, so that we could all eat together. Because this reunion also calls for a celebration. Did you know that we will soon be grandparents?"

Ezel stared at his wife with mixed feelings.

The women kissed each other, laughing and crying as they got up to fry the bombils.

Reluctantly Ezel stood up, opened the fridge, and pulled out two bottles of beer and poured a glass each for himself and Moses.

When the food was served, Malkha noticed that Ezel had not spoken to Tamar.

Malkha smiled, "Come Ezel, it is time to rejoice, soon you are going to be a father!"

The drink and the food seemed to relax Ezel; he leaned forward and offered a bombil to Tamar.

They were kissing, laughing, and crying together.

Late that night, when Moses dropped Tamar and Ezel at the entrance to their apartment, he was relieved to see them walk back home arm in arm.

Ezel opened the door and sat down to see the final score of the cricket match, while Tamar changed and went to bed. Later, when he went to the kitchen to get a glass of water, he saw the extra key Malkha had left behind on the dining table.

Malkha never visited Ezel and Tamar. Instead, like before, they visited her regularly every other weekend, or sometimes Ezel went to see her alone.

When Amy was born, Malkha went to the hospital with silver anklets for the baby and a basket of fruit for the mother. The relationship between the women was cordial, but they never became close. This continued till Benny was born and Ezel was made divisional director of his company and transferred to Ahmedabad.

Once Ezel and his family shifted to Ahmedabad, Malkha rarely saw them, but Ezel called her on Sunday mornings. Whenever he was in Bombay, he tried to spend a day with his mother. Once a year, Ezel, Tamar, and the children went to Bombay for their summer vacations and spent a week with Tamar's father and a week with Malkha.

Things changed one hot summer afternoon when Malkha stumbled over a stone in her garden while hanging out the clothes. She broke her heel and Ezel had to rush to Alibaug.

Malkha was admitted to the Alibaug civil hospital and it was five long months before she could move around with a walker. Those were harrowing days for Ezel as he traveled back and forth between the two cities. It was telling on his finances. To add to it, Tamar was irritable about his long absences and suggested that he bring Malkha to Ahmedabad.

This was in the winter, when they were still in the company apartment. Ezel booked a three-bedroom apartment in Shalom India Housing Society, so that Malkha could have a room to herself.

When Ezel brought Malkha to Ahmedabad, the first day ended in disaster.

Before she left for Ahmedabad, the big coconut tree at the entrance to Malkha's Alibaug house had been cut down and the laborer had presented her with its womb, oti chi poti. Malkha had carefully placed it in a cloth bag and brought it along, hoping to introduce a new flavor to the children.

The coconut tree was her favorite, which she had nurtured from sapling to young tree to fertile tree to old tree which was eventually felled.

That the tree had a womb proved that it was female. But Malkha had always assumed it was male as it had all the attributes of her husband, Samson.

Samson was a farmer and had the biggest holdings of coconut and areca nut in the entire Raigadh district. When his family had sent a proposal of marriage for Malkha, she refused, because she had seen him at the synagogue and her first reaction was that he looked uncouth. Like a village bumpkin, she smiled.

Malkha had just returned from Poona after getting a degree in education. She was petite, had a small round face, and wore round gold-rimmed glasses. Her hair was plaited in two long braids and rolled into a neat bun and she wore loosely draped synthetic saris or Punjabi suits. She wore brocade saris for special occasions and a special white sari for Yom Kippur, a fast she had never missed since she was eleven. On first impression, she looked neat, clean, and educated.

In contrast, Samson was big-built and rough in both appearance and character. He had a fiery temper, yet he was also caring and affectionate. Whenever Malkha saw him at the synagogue or on his motorbike as he whizzed past in the Alibaug marketplace, he looked bizarre in his crew cut, thick bifocals, and Pathani dress worn with mojdis. When she saw him wearing a lungi and riding his bike, the lungi hitched up to his knees, she decided that he was not for her. The groom of her dreams wore regular trousers, shirts, and shoes, like normal young men.

After she refused the proposal, the impossible happened.

On the night of Nariel Purnima at the end of the monsoon, the fisherfolk went out to sea in boats with colorful sails. There was a small festival on the Alibaug beach near the Durga temple. Women sang traditional songs to the beat of the drums as half-naked men wrestled and broke coconuts. The man who broke the largest number of coconuts, holding one in each hand and clashing them against each other like cymbals, was declared hero of Nariel Purnima. There were people everywhere, walking, talking, joking, laughing, eating bhel puri, paani puri, and drinking S. David's famous ice-cream soda.

Malkha never missed going to the festival.

While walking past the coconut "boxing ring," Malkha saw a

figure that looked familiar. It was Samson. He looked different without his glasses. His head looked like a gigantic areca nut and he was wearing just a small loincloth, exposing his muscular legs and bullish shoulders. Every possible muscle in his body was rippling and he exuded so much male energy that she stood staring at him, mesmerized. There was a crowd, and one of her friends nudged her and giggled. Malkha moved away embarrassed, when a strange voice called out to her, "Aye . . . " he said. She was annoyed and turned back with an angry retort, but stopped when she saw it was Samson. "Uncouth idiot," she whispered to her friend, and regretted it when he respectfully offered her an enormous green coconut, moist with five new leaves which had burst out from its half-open lips.

It was the coconut sapling he had won after breaking a hundred and one coconut shells and being declared the hero of Nariel Purnima.

Eyes lowered, Malkha accepted the sapling.

There was so much beauty in his offering that she returned home and told her mother that she would accept Samson's proposal of marriage.

On their wedding night, they had planted the sapling at the entrance to their home. And, as long as he lived, he never called her by her first name, but "Aye," much to her pleasure.

During her illness, sitting in her armchair in the veranda of her Alibaug house, Malkha noticed that the coconut tree had died.

Its trunk leaned against the roof, ready to fall and damage the house.

So, before leaving for Ahmedabad, she had called for some laborers to fell it and one of them had returned with the womb, oti chi poti.

He had brought it to her like an offering, holding it delicately in the cup of his palms. He had found it in the center of the trunk. Strangely phallus-like in shape, ten inches long, white like her wedding veil, soft like a virgin's hymen, and sweet like the taste of a first kiss.

The day Malkha arrived, Tamar noticed her sitting on a chair in the balcony, showing something to Amy. She did not bother about it, as they were laughing.

But that night Amy suddenly fell ill and was admitted to the Child Care Hospital in Naranpura. When they brought her back home, a seed of doubt had stirred in Tamar's mind.

Tamar and Malkha sat next to Amy waiting for her to open her eyes. They were worried; the child had not said a word since she was brought home.

An hour later, Amy opened her eyes, winked at Malkha, smiled and whispered, "Oti chi poti."

Tamar looked suspicious. "What on earth is that?"

Malkha smiled, "Don't you know?"

"No, what is that?"

"It is the womb of the coconut tree, very delicious."

"Is that what you gave Amy without asking me? I am sure it made her sick. I don't want you to give all this village mumbo-jumbo to my daughter without asking me."

"Really, it is harmless, ask Ezel."

"Then why didn't you give some of that tree stuff to me or Ezel?"

"It's not tree stuff, it is oti chi poti and Ezel knows it very well."

"Why didn't you give some to me?"

"Because there was no time, as soon as I arrived, Amy was sick."

Tamar was furious. " . . . sick, because you poisoned her. By the way, where is it? I want to see it."

"Look inside the fridge, next to the chocolate, it is wrapped in a wet cloth."

In a fury, Tamar rushed to the kitchen, opened the fridge, and found the oti chi poti. It looked like a slice of rotting cheese and she threw it into the dustbin, as Malkha cried out, "Please don't throw it away, Ezel loves it and throwing it away only brings misfortune."

"It looks poisonous and almost killed my daughter."

"Tamar, please don't hurt me! Do you really think I would poison my own granddaughter? Ezel has grown up eating oti chi poti. Has it brought any harm to him? You say all this because you hate me, just because I come from a village. You forget that we all belong to these villages. This is where our ancestors were shipwrecked. It is the land of the ancestors. We still carry the name of these villages in our surnames. And, by the way, do you know that every second millionaire from Bombay has a farmhouse in Alibaug?"

"I don't care, but please do not give anything to Amy without asking me."

Malkha watched Tamar, feeling helpless, as she stood in the doorway supporting herself on the walker.

After the episode of oti chi poti, other incidents followed, like the mysterious appearance of a black cat in the apartment. Then Tamar found a small rag doll under her mattress and a dead blue butterfly pinned to her favorite black kurta. This was proof enough that Malkha was practicing black magic to get rid of her daughter-in-law.

To add to it, that month when Tamar's reports came from the gynecologist, she realized to her horror that she was pregnant.

She was sure that it was the fragrance of Malkha's evil oti chi poti which had made her pregnant.

Although Tamar hesitated before telling Ezel that his mother was a witch, she did not realize it would bring things to a dead end. When she told her husband about his mother's village witchcraft, he slapped her and she left the apartment that very night with both children.

On reaching Bombay, she phoned Ezel to say she was pregnant, but did not want another child, especially his child. She banged the phone down on him and after that it was impossible to contact her. It was much later that her father Moses informed Ezel about the abortion and her decision to leave India.

Tamar wanted to study art education in Israel, because she felt there was no future for her in India.

Malkha was guilt-ridden about Tamar's departure, and regretted that she had made an issue about something so insignificant as the womb of a tree. She held herself responsible for the discord between the couple and quickly returned to Alibaug. She got herself admitted to the Alibaug civil hospital till she could walk around without a walker.

Every evening, at sunset, she prayed to the prophet Elijah to unite Ezel with his family.

At last the prophet sent a halfhearted reply to her prayers. When the train reached Bombay Central, Ezel called his mother from his cell phone and gave her the news about the abortion and Tamar's decision to leave for Israel, and that she was leaving the children in his care. He said Tamar wanted to study art, learn Hebrew, find herself a job, and then send for the children, as Tamar's father had refused to look after them.

Malkha sighed as she listened and wished Tamar had not thrown the oti chi poti into the dustbin. It was the beginning of all their troubles, even the loss of another child. Tamar had literally thrown her own unborn child into the dustbin.

Without thinking, Ezel had agreed to Tamar's demands, as he wanted to see Benny and Amy as soon as possible. From Bombay Central, he again phoned his mother and asked her to join him in Ahmedabad and help with the children.

Malkha hesitated, then sighed and said, "If that is the will of Eliyahu Hannabi, I will come."

13 Tamar

Ezra was depressed. Lolo had ditched Ben Hur, Diana had eloped with Manav, Tamar had left Ezel, strange rumors were doing the rounds about Ruby and Franco Fernandes, Juliet had asked Ezra to sell her apartment, Raghubir Chopra had agreed to buy it, but then died of a sudden heart attack. Shoshanah had said that she wanted to buy Juliet's apartment for her daughter Miriam but had never finalized the deal, and one of Ezra's housing societies had run into trouble.

It appeared to be a bad year. The only silver lining was that Rachel and Yacov were in love and were preparing for their future in Israel by learning Hebrew from Shoshanah.

Ezra did not know where all this was leading. The mini-microscopic Bene Israel community of Ahmedabad seemed to be falling apart. They were like his family, he felt responsible for them. Unable to cope with the stress, he joined the Shalom India Laughing Club.

Franco Fernandes was the president of the club. When Ruby rejected him, he had been depressed and his doctor had prescribed a mild sedative with the simple advice, "Why don't you laugh like before, then you will be okay."

Franco had discovered the laughing club idea by accident. On his way back home after his music classes he often passed the municipal gardens, where he saw the placard of the Satellite Laughing

Club, FREE FOR ALL, 6:00–7:00 a.m. and 6:00–7:00 p.m.

Franco had joined the club with some apprehension.

The session started with warming up, simple yoga and breathing exercises conducted by a leader. After this, the entire group started laughing together, almost for a full half-hour.

Franco returned feeling happy and light-headed; he had not laughed like this in days. And he became addicted to the laughing garden, as he called it. Laughter seemed to heal him, so much so that he had stopped mooning after Ruby.

On one such evening, when Franco was returning home happily whistling an old Elvis number, he met Ben Hur at the gates of Shalom India Housing Society.

Ben Hur looked drawn and thin. Franco stopped his scooter and asked, "Hi Ben, are you okay? Why don't I see your sexy friends around here, the blonde was a real bomb."

Ben Hur shrugged his shoulders, "I'm okay, Uncle, just low . . . life is sad and boring."

"Why don't you start laughing?"

"How can I laugh without reason?"

"Well, young man, you can. If you want to learn to laugh, come with me to the laughing club."

Next morning, Franco introduced Ben Hur to the pleasures of the laughing club. Ben Hur enjoyed it so much that on the way back, they decided to start a laughing club at Shalom India Housing Society.

With Ezra's permission, the club was formed with Franco as the president. It was a branch of the larger Satellite Laughing Club.

Every morning, residents from Blocks A and B, dressed in tracksuits and sneakers, stood in rows on the lawns, laughing.

However much she wanted to, Ruby did not join the club for obvious reasons and Ezra had not joined as he felt it was silly to laugh for no reason at all. With his morning cup of tea, he watched the laughing club. And eventually he joined it as he realized he had forgotten how to laugh.

As a rule, when Ezra returned home laughing he often found a solution to his problems. Like when he returned from the club and found a letter from Israel waiting for him. It was not from Juliet, but Tamar.

Tamar's letter was from a Haifa address and was written in a neat, small, curved hand, which betrayed her convent education.

Dear Brother Ezra,

I am sure you are surprised to receive this letter from me. I am writing to you after a lot of thought and introspection. As you know, Ezel and I have separated. I have left the children with him, as I am studying art education in Israel. I will send for them after I find a job.

In the mornings, I go to class and in the afternoons I work with children at a daycare. I play with them, feed them, clean them, sing songs, and tell them stories. It is a well-paid job. Every evening, when I return to my hostel, I feel miserable, as the children remind me of Benny and Amy. I worry about them, because Ezel has long working hours and sometimes I wonder if I did the right thing in leaving them in India.

This year, I have a long vacation and Papa is sending me an airline ticket. So, I will be in India for the New Year. But, I have a small problem for which I need your help.

When I return to India I will stay for a week with my father in Bombay. After which I will come to Ahmedabad but I will not be staying with Ezel. Instead, I have made other arrangements, for which I need your help.

On weekends I often meet Juliet and Romiel. I know they have big financial problems, but are generally okay, as two are better than one. As for me, I prefer to fight it out alone.

Juliet has told me about her decision to sell her apartment at Shalom India Housing Society. I believe you had a buyer, but he died, and the apartment is still empty. So, I asked her to rent it out to me. I will be paying her the rent in Israel in advance. She has agreed. Herewith, I am enclosing her letter asking you to rent the apartment to me. I will be arriving on August 5th, after meeting Papa in Bombay. I have sent an e-mail to Ezel informing him about my travel plans. I will phone him on arrival.

I hope this letter finds you in the best of health and my best wishes to you and sister Sigaut,

Yours sincerely,

Tamar

Ezra filed the letter with Juliet's documents.

It was not going to be easy to speak to Ezel about such a delicate matter.

He did not like Ezel. And ever since Tamar left it was not easy to have a conversation with him. He was secretive, sarcastic, and often rude.

Ezra wondered why the good prophet Elijah had decided to dump all the problems of Shalom India on his head.

Didn't he have enough problems of his own? Ezra went through his daily routine and went to bed early, as he needed to wake up early and find release for his tensions at the laughing club. After that he would be strong enough to handle Ezel.

Next morning, after his session at the laughing club, Ezra ran up the stairs and rang Ezel's doorbell.

Ezel was watching the news and his mother Malkha, that nice kind lady from Alibaug who resembled his own mother, was combing Amy's hair and Benny was tying his shoelaces. It was a pleasant domestic scene. He noticed Ezel did not look haggard, but fresh like a green coconut, as he switched off the television and asked Ezra to make himself comfortable on the sofa and poured him a cup of tea from the teapot on the side table.

Ezra accepted the cup and smiled, while Ezel watched him intently and said, "Ezra, let's come to the point, you haven't come here for a cup of tea . . . "

Ezra threw a meaningful look at Malkha, Ezel understood and said, "They will leave in a second."

The children kissed their father and left for school with Malkha.

Ezra cleared his throat and said, "Tamar is coming back."

"I know, so what?"

"Nothing really, I do not want to interfere in your family matters, but she is returning to Ahmedabad."

"Not to my apartment."

"No, to Juliet's apartment. She is renting it, so that she can be closer to the children. She will be here on Tuesday morning."

"Tell her to call me and we will see. Of course, she is free to see the children and create as many scenes as she wants . . . "

"I know Ezel, this is going to be an embarrassing situation for you. But, what can I do? She is paying the rent to Juliet in advance and in dollars, so I have to give her the key to the apartment."

"She is welcome to Ahmedabad, after all she is the mother of the children and they often ask about her. So far she has written ten letters to them and called them twice."

"So, shall I give her the key?"

"Do as you like." Ezel stood up abruptly, shook hands with Ezra and said he had to go to work.

Ezel spent the day feeling agitated, not knowing how to cope with Tamar's arrival.

Like every other evening, Malkha picked up the children at the bus stop, gave them a glass of milk and a snack, helped them change, and sent them downstairs to play. On return, they were supposed to finish their homework before dinner, after which they watched the cartoon network on television and went to bed at nine.

Feeling content and peaceful, Malkha changed her sari, combed her hair, and stood in the balcony watching Amy and Benny, when, much to her surprise, she saw Ezel's car. He was back early. He parked his car and stopped to watch the Shalom India Laughing Club.

Ezel exchanged a word with Franco and started laughing as though he had gone mad. Then suddenly he stopped, wiped his face with a handkerchief, and walked towards the elevator, while his mother rushed to open the door, wondering if he was sick.

Ezel walked in with a stoop and instinctively she knew something was wrong, "What is the problem?" she asked.

He threw his bag on the sofa, washed his face, slumped down in the sofa, and said, "Ezra was here this morning. Last night I told you about Tamar's e-mail. She knows very well that I hate middlemen, but she has written to Ezra that she is returning to India. She will stop in Bombay to meet her father and then come to Ahmedabad. Now, hold your breath mother, she is not going to stay with us, but in A-107."

"That is Juliet's apartment, right?"

"Yes."

"Does it really matter, as long as the children get to see their mother? They are always waiting for her return. Today I will give them the good news about Tamar's arrival, then light a candle and thank Eliyahu Hannabi."

Ezel looked at her sharply. "Thank the prophet, for the scandal?"

"No, for uniting the children with their mother."

That night, Malkha decided to return to Alibaug. She was attached to the children and it broke her heart to leave them, but she knew it was best for Ezel's little family.

When Tamar arrived, she left her baggage with Salome and went to A-111, Ezra's apartment, and rang the doorbell.

Tamar stood framed in the doorway and Ezra noticed she looked charming and beautiful. Nobody would have ever guessed that she was the mother of two children. He noticed her eyes looked different. He remembered she often wore spectacles and that she had black eyes. Ezra was sure the morning light was playing tricks upon him, because the woman standing in front of him had emerald-green eyes. It took him some time to realize that she was wearing green contact lenses, which suited her.

Tamar was wearing a tight black pantsuit, and the last button of her coat was at her navel, exposing the silver ring piercing it. Ezra found it hard to keep his gaze at eye level as he gave her the keys to Juliet's apartment, feeling an irrepressible desire to possess her. Perhaps she would not mind having a fling with him. She looked vulnerable and lonely; the scenario was perfect to seduce her. Perhaps he could have a secret rendezvous with her in Juliet's apartment on the pretext of discussing the broken window, nobody would ever guess. . . .

Alarmed at his own desires, Ezra put a full stop to his evil designs, telling himself that he was a happily married man and did not need to complicate his life.

Anyway, Tamar was already between the devil and the deep blue sea and she was not exactly his type. That she had confided in him did not mean that she was inviting him to have an affair; perhaps she looked up to him as an elder brother. How could he ever think of misusing Juliet's apartment for an illicit relationship with a married woman, one who also belonged to his tribe? He had a flash of memory; Ben Hur had often used the apartment to meet Lolo, and now he was thinking along similar lines. . . .

After she left, he was so disturbed that he decided to laugh off his desires at the laughing club.

If Ezel had imagined that Tamar's presence in Shalom India Housing Society would become a scandal, it did not.

By the time Tamar arrived, Malkha had left, and the whole apartment was in a mess. Ezel could only just about manage to send the children to school and reach his office on time. This was for just a day or two, because after that Tamar stepped back into his life.

As soon as Tamar landed in Ahmedabad, her heart beat wildly at the thought of meeting Benny and Amy. But she had decided that she would not rush to meet them. She would rest, organize herself, and then call Ezel and fix a time to meet the children.

When Tamar entered Juliet's apartment, she was overcome by emotion and sat on the packing case where the prophet had sat on the first day of Passover. She sat there with tears flowing down her cheeks and Eliyahu Hannabi looked down upon her sympathetically, a benign expression on his face.

Tamar sobbed; the children were so close and yet so far. It was her fault, she cursed herself, she had given the children away to Ezel as though they were her excess baggage.

Right then, she heard the doorbell and wondered if it was Ezel. Quickly she wiped her face, opened the door, and saw Aunt Salome, big, motherly, and comforting, standing there with a flask of coffee. Ezra had asked Salome and Sippora to help lessen the tension between Ezel and Tamar, sure it was going to be an embarrassing situation for Ezel.

Salome saw Tamar had been crying, so she put the flask down on the packing case and held her in her arms. Tamar wept, telling her how she longed to see Benny and Amy.

Salome also wept, telling her how unfortunate she was that she did not have children, but Tamar was lucky to have such lovely children.

Tamar did not protest as Salome led her to Ezel's door and whispered, "Go, ring the bell and hold your children in your arms. That is what you want, isn't it?"

Salome left her standing there, giving her the space and time to make her own decision.

When Tamar rang the doorbell, she was trembling, certain that Ezel would not allow her to see the children.

But he did.

Amy and Benny ran towards her, laughing, shouting, and hanging around her neck, making her face wet with kisses. Tamar was crying and laughing as she kneeled down at the door with the children in her arms.

The year away from them had not been easy.

Amy wiped Tamar's tears and Benny held her head in his arms.

That is when she felt two strong hands guiding her into the apartment.

She was following Ezel like one in a trance, remembering how he had stood in the synagogue on their wedding day, singing to her and inviting her to join him in the journey of life.

A year later, Ezel, Tamar, Benny, and Amy immigrated to Israel and Malkha returned to Ahmedabad. Ezel and Tamar had given her their apartment at Shalom India Housing Society as she had made many friends there. She had also retired from the school in Alibaug and Noah had offered her the post of supervisor at his Beth Shalom Primary School, where she took over from where Sara had left, organizing cultural activities and taking charge of the parent–teacher association. On Saturday evenings, Ezel called Malkha from Israel, and after she had spoken to him and the children, she would light a candle to thank Eliyahu Hannabi for having blessed her son with a happy married life.

14 Noah

Noah had noticed that whenever there was a fancy dress party at the synagogue, his daughter Ilana chose to be a policewoman. She insisted on wearing his mother's old clothes, altered to her size. Watching her, Noah would then be transported back in time and would light a candle in his mother Sara's memory.

Ilana had decided to join the national police academy after graduation.

Noah was the principal of Beth Shalom Primary School. A huge photograph of his mother in a gilded frame had pride of place in his office. She had been a pioneer. Mother and son had set up the school together, close to Shalom India Housing Society. It was one of the first English-language secular schools of the city. When other Jews had seen Noah's success, they had followed suit and Ahmedabad had seven more family-run English schools.

Sara's photograph in Noah's office showed a sturdy, square-faced policewoman dressed in a khaki sari, her hair pulled back into a tight chignon, sari pallav held in place at the shoulder with a brooch, wearing a belt with a revolver holster and decorated with medals.

She looked severe and so did Noah.

Sara had been a big influence in his life. Even while his father, Solomon, was alive, she had been like a single parent, ever since Noah was seven and his sister Rose five.

Solomon had been injured during the 1948 Bombay dock explosion. He was a security officer at the docks. When the bomb exploded, the city was ripped apart, strewn with mangled bodies and shards of metal. Solomon could not be traced in the melee.

When the explosion rocked Bombay, Sara had a foreboding. Solomon had promised to return home early for lunch and she had made fried fish with dal and rice. Everything was ready and the fresh pomfret rolled in rice flour was left lying on a plate, to be fried as soon as Solomon reached home. Sara fed the children and spent the whole day waiting on the balcony.

So far, they had led a happy but uneventful life and she prayed to the prophet Elijah to protect her home.

He did not.

That afternoon the phone had been silent for so long that Sara began to think it was out of order. If Solomon was late, he always called and asked her not to wait for him. Around four thirty, the phone suddenly rang, breaking the day-long silence. Sara rushed to pick it up. She was sure it was Solomon. It was Solomon's boss. In a matter-of-fact voice he gave her the news about the bomb explosion and said Solomon was missing from his post. They would inform her if they found him.

Sara slumped on the floor and cried as the children clung to her, not knowing what had happened. News spread quickly about Solomon's disappearance and soon their apartment in the staff quarters filled up with neighbors and relatives. Sara was annoyed as they sat in the drawing room, long-faced as though they had come for Solomon's funeral. They seemed to be sure that Solomon was dead. Sara knew that they were only trying to be helpful, as they looked after the children and whispered amongst themselves about the arrangements for a possible funeral. But she refused to believe that Solomon was dead.

A week later, when everybody had given up hope, Solomon arrived in an ambulance. They had found him unconscious, on a raft floating in the Arabian Sea.

Sara sighed and thanked Eliyahu Hannabi for having found her husband, knowing very well that Solomon would never recover.

Solomon was alive, but brain-dead. He lay in bed, staring blankly at the ceiling, eyes wide open, and breathing lightly. If Sara helped him sit down, he remained sitting all day.

He ate when he was fed, went to the toilet when he was taken there, often soiling the bed, which she cleaned without complaint.

When he was stronger, Sara saw to it that he spent the day sitting in a straight-backed chair in front of the television. She felt better, as he appeared to be watching television. Sara had made a timetable for breakfast, lunch, and dinner with four to five visits to the bathroom and a bath. For these rituals, Noah helped her, and he grew up with his father's smell of decay.

Rose helped her mother with household chores and slowly took over the organization of the kitchen so that her mother was free to look after her father.

At the end of the day, Sara sponged Solomon, changed his clothes, led him to the bed, spread plastic sheets under the bed sheet, changed into her nightgown, lay down next to him, held him close to her breast, and cried as he stared at the ceiling fan.

So far, Solomon had always been there for her and she had led a sheltered existence. Before marriage, she had lived under the protection of parents and brothers. In both homes, except for family trips, she had never stepped out even to buy a potato on her own. The bomb blast forced Sara to become independent and she learned to do everything on her own, from paying bills to buying groceries, vegetables, and fish.

Although both children helped her, she made sure that they did their homework regularly and did not lag behind in their studies. That particular year, much to Sara's pleasure, Noah stood second in class and she bought him a wristwatch in appreciation of his hard work.

As a release from the oppressive atmosphere in the apartment, they often went to the synagogue for festivals, sometimes locking up Solomon in the apartment. But thrice a year, on New Year, Yom Kippur, and Hanukah, she made arrangements with her brother to take Solomon to the synagogue in the folding wheelchair. It warmed her heart to see him seated there, in ironed clothes with the skullcap pinned to his head, staring at the ark.

The dull routine of their daily life changed when Sara realized that her bank balance had dwindled and they would soon have to vacate staff quarters. The money she had received from the dock office was put away in fixed deposits for the children's education and she knew that she had to do something with her own life.

She registered with the public service commission and often went to the employment office looking for possible posts. She also met Solomon's boss and asked him to find her employment. He suggested she apply for the post of warden in Ahmedabad's Sabarmati Jail, and promised to recommend her for the job.

The idea of power appealed to Sara.

Since Solomon had become a liability, she was uncomfortable with the idea of living without male protection, so the description of the job attracted her. The warden would be in charge of women prisoners, and would be given free accommodations and a vehicle.

Sara saw herself dressed in a uniform and wearing a pistol at her waist. The idea of transforming from timid wife into an officer made her feel secure, fearless, and happy. As she wrote out the application and posted it, she prayed to Prophet Elijah to make sure that she got the job.

She did.

Sara had to undergo a brief period of training before she was sent to Ahmedabad. Having led a protected life, she was not sure how she would cope with such rigorous duties, but she knew her priorities. She prayed to the prophet to give her strength to overcome all doubts and difficulties. She knew if she did not take this godsent opportunity she would have to live on charity.

After the training, Sara sent her belongings to Ahmedabad by truck and settled down in the house allotted to her, a small bungalow with a garden. Painstakingly, she organized her home in such a way that it was easy for her to work, look after Solomon, and attend to her household duties. The fact that she lived near the prison helped her to ensure that all was well at home. She had also made arrangements with the jail doctor to do a checkup of Solomon once a week, to make sure that his condition was not deteriorating.

Slowly, Sara started enjoying the fact that she was a powerful woman, in control of her own life.

Every morning, as she dressed to leave for work, Sara stopped to look at her reflection in the mirror, and liked what she saw. She had always been a big-boned woman and looked bigger when she wore her uniform of khaki trousers, shirt, cap, and shoes. But she preferred the option of wearing khaki saris, starched, ironed, the pallav pinned on her left shoulder with a brooch, with her hair neatly plaited, rolled at the nape of her neck and held in place with a net under the cap.

With her uniform, she always wore her wedding ring, a delicate ladies' wristwatch, and the mangalsutra hidden in her sports brassiere.

Later the homely Sara discovered that trousers were more comfortable than saris and she often wore well-cut trousers with her husband's old shirts. Women like Sippora and Tamar would look at Sara with admiration and she became a role model for the younger generation of Jewish women.

When not on duty, Sara applied powder on her face, touched perfume between her breasts, and wore four gold bangles on her right wrist, a gift she had received from Solomon on their wedding night.

She liked her appearance; it was strict, disciplined, and unapproachable.

The tough exterior cracked only at night, when she changed into her nightgown and crept into the skin of the earlier helpless Sara. She held the still body of her husband in her arms and cried. It was as though the weak woman within her was connected to the nightgown and the strong woman emerged as soon as she wore her uniform and tucked the revolver into the holster on her belt.

Sara kept her personal life a secret and had hardly any friends. Her main aim in life was to make something out of Noah and Rose.

The only outing they had was to the synagogue during festivals or for a malida. She never left Solomon alone at home, but took him everywhere in a wheelchair. This earned her a lot of respect in the Jewish community of Ahmedabad. They respected this tough-looking woman who had made Ahmedabad her home. As soon as Sara's jeep arrived at the synagogue gates, they went forward to help her bring Solomon into the synagogue. They made kind inquiries about his health and helped Noah pin the kippa on his father's head. The Ahmedabad Jews marveled at Sara and often visited her, asking if she needed something. She was cordial and friendly, but made it clear that she was an independent woman and did not need either pity or sympathy.

But she did ask Daniyal to teach the bar mitzvah prayers to Noah and took Salome's help to organize the event. When Noah was thirteen years old and ready for his bar mitzvah, the whole community was present to see Noah receive the prayer shawl from the cantor Saul Ezekiel as tears flowed from his father's eyes and Sara hastened to wipe them with a handkerchief.

At such moments, she was sure that Solomon was improving and registering events much better than before; perhaps the medication was working. Sara weakened and looked in the direction of the covered chair of the prophet Elijah and pleaded that he cure her husband as soon as possible.

Sara was supposed to be efficient, an officer both strict and compassionate. She was known to be a kind woman who organized numerous activities for the women prisoners like biscuit-making and weaving. She even opened a counter at the Gandhi Ashram to sell their products. She also helped them with pending cases, and in appreciation she received the president's medal for her services to the department. From the dais she saw to her amazement that Solomon, sitting in his wheelchair in the front row next to the wife of the Governor of Gujarat, was smiling.

Later, when Sara retired, they shifted to a rented house next to Daniyal's. Noah was then studying for his bachelor's degree in education.

When he passed his master's degree in education at the top of his class, Sara organized a special malida for him and bought him an old house in Satellite to start a school.

Sara helped Noah run the school with an iron hand. She had a special cabin with an ornate nameplate on the door, from where she organized cultural activities and ran the parent–teacher association. Although she always wore a severe expression, the children loved her and their parents respected both her discipline and compassion.

Soon after Beth Shalom Primary School was established, Sara found a bride for Noah, her niece Leah, a primary school teacher and according to her a good Jewish woman.

That year, Rose left for Bombay to study at the catering college and stayed with the Gerard family, distant cousins of Solomon. The Gerards' nephew Elias fell in love with Rose and they married at the Magen Abraham Synagogue in Ahmedabad.

Rose and Elias left for Israel where she worked in the kitchen of an aircraft factory, and after finishing his term in the army, Elias joined the Israeli police force. Once in two years Rose returned to India with gifts for the family and Sara was content that both her children were well settled and her task as a single mother of sorts had been accomplished.

Noah's story could end here, but does not.

One morning Sara died in her sleep and Noah felt cheated that his father had outlived his mother. When he saw her lying dead next to her husband, he hoped that Solomon, sleeping there with his mouth wide open, was also dead.

Much to Noah's resentment, Solomon lived for ten more years. Noah spent the next ten years of his life washing his father, cleaning him, and feeding him only in respect for his mother's memory. Often he woke up in the morning hoping to find his father dead.

But, day after day, the old man sat in his wheelchair in front of the television, his eyes closed and his head tilted towards the fan.

When his father eventually died, Noah suffered guilt at feeling relieved of a great burden.

Liberated at last from the stale smell of death which had filled his existence since he was a child, Noah bought an apartment at Shalom India Housing Society and tried to forget the past.

After the death of both parents, Rose did not return to India.

She always felt there was a certain distance between her and Noah. They exchanged greeting cards at New Year or sometimes, if they remembered birthdays, they sent e-greetings to each other. And they announced the birth of children through short messages written on greeting cards with a pasted photograph of the new arrival.

Once a year, on their mother's death anniversary, Rose called Noah and they chatted about Hindi films.

And if, for some reason, Rose did not call Noah on that particular day, he called her, more out of habit than need.

On one particular New Year he sent a greeting card to Rose, but did not receive the customary reply, which worried him. He even contemplated calling her, although he was not really a phone person.

A month later, he received a letter from her, written in a small neat hand on white, ruled paper torn from a school notebook.

Dear Noah,

Thank you for your greeting card. But it saddens me to inform you that we are in mourning. On August 20th at about 11:00 p.m. a very horrible incident took place. My husband Elias was shot dead by his girlfriend's brother. When the doorbell rang, we thought it was cousin Nathan who often dropped in for a nightcap. As soon as Elias opened the door, the brother fired without warning, pumping eight bullets into his body, brutally murdering Elias.

I am in shock, as I did not know Elias had a girlfriend, because he was a loving husband. Nothing more for the present,

Your loving sister,

Rose

A month later, another letter followed, written on the same paper.

Dear Noah,

Since Elias was murdered, it has been hard to make ends meet. I went to meet his boss and the Israeli police force has offered me the post of security guard at the Ben Gurion Airport.

I am posting a photograph of myself in uniform. Hope you like it. Nothing more at present,

Your loving sister,

Rose

Noah sat in his office studying the photograph; Rose was dressed in the Israeli police uniform with a cap on her head and a revolver at her waist.

Filled with mixed emotions, Noah called Rose but did not know what to say. So he chatted about the last Hindi film he had seen. She listened quietly and asked him to send her a DVD of the film.

Before he hung up, all he could say was, "By the way, in the photograph you sent me, you look exactly like Mama."

He heard her laugh and had a funny feeling that she was crying.

All these experiences had shaken Noah and made him into a bit of a tyrant who ran his school like the army.

15 Shoshanah

Shoshanah choked with emotion whenever she saw a picture of Mother Mary. It reminded her of Miriam, her only child.

Their last year in Poona before they immigrated to Israel, Miriam was five years old and had dressed as the Madonna for the Hanukah fancy dress party at the synagogue.

Shoshanah had dressed her in flowing white robes. To dress as Mother Mary had been Miriam's choice. She was fascinated by the image of the Mother in the chapel of her convent school. Shoshanah had her doubts about the Christian nature of Miriam's choice, but never stopped her. She wanted her to grow into an independent woman who made her own decisions.

That year Miriam won the first prize with compassionate expression just like Mother Mary's. In fact, everybody agreed that Miriam resembled the Madonna.

Soon after, Shoshanah and Yonathan had immigrated to Israel and Miriam had grown up there like any other Israeli girl.

Trouble began when she was twenty and engaged to Aaron, a bright young Israeli lawyer of Indian origin.

Miriam was beautiful: built delicately like a porcelain doll, slim, fair, mild-mannered, and shy. She was also very religious and since the age of eleven had always observed the fast on the Day of Atonement.

She had studied the Torah in school and when she was asked her choice of career she invariably said, "A woman rabbi," like the one she had seen at her cousin Benjamin's bar mitzvah. In her teens, Miriam had asked her mother to teach her how to follow the Jewish religion correctly. Shoshanah was impressed and had made a list of do's and don'ts. Miriam followed the rituals strictly, and, by the time she finished school, she was wearing clothes which covered her from neck to toe. She also tied a scarf around her head like the religious women she saw in the street. She studied the Torah regularly and never wore shorts or small dresses like most youngsters of her age. She even got an exemption from compulsory army training because she was doing religious studies and preparing for her wedding.

Aaron was a young Bene Israel Jew, born and brought up in Israel. Their parents had known each other since their Poona days and had decided on a date for the wedding.

Aaron and Miriam met often, and whenever alone in one house or the other would indulge in heavy petting. Miriam was a passionate woman. Even when they went for a stroll, or to a café on Dizengoff Square or to the beach, they could hardly keep their hands off each other.

Unlike most Bene Israel girls who preferred wedding gowns to saris, Miriam dreamt of wearing a sari for her wedding and decided to shop for her trousseau in India.

Neither Yonathan nor Shoshanah could accompany her, because they needed all their hard-earned leave and finances for Miriam's wedding. It was decided that she would travel alone to India and stay with Yonathan's cousin Cyril in Bombay.

Aaron dropped Miriam at Ben Gurion Airport. They kissed passionately and Miriam clung to him saying she would miss him.

But when the El Al flight took off, he did not know that he would never see her again.

No, nothing untoward happened during the flight, in fact Miriam had a safe landing at Bombay's Chhatrapati Shivaji Airport, where Uncle Cyril and Aunt Agatha were waiting for her. They drove her to their apartment in Bandra.

This was Miriam's first visit to India after her family had immigrated to Israel. It was late when she arrived in Bombay, and she was

Shoshanah

not sure if she liked India. But the next day, when she woke up to the call of the koel, Miriam stretched and felt happy.

At the breakfast table she met cousins Ralphi and Serena who wanted to know all the details of her engagement, while Aunt Agatha had lined up a shopping schedule for her.

Miriam had a passion for Hindi films and saw one film a day with her cousins, if not in the cinema hall then on television or on DVD at home.

Miriam was in Bombay for almost a month, with just one brief trip to Poona to meet her parents' friends Ehsan and Afsana Pathan. Sometimes she went shopping with her cousins, otherwise she preferred to be out on her own, saying it was an Israeli habit.

Shortly before Miriam's departure, Agatha went to her room to wake her up, as they had an appointment at the jewelers.

She was shocked when she realized that the bed had not been slept in, and found a hastily scribbled note under the pillow.

Dear Aunt Agatha and Uncle Cyril, please inform my parents that last night I married Zulfikar and will be in Pakistan by the time you receive this letter. Thanks for everything. Affectionately, Mariam Zulfikar Sheikh.

Agatha noticed that she had changed her name from Miriam to Mariam.

Agatha looked shellshocked as she ran with the letter to Cyril, screaming, asking him to call Shoshanah and Yonathan immediately and inform them about Miriam's elopement. For a while, she even thought that Zulfikar was a Palestinian boyfriend who had followed her to India and that the elopement had been pre-planned.

All doubts were laid to rest when Cyril folded the newspaper, lowered his spectacles, and said that the Pathans were old friends of Shoshanah and Yonathan. They had a sari shop in Poona and Miriam had stayed with them for four days. Perhaps Zulfikar was their son or a relative. Cyril felt they had been rather stupid in not double-checking details about the family and scolded Agatha for not accompanying her to Poona. After all, Miriam had been their responsibility.

Agatha remembered that Miriam had returned from Poona looking radiant; the Pathans had taken very good care of her and had gifted her with a rich green brocade sari for the mehendi ceremony.

In two days, Shoshanah and Yonathan reached Bombay by an El Al flight. As soon as they landed they wanted to file a police complaint. Instead, Cyril advised them to meet the Pathans before they took any action. Perhaps they held the key to the mystery of Miriam's elopement.

Shoshanah remembered that the Pathans did not have a son named Zulfikar. They had three daughters and a son born to them late in life, who was just about seven years old.

Shoshanah and Yonathan left for Poona and returned in a day, dejected and sad. They did not file a police complaint since it seemed Miriam had eloped with Zulfikar of her own free will.

They said the Pathans were also distressed, because Zulfikar was the fiancé of their elder daughter Soha, Miriam's childhood friend. They had been most apologetic about the matter, and said they had never guessed that Miriam and Zulfikar were planning a runaway marriage. To all appearances, Miriam was preparing for her wedding and Soha for hers.

Miriam and Soha had been inseparable as kids and were meeting for the first time since they had grown up. Zulfikar had a sari shop in Islamabad with a branch in London, but was also a poet of sorts. He wrote Urdu couplets and sang ghazals at family get-togethers.

To welcome Miriam and celebrate Soha's engagement to Zulfikar, the Pathans had organized a small garden party with close friends and relatives, followed by a night of ghazals.

A well-known poet, a friend of the Pathans, was reciting Urdu couplets, but as Miriam did not understand the language, Zulfikar sat next to her explaining the meaning of each word, much to Soha's discomfort. It was a full-moon night and Miriam was wearing one of Soha's embroidered shararas. It was the color of mother-of-pearl and was embellished with sequins and worn with a transparent dupatta of the same color. It suited Miriam and in Zulfikar's eyes she looked like a houri under the full moon. And, like one intoxicated, he too recited couplets and sang ghazals, playing the harmonium.

It was something Miriam had never experienced before. It was in complete contrast to the rather harsh life she led in Israel. There was an unreal quality to the night and she loved it, wanting more and more, as glasses of almond milk and cool rose sherbet were passed around with plates of sweets.

It was like a scene from one of her favorite Hindi films. Zulfikar was different from the men she had known. She noticed his tousled black hair and grey-green eyes. She could feel herself sinking into their depths and knew she was falling in love, perhaps for the first time in her life. Family, country, Judaism, Islam, India, Israel, Pakistan, nothing seemed to matter. She knew she was being drawn to her destiny. Zulfikar was the unknown poet of her unrealized dreams. And, try as she might, she could not remember what Aaron looked like.

That night, when everybody had gone to bed, Miriam changed into a simple salwar-kameez suit and lay on the terrace, thinking about her future with Aaron.

Between work as a primary school teacher and Aaron, life was a roller-coaster ride. She knew that even the lovemaking with Aaron had been animal-like and mechanical.

In Israel she always felt like a machine, but under Zulfikar's passionate gaze she felt like a woman.

But she knew she could not even think about him.

They belonged to different worlds and Miriam had no intention of breaking Soha's heart.

Lost in thought, she was not aware when Zulfikar knelt down beside her. Without a word they looked at each other, and kissed, at first tenderly, then passionately, and lay on the terrace, groping, touching, caressing, and making love as though they had known each other for years.

When she returned to Bombay, Miriam and Zulfikar kept in touch through text messages. Then, unable to stay away from her, Zulfikar followed her to Bombay on the pretext of receiving a consignment of saris. Unknown to the rest of the family, he stayed in a hotel near Uncle Cyril's apartment. And Miriam spent many an afternoon in Zulfikar's arms, just a block away from Aunt Agatha's ever-watchful eyes.

As the day of departure drew closer, Miriam knew she did not want to return to Israel. Zulfikar was her world. A week later, they were on the flight to Islamabad. Miriam never understood how Zulfikar had organized their marriage or her new Indian passport.

Shoshanah never heard from her daughter again and did not even know if she was dead or alive.

When Shoshanah called Aaron from India, he was shocked that Miriam had eloped with her Pakistani lover. Yet, strangely, he felt relieved. He had always been a trifle uneasy about her craze for Hindi films and Jewish rituals. As long as he had been engaged to Miriam, he felt she was pulling him backwards in time, while he wanted to move ahead and conquer time. After all, in Israel, one understood the fragility of both life and time. For a few days Aaron went around with a deflated ego; then he shrugged it off, as he was already seeing an American law student, Judy, whom he had met at a party. He threatened his parents that he would no longer consider another Bene Israel girl ever again.

Shoshanah was depressed for a long time and did not return to Israel. She felt comforted in India. On the Sabbath every Friday evening, Shoshanah prayed to the prophet Elijah, asking him to protect her daughter against evil and if possible bring her back to the fold in his chariot of fire. She was sure she would meet someone from Pakistan who would bring her news about Miriam.

Often she asked acquaintances who had been to Pakistan if they had ever met a girl named Miriam or Mariam.

But then Pakistan had so many Mariams that she never met anybody who could give her information about her Miriam.

When Yonathan tried persuading Shoshanah to return to Israel, she refused. She kept repeating that the prophet Elijah had not answered her prayers, so she did not want to go back.

Yonathan continued working in a knitwear company in Israel for five more years and would come to India on his yearly leave. But it was taking a toll on him financially and emotionally. Eventually, he was compelled to leave his job and return to India. He rented out their house in Israel and worked as a management consultant for knitwear. They led a fairly comfortable life in a rented apartment in Poona.

Shoshanah was close to her sister Eve, who lived with her family in Ahmedabad. So whenever Shoshanah felt distressed about Miriam she would visit Eve, and she eventually set up home in a rented apartment in Ahmedabad to be closer to her sister. All over again, Yonathan made contacts in the knitwear industry, and luckily he found work as manager of a small factory which specialized in socks.

It was with Eve that Shoshanah first saw Shalom India Housing Society. The idea of living in a Jewish housing society appealed to her and she persuaded Yonathan to buy an apartment there. She liked it so much that she even considered buying Juliet's apartment for Miriam, just in case . . .

Shoshanah tried to locate Miriam through the Pakistan Embassy and gave the official a letter for her, saying that she had property in India and could return whenever she wanted to. Her mother was always waiting for her.

Shoshanah hoped the bait would work and she would at last see her daughter. It did not matter anymore if she had converted and returned with a Muslim husband.

What was purity anyway? As long as one had a pure heart, nothing mattered. Look at the Bible or the history of the Jews, she argued with herself; Jewish life was after all a huge melting pot of all cultures and people.

Eve ran an English medium school in Ahmedabad and Shoshanah became the principal of the primary section, because in every little girl there she saw the reflection of her daughter Miriam.

16 Miriam

My dearest Mama,

I am sure you are surprised to receive this letter from me. It has been so many years since we have spoken to each other. I received the letter you sent me through the Pakistan embassy in New Delhi. It brought tears to my eyes. I was so relieved, I did not know where you were, so I was relieved to know that you have left Israel and settled in India, and that I can call you and we can at least speak to each other.

I read in detail about the apartment in Shalom India Housing Society, where you stay in Ahmedabad. It was interesting to read about a Jewish housing society, and about the apartment which belongs to Juliet who has married a Hindu man who has converted to Judaism and that they have immigrated to Israel. I was touched to read how the community has accepted Rahul or Romiel Abhiram, but wonder if they will accept me in the same way. We have a similar story, with different endings. But then, I suppose I should not worry, as you have written that if the mother is Jewish the children are automatically Jewish and the community will accept me. I appreciate your sentiments. Now that I am a mother, I understand how you feel.

Thank you, Mama, for offering me the apartment in Shalom India Housing Society. But I am not sure if I can accept your gift.

I have read the newspapers and seen the television reports about the Hindu-Muslim riots in Gujarat. I have also seen on television the reports on Ahmedabad. You have written that you tried to contact me for many years, while I had assumed you never wanted to see me again. I feel so sad that perhaps all your letters went to the dead letter office or were returned "undeliverable." So, when I did receive this letter from you about the apartment, I felt it was too late. Perhaps, if I had received your letter even at the millennium, I would have accepted the apartment. I feel now it is late, because I have seen the killing, beheading, and burning of Muslims in Ahmedabad, a city which is now your home. And by some quirk of fate it so happens that my family and I, we are Muslims. So, I would never dare to make Ahmedabad my home after the riots of 2002.

The other day, there was a report on television and I heard a young woman recounting how her family was massacred. She said she was saved because she was raped and left for dead. I was shocked when she spoke about her four-year-old son, who was beheaded in front of her very eyes. She was dry-eyed and had a deadpan expression. Your granddaughter and my younger child, Sheena, whom you have not yet seen, is also four years old. My son Omar is five years old. Since I saw this television report, I think I would be afraid to come to Ahmedabad. Because it is possible that something like this could have happened to us had we been living in Ahmedabad. I know that in the aftermath of a riot life does become normal in India or even Pakistan, so some day I will come to India to see you. But owning an apartment and living in Ahmedabad is another matter.

It has been so many years and so much has happened since I saw you last.

You will not believe this, but on Friday evenings, I light the Sabbath candle and make a special plea to the prophet Elijah that we meet as soon as possible.

I remember how much you believe in Eliyahu Hannabi. I also read and re-read the part in your letter about the prophet appearing in your dream like a silver cloud and planting the idea in your mind to buy that apartment for me near yours. Which also means that the prophet Elijah is making efforts for our reunion. I understand. In a way it is a miracle. We all know that he is often known to reveal himself to the devout, and soon after, you decided to find me through the Pakistan embassy and your letter reached me! So, in an indirect way, he did bring us together. So, now our meeting is just a matter of time and I am sure we will have a family reunion as soon as possible, although I feel sad that I do not have the courage to accept the gift of a home in India. Had things been different in Ahmedabad, perhaps I would have accepted your offer and set up another apartment in Ahmedabad, and we could have visited you once a year and stayed in the apartment for a month or so. But, if the prophet wishes, I am sure we will meet as soon as possible. The day we meet, I have decided, I will offer prayers to Eliyahu Hannabi.

But Mama, as the time when we may meet comes closer, you must prepare yourself and Papa to accept the fact that I am now a Muslim. Truthfully, this is nothing to feel upset about, as I follow both faiths. You will be happy to know that I still wear the Star of David chain you had given me on my bat mitzvah. I was wearing it when I left with Zulfi. You may feel angry and ashamed that I hide it under my kurta. You know how it is in Pakistan. Except for a few Jews who live here as Parsis and Aunt Rachel who looks after the graveyard, there are almost no Jews in Pakistan; as you know, it is an anti-Zionist state.

The Star of David was the only thing I had besides my Israeli passport and dollars. In fact the Star came with me only because I was wearing it when I left India with Zulfi.

The Star stayed with me, but the passport was useless. It is still with me. When we eloped, Zulfi had worked out everything.

I was a little shocked when he gave me the Pakistani passport in which my name was Mariam Zulfikar Sheikh, instead of Miriam. Till then, it had not even crossed my mind that I could not travel to Pakistan on an Israeli passport. I admit we were already at the airport and I was standing in the queue for immigration at Indira Gandhi Airport after a quick nikah at Zulfi's friend's place. Zulfi saw the shadow of doubt and noticed that I was not moving forward, nor was I smiling and joking as usual, so he held my hand and we stood for a moment to one side, as he asked if I was afraid. I said I was, as I had not given a thought to the larger implications of a Jew migrating to a Muslim country which was hostile to a Zionist state like Israel.

Zulfi is a good man, so he smiled and said if I had changed my mind, I was free to return to Uncle Cyril's apartment in Bombay and return to Israel.

Suddenly I felt torn between two worlds. As if I was in a no man's land and did not know which direction to take. I could see the intensity of his love and honesty in his eyes. No doubt, we had fallen in love much too quickly, but in that short time here was a man, who was in all principles my husband, yet had the courage to offer me the chance to choose my life. I asked myself if I really wanted to return to Israel and go through with a loveless marriage with Aaron. And, if I did return, perhaps he would refuse to marry me because of Zulfi. He was like that. And there was no guarantee that I would love the next Jewish man in my life as much as I loved Zulfi. So I held his hand and confidently walked towards immigration.

Of course, there were moments when I felt guilt, remorse, and loss. There were also feelings of mixed loyalties when I saw on television the Palestinian suicide bombers killing so many Jews in Israel.

On such days I would be a wreck and worried about you and Papa.

Every time I saw or read the news about suicide bombers in Israel, I was desperate to speak to you and wanted news from you, Papa, our relatives, friends, and my best friend Myrrh. But whenever I called all I got was this Russian woman telling me some vague story about India in her heavily accented Hebrew, till I started hating her voice.

Remember Mama, I used to have a good memory for numbers. But, believe me Mama, after I arrived in Pakistan I could not remember the phone numbers I used to know so well. I only remembered our number, nothing else.

Life has been comfortable in Pakistan, but Mama, I missed you very much during both my pregnancies, although Aunt Rachel was always there, helping me with the house. I will write a longer letter about her later. Yet I was often sad; unhappy that ever since I made my life with Zulfi I had become a stranger and could no longer be part of the family and community I had known since my childhood.

We live in Karachi and have a bungalow in the suburbs. We also have a small apartment in London, as Zulfi has two sari shops, one in Karachi and the other in London. In fact, eventually we plan to move to London. Remember Mama, how you always wanted me to study and take up a profession, but I was never interested and you were disappointed that I was not highly educated like most Indian girls? Women of your generation always stressed the need for higher education. You will be happy to know that here in Pakistan I have done my post-graduate degree in political science and have applied to a British university for a doctorate on cross-cultural conflicts in minority communities. One of the communities I am working on is the tiny Jewish community that still lives in Pakistan.

Someday, I hope you will visit us.

Zulfi is a good husband, a good father, and we are happy.

Believe me, Mama, I have often thought of communicating with you, but did not know how. I am happy, but I do suffer when I think about you and feel guilty about abandoning you. But since I received your letter I feel better.

I do not know how and when we will meet, but thanks to your perseverance, we can at least communicate through letters, phone calls, and e-mails. We will work out a way of meeting some day. I hope Papa has forgiven me. I remember his views on the Arab-Israel conflict and his hatred of the Palestinians, although one of his best friends was a Bedouin who sold us watermelons. Remember how he used to wait for me if I was late. And when I returned he always lit a candle and thanked Prophet Elijah that I had returned home safe and sound. I wonder if his political opinions have changed, since I, his only daughter, became a Muslim.

The last time I was in London, I thought of flying down to Israel and meeting you, even at the risk of using my Israeli passport. But then, every time I opened my Israeli passport, I was afraid to use it, as I know the Israelis and their vigilance department.

Once, during the first year of my marriage to Zulfi, when I was pregnant, I booked a ticket to Israel on a British Airways flight, but before that called you on our Israel phone number. I was surprised to hear the woman with the heavy Russian accent and when I insistently asked for you, she said something about India.

That really created a problem, as I did not have the courage to call either Aunt Agatha and Uncle Cyril, or Aunt Afsana. I am sure I am still a criminal in their eyes for having eloped with Zulfi.

Hanging onto some hope, I kept calling our home in Israel, but the same Russian voice answered me and slowly it seeped in that you had left Israel for India.

I never understood why.

I always thought you were very happy in Israel and had no reason to return to India.

Perhaps, when we meet you will tell me why you decided to return.

I hope it is not because of me and I have a sinking feeling that you are living there hoping that someday I will return to you.

When I could not reach you, I often thought about asking Zulfi's Bombay associates to find Uncle Cyril's phone number, as I vaguely remembered his address. But I did not. I was hesitant to speak to him and Aunty Agatha, as I am sure they think I am a cheat and a liar. I was also not sure if they would speak to me, as I had been their responsibility in India. So I did not dare call them, for fear of spoiling my own peace of mind. After the initial guilt and trauma of elopement, it has taken me a long time to settle down in Pakistan.

My decision was not easy, Mama.

I cannot explain how often I needed your comforting presence and missed being Papa's little girl.

Perhaps Zulfi could have asked Uncle Ehsan and Aunt Afsana your whereabouts, but since Zulfi had ditched their daughter Soha for me, we did not have the heart to open an old chapter. Although I have heard that Soha is married to a well-known industrialist of Bombay, is happy, and has three children. But after all, Zulfi was her first love, so I am sure she holds a grudge against me, as I, her best friend, ran away with her fiancé. Caught between countries, families, and life, my leaving with Zulfi sounds very romantic, but Mama, I want you to understand that it has never been easy to settle down in a new country, in a new environment, with a new religion. I hope you understand. Of course you do, or why else would you have written to me?

Mama, someday we have to meet, as there is so much I want to share with you, all those little things about my children. I have told them about you and Papa and they are looking forward to meeting you. They are too small to understand about Israel, so I keep telling them about my childhood in Poona.

The other day, I was at Sheena's convent school and during the parent-teacher meeting, I almost choked when I saw a picture of Mother Mary in the conference room. On the way back home, Sheena was chattering away about her school and her friends and I felt I was seeing myself in her.

When we immigrated to Israel, I must have been five years old. And I was your only child, pampered and spoiled. Before we left, there was a Hanukah party at the synagogue and I had insisted on dressing up as Mother Mary. I had seen her idol at the chapel in school.

You had objected and said it was a non-Jewish character, but I was just a child and had thrown a tantrum. So you draped me in your best blue and white chiffon saris. While dressing me, you said that you had allowed me to make my own decision about the dress, as you wanted me to be an independent woman, my own person, a woman with my own mind. You pinned the white sari like a flowing robe and covered my head with the blue sari. I was a bundle of saris and could hardly walk, but I loved the slippery feel and texture of the saris.

That year I won the first prize, a children's Bible, which you displayed prominently in the drawing room of our house in Poona and later in our house in Netanya in Israel.

You and Papa had been so worried about my choice of a Christian theme for the fancy dress party, that you had carefully instilled in me Jewish ideals and the importance of the strict following of rituals from a young age. Slowly, I became so interested in religion that sometimes you felt sorry that I insisted on following certain rituals even when you were not willing to go through them. But I remember Papa was pleased. In fact, if I remember correctly, after we immigrated to Israel, I could feel Papa had changed and was often attending right-wing party meetings. Especially since life became tense in Israel because of the Arab conflict and Cousin Effie died in an attack by a suicide bomber in a Jerusalem bus; Papa hated Arabs and often spoke against them.

I could not understand his change of heart, as in Poona we had Hindu, Muslim, Christian, and Parsi neighbors and you were both close friends of Uncle Ehsan and Aunt Afsana. You were seen together everywhere, at the cinema, at restaurants, and had many a dinner party in one or the other's home. The circle was complete, because their daughter Soha and I were best friends as kids and continued to write to each other even after we immigrated to Israel.

As a child, a visit to their house meant Urdu poetry recitations, sweets, tall glasses of rose sherbet, and Aunt Afsana looking like a houri in an embroidered gharara and star-spangled dupatta. Their house always had a certain fragrance, which has stayed with me for years. I never knew what it was. Much later, when I was again in their house, it suddenly struck me that it was the fragrance of fresh jasmine flowers. I noticed that Uncle Ehsan had at least fifty jasmine shrubs in his garden and surprisingly the fragrance had stayed with me through the years. So, as a symbol of this fragrant house where I first met Zulfi, we have also planted jasmine bushes around our home and during the hot summer months, I arrange bowls of jasmine all over the house and also put some next to our pillows, so that my home feels as fragrant as Aunt Afsana's.

When I write this, I wonder: how could I have been so religious? For, even if you were sometimes careless, I insisted that you teach me all the Jewish rituals and the correct way of following them. And much to the surprise of many, I observed the fast of the Day of Atonement, studied the Torah, and if anybody asked me what I wanted to become when I grew up, without having to think I would answer that I wanted to become a woman rabbi. I had seen a woman rabbi at Cousin Benji's bar mitzvah. I was so impressed with her confidence, knowledge, and style that all I wanted to do was study to become a woman rabbi.

And to prepare myself for the profession of my choice, by the time I was in my teens, I was wearing plain clothes which covered me from head to toe, and tied a scarf over my long black hair. I never wore shorts or small dresses like girls of my age, nor did I go to dance parties. But I did enjoy the Indian association programs, where I loved listening to Hindi film songs and would have liked to wear the pretty Indian saris, salwar-kameez suits, and shararas. I would have also liked to dance to Hindi film songs, but I was shy and anyway, that is not how a woman rabbi should behave, so I sat still like a statue and never participated in any of the Hindi-film type dance and music parties. Though I must admit that one side of me was attracted to it. I stopped myself from doing things which were natural for girls of my age. The only liberty I allowed myself was an addiction to Bollywood films.

When I switched on the DVD player, I was transported to another world, a world I wanted to know better. My all-time favorite was the film *Mughal-e-Azam*. If I could I would watch it every day. There was something spectacular about that one single scene in color with Madhubala dancing in the sheesh mahal. It caught my imagination. The other film that amused me was the Madhuri Dixit film *Hum Aapke Hain Kaun*. I loved the family rituals of a wedding and imagined myself as the heroine, but I was appalled when I could not imagine Aaron as the hero Salman Khan. And, I would force myself to imagine that Aaron and I were the main actors of the film.

Aaron was different and somehow never seemed to fit into my romantic dreams.

When he came to drop me at Ben Gurion Airport, we hugged, and I was in tears, sure that I could not survive a day without Aaron.

Although I had grown up in Israel like any other teenager, there was something within me which I never understood till I met Zulfi.

But, before that there was Aaron. That was the beginning of all my troubles.

I still remember how Aaron, who had grown up in Israel and never seen India, saw me at an Indian dance program and liked me, sat next to me and chatted about this and that. Mama, I could see you were pleased when within a week we received a proposal of marriage from Aaron's family.

You convinced me that it was a great catch, but had informed Aaron's family that I was exempt from the army and was studying to become a woman rabbi. They did not have a problem, in fact they said they felt impressed that a young woman like me had such high ideals as wanting to become a rabbi.

I agreed, because you convinced me that women rabbis did not keep away from matrimony and that most were married. You said that if married, a woman understood life better and could make a perfect Jewish home.

As soon as we were engaged, I realized I had another side to myself. I am sure it will embarrass you, but I discovered that I liked to spend time with Aaron. Even if we went for a walk or were at one or another café, we could hardly keep away from each other. We were in a great hurry to get married, so we fixed a date quickly, decided upon the synagogue, booked a hall, and fixed the menu for the reception.

I remember the surprise on your face when I suddenly announced that I preferred saris to wedding gowns and would like to shop for my trousseau in India. So, it was decided that I should travel alone to India and stay with Uncle Cyril and Aunt Agatha in Bombay.

I was in fact going to Bombay for the first time after we immigrated.

I was looking forward to shopping and seeing all the latest Hindi films. I was excited.

But when I landed at the airport in Bombay, I was not sure if I liked India. As soon as the doors of the plane opened a stink hit me, and I felt disillusioned and cheated of the rose and jasmine fragrances.

Uncle Cyril and Aunt Agatha received me with warm hugs, but I was still not sure if I was going to like India.

The next morning, I woke up to the call of the koel on the gulmohur tree outside my window; I felt happy, looking forward to endless days of shopping and cinema.

Suddenly Israel was very far away and India had entered my heart.

It was summer and the kitchen had a big basket of mangoes. With the heady, tangy fragrance of mangoes, I was transported to another world, the first few years of my life in India.

Mama, do you remember when a truck full of mangoes overturned in the lane next to our house in Poona?

In Aunt Agatha's house, we had mangoes for breakfast. When I cut the golden fruit in two and licked the juice from my hands, I was thinking of that afternoon when you had bought pounds of mangoes from the overturned truck. They were enough to fill an entire room and the whole house was filled with the heady fragrance of mangoes.

When the truck overturned, from our veranda the mangoes looked like golden orbs full of nectar. They were in all shapes and sizes and colors, from dark green to lighter tones of green to lemon yellow to dark yellow to red to deep mango-yellow. Some were ripe, others unripe, so there was always a sour-sweet fragrance around us. You sat on the cane chair in the veranda, sorting the mangoes, identifying them, and telling me their names, like Hafooz, Alphonso, Gulab, Langda, Totapuri, Kesar, and Junglee, which you said was very good for making aam-ras. This was a season when we had mango on the mind and nothing else, and since I rediscovered mangoes in India and Pakistan, I am euphoric about mangoes and think of nothing else. Mama, you will be happy to know that, like you, I keep making every possible pickle, chutney, and papad. I also put raw mango in dal and vegetables and my mango soufflé is supposed to be the best in the neighborhood.

Living on this side of the world, which is similar to India in many ways, I have become addicted to the smell of mango flowers in spring. At the onset of spring, I like to make a trip to the mango orchards in the suburbs, where the air is heavy with the tangy fragrance of mango blossoms. Later, as the mangoes start coming to the market, I enjoy exploring various mangoes. Full, round, golden-yellow, voluptuous, sensuous, plump, tactile, they make summer bearable as I practically live on them, raw, cooked, or ripe. And, like you, I also make gallons of green mango sherbet; it is amazing how it helps beat the summer heat. I also discovered that I have good pickle hands. I did not know I could make pickles, till I once tried and since then it is like a home industry for me. My favorites are the sweet Bene Israel muramba and a delicious chutney with mint, green chilies, coriander, green mango, and coconut. I remember your mango chutney was the best. You even made it in Israel, that is, if by chance you found raw mangoes in the Beersheba open market. You made the chutney, bottled it, and as long as it lasted, we ate it in pita bread sandwiches and with our daily curry and rice.

Much to Zulfi and the children's amusement, I still like eating my mangoes straight or drinking those endless bowls of aam-ras, till I feel I am going to burst like an over-ripe mango balloon. For me, mangoes are so precious that I do not spare even the seed and like you, I often preserve extra aam-ras as sweet mango papad. You said you had learned it from your sister, Aunt Eve, who lived in Gujarat. No wonder you have decided to live there, close to Aunt Eve and eating all those mangoes and chutney sandwiches.

There is something ethereal about mangoes, especially when I cut open an Alphonso mango. I think mangoes have names which sound like Urdu verse—Gulab, Badam, Kesar, Gola, Rajapuri, Totapuri, Sundari, Desi, Dusseri. The names of mangoes are almost the same in Pakistan, sometimes there is a difference, but the last time I was in London, I picked up a small booklet on mangoes from a Gujarati store, and I know the names by heart!

After the mango truck overturned and you bought your share from the trader, you emptied the guest room of all furniture, spread dry grass on the floor, and arranged the mangoes in different stages of ripeness. You often talked about it later in Israel, remembering it as your house of mangoes.

Some mangoes you kept aside to make pickles, some to give away, some for the cook, but the overdone mangoes were for aam-ras, which was kept bottled or frozen in the fridge.

That afternoon you had invited all your women friends for a dinner of aam-ras, puris and potato spiced merely with cumin, turmeric, salt, and green chilies.

I was helping you make the juice. You were sitting on the low stool, your sari hitched above your knees and laughing like a little girl because I had plastered myself with mango juice. My face was covered with the golden juice, I was sitting cross-legged, licking my fingers, and asking you to fill a tub with mango juice, so that I could swim in it.

That week, I ate so many mangoes that naturally I was sick.

That afternoon in Poona, mangoes entered my being. If I breathe deep, I can still inhale the fragrance of mangoes rising from within me.

You had so many mangoes, and as the date of our departure was coming closer you did not have the heart to give them away, so you tried every possible trick to take the mangoes to Israel in different forms: dried and powdered to add to dal and vegetables, pickled in five different ways, and also made into papads. For years I thought of India as one big fat juicy mango. So whenever somebody asked me to draw a picture of India, I invariably drew a mango!

The mangoes for breakfast at Aunt Agatha's table disturbed me. I tried to distract myself with the shopping and regular visits to the cinema or with soaps on television or sometimes old classics on DVD. My cousins thought I had old-fashioned tastes in films and dress. Late at night, I sat alone in the dark drawing room, watching films like *Pakeezah, Mughal-e-Azam, Umrao Jaan, Pyaasa,* and *Kagaaz ke Phool.* Aunt Agatha had similar tastes and often joined me and I am sure she thought I was a very nice sentimental girl, till I eloped with Zulfi and left that teary letter, very filmy, *Pakeezah* style. In the same way that Rajkumar leaves the letter between Meena Kumari's beautiful toes in the train scene. Well, Aunty Agatha's swollen feet with spread-out toes and thick nails were not so beautiful, but then, as she also liked my sort of films, she cannot deny that it was a poetic way of disappearing from my Jewish avatar.

Aunt Agatha must have really thought I was very stupid and filmy and my head was full of nonsense, or why else would a nice, well brought-up Bene Israel girl from Israel, engaged to be married to one of the most eligible Israeli suitors, be crazy about Urdu couplets and elope with a Pakistani named Zulfi! She must have thanked the Lord that I did not find an Arab in Israel or it would have been disastrous for the family. With Zulfi, as he is a Muslim from the East, there is still a possibility that we could be accepted by family and community. At least, with your support there is a possibility we could be accepted as part of the family. It does not happen often, but with an Arab it would have been impossible, even if he looked like Omar Sharif.

But, when I think about my life in Israel, I do not think I would have ever fallen in love with an Arab. We grew up with Muslims in India and have good friends in the Muslim community, the way you and Aunty Afsana have kept up a lifelong friendship, yet the conditioning is such in the Israeli way of life that one automatically treats Arabs as enemies. In those days, I would get goose pimples with fear if I found an Arab staring at me on the bus to Jerusalem.

But then, what happened with Zulfi at Aunt Afsana's place was out of the blue. I had neither expected it, nor planned it. No doubt, Zulfi resembles Omar Sharif. As luck would have it, I met him at Aunt Afsana's house.

Before I left, you had told me in detail about their sari shop in

Poona. You had said they had the best wedding saris. After I reached Bombay, Aunt Afsana called me at Uncle Cyril's, inquiring about you and inviting me to Poona to look at wedding saris. Then Soha came on the line and, much to my excitement, invited me to her engagement party.

Normally, somebody or the other accompanied me when I went shopping, but as Aunt Afsana was going to receive me at the station, Uncle Cyril thought I was in safe hands. Aunt Afsana had said that she would wait for me at the book stall.

Hardly did anybody imagine that when Aunt Afsana called me, it was my destiny calling me to Poona, where I was to meet Zulfi.

Soha was there at the station with Aunt Afsana. Meeting them after so many years, I had no idea what they looked like, but as soon as I got off the train, I saw them standing at the book stall, dressed in the latest salwar-kameez suits, looking stately, tall, and so breathtakingly beautiful that I felt awkward in my jeans. When I introduced myself, they gave me a warm welcome and Soha and I were chattering away in the car as though we had never parted.

On my first day in Poona, I did not see Zulfi. I just saw his photograph on Soha's dressing table and she demanded that I show her Aaron's photograph. She was shocked that I had forgotten it in Bombay. Actually, I lied and did not tell her that when I left Israel it had never crossed my mind that I should carry Aaron's photograph in my purse; after all, he had enlarged my close-up and hung it on the wall opposite his bed, so that mine was the first face he saw in the morning.

From Zulfi's photograph, I could not make out what he really looked like. And, although he was living under the same roof, I did not ask to see him, as the house fascinated me. Soha took me on a guided tour. I studied the house in great detail. It was like a film set similar to the ones I had seen in my favorite *Mughal-e-Azam, Pakeezah,* and *Umrao Jaan.*

The façade of the house was like a fort and was surrounded by a step garden. A veranda with high pillars led to the drawing room. I liked it so much that I have designed my drawing room on similar lines. The room had carved furniture surrounded by arches and carvings. At night, these were lit with marine-blue lights and there was a red wall-to-wall Persian carpet, so soft and beautiful that with-

out being told to one was impelled to remove footwear before tread-
ing on it. The sofas were colonial and had satin covers and gol takias.
In the center of the drawing room there was an enormous glass
chandelier, and there were multicolored stained-glass windows, glass
lanterns, bead curtains, and an old ancestral hookah with gold strings
on its pipe was kept in a corner as decoration. Uncle Ehsan had
bought an old haveli and done it up in a mixed style. The drawing
room had trophies of a tiger and a bear and a painting of Uncle
Ehsan's grandfather dressed in a turban, sherwani, mojdis, jewelry,
and holding a sword. I thought it was very impressive. The drawing
room led to a courtyard, which had a fountain, and the other rooms
and kitchen were built around the courtyard. There was a beautifully laid-out garden with a swing, around which were garden chairs
and a table. It was a pleasure to sit there and drink tea to the music
of the songbirds. The dining room was a platform with a portico
extending up to the fountain and had ornate carved furniture, tall
chairs with red upholstery, and bowls filled with flower petals. The
kitchen was the most amazing place in the house. At all times I felt
the flavors of Arabia wafting from the many dishes that their old
cook made for the family. There were ancient vessels of copper and
brass arranged on the upper shelves and modern casseroles on the
lower shelves and in the cupboards. They also had an old dining set
of Chinese ceramics. There were chikh curtains almost everywhere,
especially along the courtyard, which according to the time of the
day were pulled down to shade the house from the harsh sun. Only
Aunt Afsana and Uncle Ehsan's bedroom was downstairs; the other
bedrooms were upstairs and each had a balcony overlooking the garden. All the rooms were done up in the Oriental style and had colored glass windows and lanterns. If Aunt Afsana's room had a
tapestry of Omar Khayyam, Soha had Aishwarya Rai, her younger
sister Ayesha had her own fashion drawings, pieces of textile, and
pictures of models, as she was studying for a diploma in fashion
design, while their teenage brother Shiraz had covered his walls with
pictures of cricket stars. The guest rooms were on the same lines and
had Ayesha's watercolors of flowers.

Believe me, Mama, I was so fascinated by the house that it was
not deliberate and I had no intention of falling in love with Zulfi or
anybody else at that. I was there to shop for saris for my own wed-

ding to Aaron. Yes, till that very point, I was serious about Aaron, and was wondering how much we would have to earn to build a house like that.

But, I suppose it was destined that the night of Soha's engagement party was to change the course of my fate. I know you will never believe this, but it is true.

All day as I walked through the house, I did not see Zulfi. He did not even appear at lunchtime, after which the preparations for the party began and I was worried stiff about what I would wear, because all I had brought for the party was a black gown to be worn with a golden stole, a little jewelry, and high-heeled shoes. My heart sank when Soha laid out all her shimmering ghararas, shararas, kurtis, and ghaghras on her bed. I felt the black dress which would have been all right for a party in Israel was not adequate for Soha's engagement party. I kicked myself as I could have at least borrowed one of Aunt Agatha's mirror-work dupattas, which I could have worn with my old red mirror-work kurta. When Soha suggested we go to the beauty parlor for shaping our eyebrows, waxing our legs and arms, and applying makeup and mehendi, I was enthusiastic, as I had come to enjoy the Indian beauty parlor, where you felt like a queen with girls attending to you and making you look like Cleopatra. But as we reached Soha's beauty parlor, I confided in Soha that I would skip the beauty treatment and instead go looking for something to wear for the party. She refused, and that night, at her insistence, I wore her silk sharara and a silver-spangled chiffon dupatta of the same color. I was wearing my silver anklets, long chandelier earrings, colored glass bangles up to my elbows, my palms were the deep orange color of mehendi. I had strings of jasmine flowers in my hair, and a touch of Anais-Anais behind my ears. I wore lipstick, applied kohl to my eyes, arranged the dupatta, and could not recognize myself in the mirror. I felt I had walked off the sets of *Mughal-e-Azam*. All I had to do was to start dancing and that was exactly the mood of the evening. But when I saw Soha decked out in her shimmering shot-silk marine-blue sharara, I felt nobody could compare to her in beauty.

The house was alight with a thousand diyas. The chandeliers and lanterns were lit, the glass windows glowed with subdued reflected light. There was a touch of romance in the atmosphere with beautiful people floating in the garden amidst bowls of flower petals, around the fountain, in silk, chif-fons, saris, ghararas, shararas, embroidered Lucknowi kurtas, tinkling anklets, shining jewelry, all to the sound of a live shehnai.

An early dinner of biryani, both meat and vegetable, was served in the inner courtyard with tall glasses of fruit juice, chicken tikkas, sizzling kebabs, paneer masala, butter-soft naans, roomali rotis, kofta curries, phirni with rose petals, and platters of sweets.

That was when Uncle Ehsan introduced me to Zulfi.

"Oh, so you come from Israel, I cannot believe it. You look like an Indian," he laughed. I swallowed the biryani and smiled, "But, you do look like a Pakistani." Zulfi looked handsome in a white kurta embroidered with subtle motifs, a churidar, a red velvet cap arranged at an oblique angle, and long black hair. At that very moment something sparked between us, although I was not half as beautiful as Soha. There was an instant chemistry, but I could not figure him out, as he was teasing Soha and they often stood holding hands.

For some reason, I sensed that I was jealous of Soha.

I did not have the same feeling with Aaron.

I blamed my feelings on the atmosphere.

With Aaron, it always ended up with coffee at Tel Aviv's Dizengoff square, a late night movie or the beach. I was back in Israel, imagining a bleak future.

Then, I wiped out my black mood and forced myself to enjoy the evening.

Later that night, there was a recital by a well-known Urdu poet in the open pavilion of the garden. White sheets were spread out on the lawns, where the guests reclined on gol takias.

It was a magical evening, with Soha on my right and Zulfi on my left, explaining the meaning of the words. I was uncomfortable that something was happening between Zulfi and me and Soha was not even aware of the attraction. I felt sorry for her, as she was lost in her own dreams. Once in a while she lowered her kohl-filled eyes, raised her arched eyebrows, and threw a shy sideways glance at Zulfi, who merely winked back at her, much to her annoyance.

It was almost two in the morning when the party broke up. I was so happy and elated that I could not sleep, so I took a durrie and went to the terrace and lay down there. Far away, I could hear the call of a bird I could not identify. It was a full-moon night and the dome of the sky seemed so close that I felt I could have touched the stars. I lay there, half asleep, with the music of the Urdu words still echoing in my ears. I was transported into another world.

It was then that I felt a feather-like touch on my feet and for some strange reason, I remembered that ostrich feather scene from *Mughal-e-Azam*, when the hero kisses the heroine, tenderly touching her lips with a feather. But this touch was not part of my dreams, so I looked towards my feet and saw Zulfi caressing them and kissing them. I allowed him to as he made me feel that I was the most beautiful woman on earth.

Mama, this sounds strange, but without exchanging a word, it was clear that we had fallen in love that night, deeply and dangerously.

And, believe me, the next morning I felt so awful about facing this beautiful family and Soha that I found some excuse and returned to Bombay.

The next week in Bombay was madness, as Zulfi followed me and sent me a text message that I should meet him at the cinema hall next to Aunt Agatha's house, where they were showing *Mughal-e-Azam*. I had to tactfully take Aunt Agatha's permission to leave the house. Zulfi and I saw the film together. The impossible romance, the songs, and the plight of the heroine made me cry. After that, one thing led to the other and I felt so guilty about Soha, Aaron, and both families, that I almost told Zulfi to leave me alone as Soha was not only more beautiful than me, but very sensitive and would not be able to bear breaking the engagement. But Zulfi insisted that he did not love Soha and a love like ours happens only once in a lifetime. That is true; in just a week, I could not imagine life without Zulfi. And, truthfully, I could not remember what Aaron looked like. So, giving up everything, we eloped. And, we have not once regretted our decision, because we are very happy.

I believe one can now see the film *Mughal-e-Azam* in color, perhaps we will see it in London or perhaps you could send us a DVD?

And yes, Mama, even if I did convert to Islam, please believe me when I say I am Jewish. As I told you, I still wear the Star of David.

I fast on the Day of Atonement, and on Fridays I always light the Sabbath candle. It is easier in London, where nobody questions me and I am free to observe the festivals and even attend prayers at the synagogue.

We often meet with the few Jewish families in Pakistan and celebrate the festivals in one home or other. Zulfi makes sure that he is always present with the children and has also learned some prayers. You must hear him singing the Passover prayers with the children. The children do not know these, as they are too small. But when they grow up they will know.

Then, there is Aunt Rachel, a pillar of strength for all of us. She is known as the only living Jew of Pakistan. Hers is such an amazing story, as she stayed on after the other Jews immigrated to Israel in the forties. She is an example to the Jews of the world, because she has proved that a Jew can survive against all odds in an Islamic country if he or she believes in the Lord, is truthful, honest, and compassionate. I take food and clothes for her. She is a sort of a caretaker of the graveyard and during festivals I help her light candles at the graves and offer flowers to the dead and together we say the Kaddish. I often meet her and feel she is my Pakistani family. So, Mama, it is not so hard to retain a Jewish identity even in a Muslim or Arab country. Believe me, Mama, I hope someday you will meet my family and I am sure you will love Zulfi and the kids.

I love you and Papa and hope to see you soon.
With love and kisses, your loving daughter,
Miriam

17 Samuel

Unless he showed an inclination to speak, nobody ever spoke to Samuel on the stairs, in the elevator, in the parking lot, at the bread shop, or at the synagogue. He was one of the few who did not join the Shalom India Laughing Club.

Samuel was a thin man of medium height, but had an autocratic bearing in the way he dressed, walked, and spoke. He made the perfect picture of a Jewish patriarch. Often people mistook him for a foreigner as he was very fair, sported a French beard, had pink cheeks and a long sharp nose which was always red at the tip.

Actually, if one looked at the family photographs in his drawing room, it was easy to see that he resembled his mother. Except for a photograph of his parents, the rest of the photographs arranged in rows at lintel-level were of the men of the family, all male twins. There were photographs of his grandfather with his twin brother, his father with his twin brother, himself with his twin brother Solomon, who had died in a road accident, and his own twins Abel and Albert. Samuel and his parents had left for Israel after Solomon's death.

Salome, who had been friendly with his mother Lily, was of the opinion that Samuel had changed after he lost his twin. She sympathized and said he was not rude; it was just that he felt lost and forlorn without his other half.

Very few people knew that on most mornings when he woke up, he did feel lost and helpless as if he were searching for something, actually his brother.

Samuel's father Mordecai had also suffered from a similar syndrome.

In contrast to the sophisticated Samuel, his wife Sharon was a small-town girl from Junagadh. Normally, he would have said she was provincial, but since he was attracted to her, he liked her the way she was. He had first seen her at the Magen Abraham Synagogue in Ahmedabad at the New Year celebrations. Sharon looked different from the rest of the girls: she had covered her head with a golden gauze dupatta and wore a long flowing skirt and a blouse of the same color.

She was not exactly beautiful. She was beetle-browed and had full lips set in a long, thin face. That day, she was wearing gold chandelier earrings, a pearl choker, an armful of gold bangles, and anklets. So whenever she moved there was a tinkle of silver bells and a rustle of silk.

Samuel was then forty-two, over-age by Bene Israel standards, and had come to India from Israel with his parents for the New Year. They were also trying to sell their house next to the synagogue and perhaps find a bride for Samuel. When his mother Lily saw him staring at this young woman from Junagadh who spoke in strongly accented Gujarati, she asked him if he would like to consider her as a bride.

He was then working in a biscuit factory in Israel during the day and as a watchman at night. Samuel nodded his head in agreement. Sharon was attractive, appeared to be thirty-plus, looked playful and happy. Lily changed places and sat next to Salome, whispering in her ear that she wanted to speak to Sharon's mother. Salome pointed Hana out to her. Hana had noticed the fair man staring at her daughter all evening. Lily again changed places and cornered Hana, asking her for Sharon's hand as Yacov sounded the shofar, ushering in the New Year.

Hana refused, saying she did not want to send her daughter to Israel.

But Lily insisted and painted a beautiful picture of the promised land, saying her daughter would be happy with her son.

Craftily, she also hinted that Sharon had passed the age of marriage. Hana sighed, knowing very well that her daughter was almost thirty-five and had so far not received any decent proposals of marriage.

In a flash she saw endless, barren years of lonely spinsterhood for her daughter and agreed to arrange a meeting between Samuel and Sharon.

That night Hana told Sharon about the proposal and convinced her to accept it, saying this was her last chance, after which it would be difficult to get such a good proposal from a well-settled Bene Israel groom. Sharon had had a strict upbringing and did not get involved with non-Jewish males. If and when she felt attracted to someone who did not belong to the Jewish community, she stopped herself from thinking of marrying him.

Sharon agreed to meet Samuel; she had her doubts about him, but did not voice them.

Sharon would not have noticed Samuel, but since he appeared to be a stranger in the synagogue and kept staring at her, she had thrown him a glance. And instinctively she felt there was something cold and distant about him.

She gave the final consent only after she went out for lunch with Samuel. He was polite, well mannered, sometimes funny, and definitely intelligent. Though she was a musician, he admitted that he knew nothing about Indian classical music, but assured her that he would make an effort to take an interest in music so that they would have something in common.

At the end of the evening, halfheartedly Sharon came to the conclusion that she could perhaps spend a lifetime with Samuel.

It was better than living the life of a confirmed spinster.

In a week Samuel and Sharon were married. She experienced a moment of misgiving at the wedding reception.

A busload of Sharon's friends from Junagadh had come down to Ahmedabad for the reception. With them came Gautam-sir, Sharon's handsome music teacher, dressed in a spotless white kurta-pajama, his long locks falling over his high forehead, carrying a sitar.

As part of the festivity, Gautam offered to play the sitar for the couple. He played an evening raga and received a standing ovation from the guests.

Immediately, Samuel was uncomfortable with Gautam-sir. On the way back to their hotel in the car, he asked her if he was her ex-boyfriend.

Insulted, she retorted that he was her guru and a married man with a family. But she made sure that Gautam-sir never came to see them as long as they were in India, and much to her relief, Samuel never mentioned Gautam-sir until he reappeared in their lives.

Life in Israel meant hard work, accepting a different lifestyle and learning Hebrew, which was hard to master. From the day Sharon landed at Ben Gurion Airport, she knew that life would never be easy and she would have to keep making adjustments.

She also understood that she could never be Samuel's other half, as that was his dead brother's place and had been empty for so long there was no possibility of her filling it.

For those extra shekels which they always needed and her own peace of mind Sharon decided to find work. She had learned the sitar from Gautam-sir and it was not difficult for her to find work as a music teacher in the Indo-Israel cultural association.

Everything seemed all right for a few years, until she started having problems with her domineering mother-in-law Lily, and soon Samuel was faced with the problem of making separate living arrangements for them.

The family moved from north to south Israel and Samuel found a house in Beersheba which appeared to be ideal for them.

It was a duplex and he decided that his parents would take the first floor and he would live on the second floor with Sharon. There was a staircase which led to the first floor apartment from the inside of the second floor. The first floor apartment looked out onto a small garden.

But the common kitchen was on the second floor. The aging Mordecai and Lily found it difficult to climb the stairs and felt imprisoned in the first floor apartment, though every morning before she left for work, Sharon prepared their food and Samuel left it on their dining table. There was always a flask of tea, a box of sandwiches, and casseroles full of dal, rice, and vegetables. Sometimes they left extra food, if they were to return late or were invited to a party. On holidays and Saturdays, Sharon made chapatis, paranthas or poories, chicken curry, rice, salad, vegetables, and sent warm casseroles to her in-laws downstairs, always with a box of Indian sweets.

Sharon saw them once in ten days or when Samuel was away on business. When they rang the alarm, normally Samuel ran downstairs to attend to their needs; if not Sharon was always there for them. If Sharon and Samuel returned late unexpectedly, Mordecai and Lily ate the leftovers from lunch or made themselves a bowl of cornflakes. Often it happened that by the time Sharon made something simple for dinner and sent it downstairs they were fast asleep.

But Samuel was the proverbial good son; once a week, he took them for a drive or took them to the synagogue. Sometimes, he even took them to dinner parties and cultural programs hosted by the association of Indian Jews.

A situation like this could create a lot of bitterness and distance in the family and Mordecai and Lily made a pact to keep quiet on this particular topic. They never confided in Samuel that they felt trapped and suffocated in the first floor apartment with the kitchen, television, and other living spaces upstairs. They thanked the prophet Elijah that their son had not abandoned them, and instead had given them shelter in his own house.

Then the inevitable happened, early one Saturday morning, the only day he could sleep late, Samuel sat up with a start when he heard the continuous ring of the alarm-bell. He was sure something was amiss as the bell kept ringing till he reached downstairs. His father was ringing the bell and trying to wake up Lily. She had died of a heart attack in her sleep.

Ten days after the funeral, Samuel started noticing signs of disorientation in his father's behavior. Late at night, he would ring the bell, and when Samuel went downstairs he said he had seen Lily sitting next to him on the bed. He insisted that Samuel take him upstairs, as he was afraid of Lily's ghost. When Samuel suggested that he open the first floor door and take a walk in the garden, Mordecai refused, he wanted to be upstairs with Samuel. Samuel returned upstairs to speak to Sharon, but she looked away and did not say anything.

Since Lily died, Samuel was invariably late for work, as he helped his father climb the seventeen steps. He seated the panting Mordecai, breathless with the effort, in his favorite colonial chair, which they had shipped from India when they had immigrated to Israel in the fifties.

Mordecai sat in the chair and Samuel switched on ancient K.L. Saigal songs on the automated music system, which kept playing till Samuel returned home and switched it off.

The old man sat there reading the *Jerusalem Post* from one end to the other and writing poetry about India. Sharon left his breakfast and lunch on a table next to him. And even if Mordecai's routine bothered them on Saturdays, they saw Hindi films on the video, so that everybody was happy and there were no complaints.

For a year or two, life ran smoothly with occasional ups and downs, till Samuel returned home one day, and found his father sitting naked on the colonial chair talking incoherently and having lost control of his bladder. Immediately he shifted him to the hospital, and when he brought him back home he knew that it would be difficult to look after Mordecai. So they took him straight to the first floor room, where he stayed till his end, wallowing in his urine and talking to Lily, who he was sure was sitting next to him.

Religiously, every single day, Samuel went down the seventeen steps and attended to his father's needs. He employed a nurse to look after his father when he was at work. Every single day, he washed his father, changed his clothes and fed him. Not once did he ask Sharon to help him, although it created a certain distance between them.

After his father died, Samuel closed the first floor apartment, emptied the rooms of memories of his father and packed away the photographs in boxes. Samuel never descended the seventeen steps again, as he was guilt-ridden and the steps symbolized his parents' distress.

He considered renting out the first floor to students, but was worried that perhaps his mother's ghost really lived there.

In fact, he had come to believe that both his parents' dissatisfied souls lived in the house, behind the door to the first floor apartment.

Sharon was not untouched by the deaths in the family. She was unhappy that Samuel spoke to her in an offhand manner and even when they made love she knew it was a mechanical act.

But it was an eventful year. Some time after Sharon celebrated her forty-sixth birthday, she missed her periods and her gynecologist informed her that she was pregnant. Immediately Sharon went into a depression. She was sick and cried when she was at home.

Samuel was not sure whether he was happy or sad about fatherhood, till the doctor informed him that Sharon was carrying twins. Samuel smiled for the first time in years and distributed sweets to friends and family.

That evening, he saw Sharon was in bad shape, crying on the phone and telling her mother how much she missed India. On a sudden impulse, Samuel decided to return to India.

He wrote to old friends in Ahmedabad, who helped him find a good apartment and a consultancy in a biscuit factory. Eventually he took a bank loan and started his own biscuit factory in Ahmedabad, with Israeli collaboration.

Samuel sold the house in Israel for a good sum, and returned to Ahmedabad with a pregnant wife. When the twins were born he felt he needed a bigger apartment, and booked a three-bedroom apartment at Shalom India Housing Society. He argued with Sharon, saying he was a religious man and needed a community so that he could follow Jewish rituals. He understood she was trying to maneuver him, telling him that Citizen Apartments, where Juliet's parents lived, were much better. Sharon's parents had bought an apartment there, having left Junagadh so that they could be closer to Sharon.

Samuel rejected Citizen Apartments, saying they were too small, and also because he wanted to maintain some distance from Sharon's parents. Samuel had noticed they lived in Apartment 17 and he did not want to repeat parental history.

Samuel was happy to settle down in Ahmedabad. Unlike Israel, life was easy and he had more time for himself and took up photography as a hobby.

He was relieved to have the seven seas between himself and the seventeen steps in that house in Israel.

And if he saw them in his nightmares, he woke up in a sweat, drank a glass of water, prayed to Eliyahu Hannabi for relief, lit a candle, and went back to bed.

Sharon was happy to be back in India, and did all that was expected of her as a good Jewish wife. But she never told him that she was bored with their lifestyle.

SHALOM INDIA HOUSING SOCIETY

The only respite from boredom was her sitar. She gave music lessons in the drawing room in the afternoons, when Salome stepped in to look after the twins. The only silver lining was that Samuel loved the twins and believed they were incarnations of his father and brother.

Samuel's peaceful existence came to an abrupt end one morning when Sharon, who was frying eggs for breakfast, asked him chattily if he remembered her music teacher, Gautam-sir. She said he was planning to buy Juliet's apartment and start a music school there with Sharon as partner.

Samuel, who was reading the morning paper, looked up quizzically.

She had never mentioned Gautam-sir before. He did not even know she was meeting him and now they were planning to start a music school under his nose in A-107.

Samuel asked sharply, "I did not know you had met Gautam-sir. Does he live in Ahmedabad?"

Sharon was pouring the tea and gave a short answer without looking up, "Yes."

"When did you meet him?"

"Oh, as soon as we returned from Israel, I met him at Mama's."

Trying to control his temper, Samuel asked, "Why didn't you tell me? And, why do you meet him at your Mama's? Why don't you invite him home for dinner?"

"No reason," she said, "It's just because we never invite people. When did we last invite anybody to dinner? Anyway, now that we will have a class upstairs, you will see him often," she smiled coquettishly.

Samuel pretended he was deaf and continued reading the editorial page. Then he asked haltingly, "Is he going to stay in Juliet's apartment with his family?"

"No."

"Why?"

"Because he does not have one."

"But, the last time we saw him, you said he was married."

"He is. But his wife does not live with him. Sujata has been living apart for four years. They have two children and she works in a bank."

"So, does it mean he will live here all alone?"

"Yes. We will use part of the apartment as a music school."

"What do you mean, we?"

"Gautam and I."

"Since when? You never told me anything."

"He is coming to see the apartment this afternoon. In fact brother Ezra has agreed to sell it to Gautam."

"When was this decided?"

"Today."

"I see," said Samuel, folding the newspaper; he felt threatened for the first time in his life. He did not like the idea of Gautam living in Shalom India Housing Society.

Samuel started pacing the balcony and wondering how he would solve this problem.

He knew that their otherwise peaceful family life would be disrupted if Gautam came into the picture. And after the ups and downs of the seventeen steps he did not want any more problems. He started wondering whether there were seventeen steps between their apartment and Gautam-sir's apartment.

Besides, he did not want to disturb the twins; he wanted to give them a happy family life. After all, the prophet Elijah had sent them to him after innumerable prayers.

As he sat in his father's colonial chair, tying his shoelaces, he came to the conclusion that he did not want Gautam-sir's presence in his life.

In a crisis like this, Samuel surprised himself by dropping his indifference like a snakeskin, and decided to act.

Sharon had packed his lunch in a small tiffin-carrier and left it on the dining table. He slid it into his bag, kissed the twins and called out to Sharon that he was leaving. Then he closed the door behind him and went down to the parking lot and sat in his car.

He did not start the ignition, because he needed to think.

Not once had Sharon given him reason to believe that she could fall in love with anybody else. Since their wedding, they may not have been in love but she had always been there for him. Though he still held a deep grudge against her for having been distant with his parents, he could not deny that every morning at seven she had made the food ready for them, had their laundry done, and their bed sheets changed. And how could he ever forget that on weekends she made paranthas for them? She never ate sweets, but had made it a point to please his parents by making Indian sweets for them, like pedas and gulab jamuns. And if she was not expressive, he blamed himself; it was entirely his fault. In the early years of their marriage, she was lively and spontaneous, but he had snuffed it out by not responding to her gaiety.

Samuel could not imagine life without Sharon. And even if she was attracted to Gautam-sir, he knew he was responsible, as he had taken her for granted, never being really affectionate or caring.

But when she had told him in a matter-of-fact tone that she was starting a music school with Gautam-sir, instinctively he knew that she was hiding something from him.

Perhaps she was having an affair with Gautam-sir and the apartment upstairs would be their love-nest if Gautam-sir was given permission to buy it.

He felt strangely afraid of losing Sharon; he knew she was now part of his existence.

He no longer felt that strange vacuum within him that he had known ever since his twin had died, because Sharon had not only given him a new set of twins, but had taken the place of the brother he had lost.

But the seed of suspicion had been planted in Samuel's mind.

Sharon had never given him reason to be jealous; but he could not deny that she had changed after her stay in Israel.

Gone were the shiny salwar-kameez suits, shararas, ghararas, and saris, instead she wore jeans with tee shirts or long skirts with embroidered tunics, silver jewelry, and strap-sandals brought back from Israel. She was still slim and her hair was cut short, permed, and streaked red. Grudgingly, Samuel agreed that the style suited her face and she looked sexy.

He was uncomfortable about it, because he was still his old square self.

Sitting there in the car with his precious camera-phone, he had a sudden flash of memory. He rolled up the windows, switched on the air conditioner and started retrieving the images of a ceremony he had shot at the synagogue.

When the twins were two years old, a certain David Cohen, a rabbi from Israel, was invited by the trustees of Magen Abraham Synagogue to bless the firstborn male children of the Bene Israel Jews. It was an age-old custom, which ensured health, wealth, happiness, prosperity, and a long life for the child.

When Daniyal had given him the circular about David Cohen's visit, Samuel and Sharon had decided that Abel would receive the blessing as he had arrived before Albert.

Cohen was not an old man as expected, but in his thirties, and looked more like a professor than a priest with his gold-rimmed spectacles. If he had not worn his prayer shawl and kippa, one could have taken him for an Israeli tourist.

David Cohen stood on the Teva saying the prayers, as seven pairs of parents lined up with their sons.

Samuel suddenly became uncomfortable about the number seven and had half a mind to turn back, but he knew he could not, as it would lead to a scandal. So, he stood there patiently with Sharon. Then he decided to divert his attention to other matters, and started shooting the ceremony with his camera-phone. Through the lens, he saw David Cohen bending towards the mother of each child and asking a question. Only if the woman shook her head did he bless the child.

Samuel did not pay attention to the proceedings till he stood facing David Cohen, who was pleased that he spoke Hebrew. They stood chatting for a while, then David Cohen bent towards Sharon and Samuel started shooting the most memorable moment of their lives. The camera was focused on Sharon's face and Cohen was asking Sharon if she had ever had an abortion or a miscarriage before Abel was born; if she had had one, he could not bless the child.

For a moment, Sharon stood thunderstruck and did not shake her head like the rest of the women. David Cohen was looking at her and waiting for an answer, his hand suspended in mid-air to bless Abel. Assuming that Sharon did not understand the question, Samuel shook his head, but stopped when he felt Sharon's hand on his. She shook her head, signaling that he should not answer the question and then looking straight into David Cohen's eyes, she said, "Yes, I had an abortion before the twins were born."

Samuel's ears and nose turned red with shame and he quickly switched off the camera-phone and slipped it into his shirt pocket. Embarrassed, they had descended from the Teva without the blessing for Abel. Samuel had turned beetroot red as he had never known about the abortion.

Even questionable women like Sippora had passed David Cohen's test, but not his God-fearing wife Sharon. He did not know whether it had been in Israel or India, before marriage or after?

He would never know. But he was grateful that David Cohen had touched Abel's head and said a short prayer. It was not relevant to the first-born blessing, but to all appearances, Abel had received the blessing. Except Saul Ezekiel, nobody had really noticed that anything was amiss. The ritual had taken more than two hours and the congregation was restless; they were talking amongst themselves, waiting for the ceremony to end so that they could head for the refreshments table.

On the way back home, Samuel had looked at Sharon questioningly. She had looked out of the window and told him without change of expression, "In Israel."

It was a delicate moment and not knowing what to say, he looked at the reflection of the twins in the rear-view mirror and thanked Eliyahu Hannabi for small blessings.

With the memory of that particular evening, Samuel felt a black mood descend upon him. He slid the camera-phone back in his shirt pocket, switched off the air conditioner, got out of the car, locked it, and decided to speak to Ezra.

He was in a fury and to calm himself, took the stairs. He also wanted to check if there were seventeen steps between the floors. When Samuel rang the doorbell, Ezra was still in his pajamas, sitting on the balcony and reading the newspaper. He invited Samuel into the apartment and offered him a cup of tea.

He was surprised at this early-morning visit from a man with whom he had hardly exchanged seventeen sentences in seven years. Samuel sat uncomfortably in his chair, crossing and uncrossing his legs, then found the right position and said, "I believe you are planning to rent out Juliet's apartment to a certain Gautam Seth."

"Yes, the famous sitar player. Your wife had told me about him.

He is coming to see the apartment this afternoon."

"So I gather."

"Isn't it a great honor that a great sitar player will be living amongst us? You know he is very famous."

"Is he?"

"I am surprised you don't know, because he is like your wife's brother."

"Gautam Seth is not Sharon's brother, he is her guru. Sharon may not have mentioned that he is a divorcee and plans to live alone here. I feel a single man is not exactly what you are looking for, are you? You must think about our women. He is planning to start a music school. I feel this is incorrect, as this is a residential area, and especially when we have our high holidays, the classes could disturb us."

"Thank you Samuel, for bringing this point to my notice. I will have to reconsider Gautam Seth's offer. When he called me, I thought, 'At last there is a buyer for Juliet's apartment, and she can have her restaurant in Israel.' But what about your wife?"

"Nothing, she will continue holding her sitar classes in our apartment."

"Thank you, Samuel. I should have checked Gautam Seth's marital status. He is so famous, that I never thought about asking him personal details. I will have to reconsider giving the apartment to a man without a wife. But, how do I tell your wife that we cannot sell the apartment to Gautam Seth?"

"I don't know, I leave it to you."

Then he stood up, smiled, shook hands with Ezra, and left.

18 Juliet

Ezra did not know how to frame the letter to Juliet informing her that the deal with Gautam Seth had fallen through, and he had not been able to sell her apartment. He did not want to tell her about Samuel's intervention in the matter. He switched on the computer to see if there was mail and to his surprise saw Juliet's name in the inbox.

> Dear Uncle Ezra,
> Shalom.
> I received your last e-mail, in which you mentioned how every possible deal had fallen through when you were trying to sell our apartment. Aunt Tamar almost bought the apartment from me while she was here in Israel. But, that did not work out. Anyway, I am glad she made up with Uncle Ezel. I know Aunt Shoshanah wanted to buy our apartment for Miriam, but never pursued the matter. I feel sorry for Aunt Shoshanah. I hope Eliyahu Hannabi arranges a reunion between mother and daughter. I was also sad to hear about Raghubir Chopra's sudden death.
> In your last mail you had mentioned that Gautam Seth, the sitarist, was interested in buying our apartment. You said he

wanted to start a music school. We were thrilled with the idea. But, since you have not written back, I suppose he also backed out.

By the way, if you ever meet Gautam Seth, tell him that I am his fan. Do you think we could meet him when we return to India?

I know you have been trying to sell the apartment for us so that we can buy that much-prized restaurant at Jaffa gate. But obviously, that is not the will of the prophet. With his blessings, we are returning to India, just in time for Hanukah celebrations. Romiel is sure that he will be the first one to grab the holy citron in the succa at the synagogue, so that all our dreams come true. In fact, our return to India is the beginning of the realization of our dreams. We have written to our parents about our plans and they are buying us a small restaurant which is up for sale on the Sarkhej–Gandhinagar highway. We are also bringing back all our savings with us, and fortunately the apartment is still there for us.

We are planning to start a Chinese restaurant. I am sorry to say it will not be kosher, but I know the prophet Elijah will forgive us our little errors. Perhaps Ben Hur could help us with the interior design of our restaurant.

The name of the restaurant will be Ha Ajalon.

We live very near the Valley of Ajalon and Mount Gibeon. On some evenings we see the sun and the moon suspended on the horizons of the east and the west. Often I catch myself thinking, are we on Mount Gibeon or in the Valley of Ajalon? If you remember, there is mention of this in the Torah, "Sun, stand thou still upon Gibeon; and thou moon, in the Valley of Ajalon . . . and the earth stood still and the moon stayed . . . So the sun stood still in the midst of heaven, and hasted not to go down for the whole day . . . "

Watching the sun and the moon, we often discuss our future, and that's how we decided to return to India. Because when you live in a country like Israel, which is yours but not exactly yours, you have to work harder. In the beginning when Romiel and I were working different hours, we rarely saw each other and were so tense that we fought for no reason at all. Sometimes we also had fights just because we were hungry and there was no food at home waiting for us. So, we started planning our dinners in advance or buying some Chinese food on the way back home. Chinese food is closer to Indian food with its curry-based dishes, which are eaten with a bowl of rice. That is how we decided to start a Chinese restaurant in Ahmedabad. I don't have to tell you how hard it is to keep a marriage going in the face of all odds. We feel perhaps we could organize our lives better in India.

We are aware that India is not easy after the earthquake of 2001 and then the riots of 2002. But keeping all possibilities in mind, we plan to keep both doors open.

The two countries are like the sun and moon for us.

As a Jew, sometimes I wonder, are we coming or going?

Where are we going?

Where is home? Is our home within us or somewhere else? As we prepare to return to India, in a way, we are making our own law of the return . . .

Looking forward to seeing you soon, with warm regards to you and Aunt Sigaut,
Juliet

19 Hadasah

Hadasah, the author of this narrative, lives in A-114 of Shalom India Housing Society. She is often invited to judge competitions of drawing, sports, cooking, and fancy dress at the synagogue.

She particularly enjoys fancy dress competitions, because through the clothes the children choose, she interprets the latent desires of the participants and their parents, changing from one skin to the other, conflicted between their Jewish and Indian identities.

But as a child, Hadasah, named after the Persian queen Esther, had never participated in fancy dress competitions during Hanukah or Purim.

Hadasah was amused when she first met Ezra to book an apartment at Shalom India Housing Society. He had only a vague idea about her personal life and asked her the usual questions, "Are you married?"

Confused, she shook her head, "Not exactly."

He had looked at her pointedly and smiled, "So, you are still a highly eligible spinster?"

She laughed, "In a way, yes, but the booking office of my marriage bureau is closed."

Ezra had not understood the meaning of her words and asked, "So, do you need a one-bedroom apartment or two bedrooms?"

She had lit a cigarette, much to his discomfort, and said, "Two, as sometimes I have guests and family staying with me."

Ezra looked up startled, "So shall I assume you are married?"

"No," she said, confusing him further.

Ezra was thinking, "So there is a husband somewhere . . . wonder if one or two, Jewish or non-Jewish?"

He understood from the determined look on her face that he dare not ask personal questions.

Lately she was often seen inside the synagogue, but as she did not participate in the events, Ezra tried to involve her in the community by inviting her to judge the various competitions held in the court-yard of the synagogue. She seemed to enjoy fancy dress competitions and even played with the children.

For years nobody had seen her inside the synagogue. They said she had lived in Israel for a while. Nobody knew any details about her personal life, although they said she wrote novels, but never spoke about her own life.

Hadasah does not fit into the Bene-Israel-Jew mold.

She had in fact lived in Israel for years and she returned in the mid-eighties to her ancestral house in the walled city, a little distance from the synagogue, where she lived with her father.

During the riots of 2002 she was living alone in the house, as her father had died a year back.

After the riots, she moved to Shalom India Housing Society. From the half-closed window of the old house, she had seen a young woman being stripped, raped, and murdered. That was reason enough for her to book an apartment at Shalom India Housing Society, so that she was safe with her own kind.

The daily rhythm of apartment life disturbed Hadasah, so she often returned to the old house to write on her laptop.

Residents of Shalom India Housing Society had seen her novels in bookshops and on her bookshelves, but they never dared ask her to lend them.

In a way, they hesitated to read her novels as they were sure she was exposing the secrets of their lives.

Hadasah was friendly, but distant.

The only person she was close to was simple Salome. She spent hours with her, taking notes as Salome spoke about Jewish traditions, rituals, and recipes. In fact, they often cooked together some long-forgotten Bene Israel recipe.

But Hadasah knew very little about the services at the synagogue.

She did not know in which direction to turn, right or left? Rise on the heels? Or how to hold the two fingers at the temples and say the prayer, Shema Israel . . .

Hadasah was known to have her individual style of services in her apartment, inviting friends from all communities to celebrate the festivals.

She had strong views about a secular society and was at the forefront of discussions about selling Juliet's apartment to a non-Jew. It was another matter that the sale of the apartment never materialized and Juliet and Romiel were returning to India.

Hadasah had made a mental note to speak to Juliet about a delicate matter.

When Juliet and Romiel's parents had bought them the apartment at Shalom India Housing Society as a wedding gift, there had been a ceremony before they entered the apartment. Hadasah had noticed the auspicious Hindu swastika on their kitchen wall. For her, it brought back tragic memories of the Holocaust. Hadasah thought it was important to explain to Juliet the difference in the direction of arms in a Hindu swastika and a Nazi swastika. Juliet was an intelligent girl and Hadasah was sure she would understand the implications of both swastikas.

Hadasah had also objected to David Cohen asking young Jewish mothers if they had had a miscarriage or abortion before he blessed their first-born child.

She was one of the few who had noticed Sharon's discomfort when her child was not blessed. Sharon was heartened when Hadasah sat beside her and told her that women had a right over their bodies.

Soon after the blessing, David Cohen had distributed one-rupee coins to the singles of the community, to help them find Jewish life-partners as soon as possible.

Hadasah had watched, amused, as Lebana blushed when she received the coin and quickly slipped it into her purse, just in case . . .

The coins had the opposite effect on Diana and failed where Ben Hur was concerned.

When a rather confused Ezra led David Cohen to where Hadasah was sitting and gave her the coin, the synagogue resounded with her laughter.

She studied the coin, smiled at David Cohen and said she did not need one, as she intended to remain an eligible spinster forever.

But she kept it, thanking Ezra profusely and unnerving him in doing so.

When the congregation broke up for refreshments, she looked for Ben Hur, mooning under the canopy of the pomegranate tree in the courtyard of the synagogue. Hadasah kissed his forehead, slipped the coin into his palm and whispered, "Perhaps you need two for luck."

Then there was the incident of Yom Shoah, when she had a major disagreement with Ruby.

After the encounter with Franco Fernandes during her daughter's visit, Ruby had left for Canada and involved herself in Jewish activities. On her return to India, she had gone a step ahead from divining dreams and was often seen reading books on the Kabbalah.

According to Salome, Samuel was one of Ruby's first clients and often consulted her about his difficulties with the number seventeen. She had also formed a women's group at the synagogue and held classes to enlighten the women about Jewish history, the Holocaust, and Western-style festive services, sometimes teaching them to make the braided challah bread for the Sabbath and hamantashen for Purim.

Hadasah thought Ruby's classes were basically harmless, but often historically incorrect and monotonous. She always found some excuse or the other not to attend Ruby's discourses, until the time Ruby invited Hadasah for the celebration of Yom Shoah or Holocaust Day. When Ruby phoned her, Hadasah was amused at the use of the word celebration, but nevertheless agreed to attend the function. Dressed in white, she arrived at the courtyard of the synagogue and saw that Ruby had arranged an exhibition on the Holocaust with picture postcards brought back from her foreign trips.

Hadasah noticed a poster pasted on the synagogue wall which

said "Happy Yom Shoah." She also saw that the others including Ruby were dressed as though they had come for a party. They were laughing and joking, standing around a table where hot samosas and glasses of sherbet were being served. This was enough to ignite Hadasah's temper.

She stood on the steps, facing the congregation, and declared that Holocaust Day was not a festival; it was the Memorial Day for six million Jews who had died in Nazi Germany.

It did not call for samosas and sherbet.

Heads turned towards her in shock, as samosas and sherbet glasses were quickly put down.

Hadasah ripped off the poster from the wall, crumpled it, and threw it away, much to Ruby's displeasure. She then requested Saul Ezekiel to recite the Kaddish, the prayer for the dead, after which there was a solemn silence.

Later, an angry Ruby confronted Hadasah, asking what right she had to spoil her party; after all, what sort of a Jew was she? She did not even know simple Sabbath prayers. So how would she know the meaning of Yom Shoah?

This only infuriated Hadasah, who sat down on the steps, opened her wallet, and showed Ruby a photograph.

It was a photograph of Hadasah with a man much older than her, on whose arms the tattoo marks of a Nazi concentration camp were visible.

Ruby watched like one shell-shocked as Hadasah said, "I know, because my late husband was a survivor from a concentration camp and I know what it means."

Then she slumped down on the steps and wept, her face hidden in her hands, as Ruby and the others stood around her in silence, not knowing what to do, till Salome took her in her arms and comforted her.

Much later, Salome who knew Hadasah better than anybody else, opined that Hadasah's Jewishness was abstract, something which was there and not there. Actually, she said, Hadasah had learned a lot about being Jewish by sitting in front of her computer and spinning tales about the Bene Israel Jews of India.

Salome agreed that Hadasah had a knack for making everybody

feel uncomfortable. When Hadasah was around, they felt watched. Even if she never probed into anybody's life, nothing escaped her sharp eyes.

Yet they were heartened by the mere fact that she had booked her own funeral space, six feet by six, at the new Jewish cemetery on the Ahmedabad–Baroda highway, by paying an advance of rupees five hundred only.

Acknowledgments

It was at a conference in New Delhi that Ritu Menon suggested I write an anthology of Jewish short stories. I agreed and decided to weave the stories around the Bene Israel Jews of Ahmedabad. When I started writing, I realized that the lives of all the characters were making connections with each other and taking the form of a novel and that is how *Shalom India Housing Society* was created.

Around this time I was writing *Book of Rachel*, in which the Prophet Elijah has an important role, so I decided to make him the main protagonist of *Shalom India Housing Society*. While writing, I also had a distant memory of Bombay's Jacob Circle when, as a bridesmaid at my cousin Sarah's wedding, I had seen Jews living together in the same building. This was before the mass exodus of Indian Jews to Israel in the late fifties. More recently, while writing *Shalom India Housing Society*, I discovered another such society in Bombay. In the same context, many Jewish families of Ahmedabad have moved to the western side of Ahmedabad since the communal riots of 2002.

A trip to Alibaug for the ninety-third anniversary of the Magen Aboth Synagogue gave me the rare opportunity of meeting Indian Jews from all over India, Israel, and the United States. It was then that I got another insight into Jewish family life, when Irene Abraham Rohekar of Ahmedabad suggested I meet her parents in Alibaug and I stayed with Sofie and Samson David Wakrulkar. The story of oti chi poti was given to me by Sofie.

While writing I often visited Jewish homes, observed lifestyles and came closer to the Jewish communities of Ahmedabad, Bombay, and Alibaug. From these experiences I created my own characters, which are largely fictitious. *Shalom India Housing Society* also helped me to understand my own mini-microscopic community, which has held onto its Jewish roots in an Indian environment.

While constructing *Shalom India Housing Society*, it was good to have Namrata Dwivedi around, reading the text, researching, and discussing the characters with me. During this period, my late cousin Sybil often dropped in to give me some juicy tales she might have heard at the synagogue. The idea of using a fancy dress competition as a method of introducing the characters came to me when I was asked to judge one such event at the synagogue in Ahmedabad.

I gave this form to the novel when I sent the first chapter to my in-house family critics, daughter Amrita and son Robin, and they liked the concept.

The Bombay blast story was told to me by my brother-in-law Victor Elijah. And if my cousin Elizabeth Elijah hadn't driven me around Bombay's synagogues, I would have missed out on some invaluable information. I also got a rare insight into the rites and rituals followed by the Jewish community from Johny Pingle of Magen Abraham Synagogue, Ahmedabad, and Ezra Moses of Gate of Heaven Synagogue, Thane.

I wish to thank Ritu Menon for believing in me, Niharika Gupta for editing, and above all, Prophet Elijah, for guiding my hand.

Esther David

Afterword

Set in Ahmedabad, Esther David's magical tale, *Shalom India Housing Society*, is the latest of David's four novels to bring the Bene Israel of India to life. Through her stories, the reader enters the vibrant spiritual and material worlds of this community of Jews who have resided in India for thousands of years. In all her work, David transports her readers into the lives of the Bene Israel, from village India to contemporary Ahmedabad, Bombay (Mumbai), and Israel. This ancient sect of Jews initially made their homes in villages along the Arabian Sea in Maharashtra State on the west coast, an area that was lush with "coconut, supari, neem, mango, chikoo, guava, papaya, banana and banyan trees," as David writes in *Book of Esther*, a novel loosely based on her own family history. This tropical paradise was worlds apart from the congested, narrow lanes of the walled city of Ahmedabad or the commercial heart of India in Bombay where many eventually moved. The Bene Israel thrived in the cities, building synagogues, schools, and community centers, and living comfortably amidst Muslims and Hindus until the early years of the 21st century.

India has had several distinct Jewish groups, which include the Bene Israel; the Cochin Jews, also called the Malabar or Kerala Jews;

the "White Jews" from Europe; and the Baghdadi Jews from the Middle East. Each has its own separate history and culture. The Jews of Cochin, like the Bene Israel, have been in India for many centuries. They follow many Jewish traditions common to other groups, although they are known for one distinctive practice: Cochin Jews do not forbid public singing by women and have a rich culture of Jewish prayers and songs performed by women in Judeo-Malayalam, a Dravidian language that uses Hebrew words. The European Jews, who have also historically lived in the Cochin area, began arriving on the subcontinent after the Jewish expulsion from Spain; they spoke Ladino (Judeo-Spanish) for many years, but now generally use a form of Malayalam.

David and I grew up in Indian-Jewish communities at about the same time—she in the Bene Israel, I as a member of the Baghdadis; she in Ahmedabad, and I in Calcutta, on the east coast. The differences between our two versions of Judaism can be explained in part by the Bene Israel's long history in India. They are said to be the descendants of a group of Jews who were shipwrecked more than 2,000 years ago. Recent DNA testing lends some credibility to the story that the ancestors of the Bene Israel (literally "children of Israel") were a small group of hereditary Israelite priests, one of the Ten Lost Tribes of Israel. Whether in a shipwreck or not, the Bene Israel arrived in India without religious books, and over the centuries maintained only a few Jewish traditions, such as observing the Sabbath as a day of rest, reciting the *Shema*, Judaism's most holy prayer, maintaining a few dietary laws, and circumcising their male infants. Jewish festivals such as Hanukah and Purim developed long after they arrived in India but eventually became part of their rituals.

In traditional Indian style, the Bene Israel took on a specific job that only they performed; they were oil pressers, called the *Shanwar Teli*, or Saturday oilmen, an ironic reference to the fact that they would not press or sell oil on the Jewish Sabbath. This caste-like designation placed them at the lower end of the Konkan class structure. In addition to their designated occupation, they also engaged in agriculture, peddling, and carpentry. The Bene Israel generally lived in large extended families, with each family typically owning a few acres of land, cattle and chickens, an oil press, a couple of bullocks, and a two-wheeled cart that the head of the family used to peddle their surplus in small towns.

Since there were rarely more than a hundred or so Bene Israel Jews living in any village, they were unable to create extensive community structures. In the absence of prayer halls and synagogues, people performed group prayers and rituals in their homes. The family patriarch structured both religious and social life. As David writes in *The Walled City*, "in the small and orthodox community, the elders were the matchmakers and took all the major decisions." Bene Israel marriage traditions mirrored Indian ones in many ways. They incorporated the *mehndi* ceremony, in which the bride has henna designs painted on her hands and feet and wears a traditional green sari as a symbol of fertility, followed by a white sari to signify purity and virginity during the wedding. Inheritance, ceremonial food offerings, and funeral rites also followed Indian customary practices. David's ancestors spoke Konkani, the women wore the traditional *nav-vari* (nine-yard sari), and the men dressed in *dhoti* (loincloths), *kurta* (long-sleeved shirts), *chappals* (sandals), and a *topi* (hat). Virtually indistinguishable from those around them, they were welcomed into village life.

My ancestors, by contrast, were distinct from their neighbors in looks, dress, language, and formal religious practice, and for the most part, chose to maintain the distance this created. They spoke Arabic. The men wore loose clothing along with turbans just as they had in Baghdad. The women wore flowing cotton ankle-length *gowans* (gowns), and married women covered their heads with *yasmas* (scarves). They practiced a conservative Sephardic Judaism and strictly followed the Baghdadi liturgical traditions.

In the mid-eighteenth century, David Rahabi, who is thought to have been from Cochin, was the first modern Jew to encounter the Bene Israel. Rahabi introduced them to the Judaism that had developed after the destruction of the Second Temple and taught them to read and write in Hebrew. Some of those trained by Rahabi, known as *kazis,* traveled among Bene Israel families throughout the Konkan region to administer rites of passage and other rituals according to Jewish law, to judge disputes among Jews, and to teach prayers by

SHALOM INDIA HOUSING SOCIETY

rote. Over the course of the nineteenth century, Cochin and Baghdadi Jews became religious leaders among the Bene Israel and helped spur a religious revival. The Bible and some Hebrew prayer books were translated into Marathi, and a few synagogues and prayer halls were established. As a result of all this activity the Bene Israel now commemorate and celebrate the major Jewish festivals and customs while maintaining a few traditions of their own, such as their unique devotion to Elijah *Hanabi* (the prophet), who provides an organizing principle for *Shalom India Housing Society*.

The Bene Israel's powerful link to Elijah is symbolized by the belief that he ascended to heaven in his chariot from Khandalla, a Konkan village, where the hoof prints of Elijah's horses and the ruts of his chariot wheels are said to be embedded in a sacred rock. Bene Israel Jews give thanksgiving offerings and make fulfillment vows at this sacred site, which they share with Muslims and Hindus, who also consider it a holy place.

In 1674 the British East India Company moved its headquarters from Surat, in Gujarat, to the Islands of Bombay. The natural harbor and the fishing villages on these islands quickly became the busy metropolis and port of Bombay, offering numerous opportunities for employment and education. Some time around the middle of the eighteenth century, a junior commissioned officer in the service of the British Indian Army, Samaji Hassaji (Anglicized to Samuel Ezekiel Divekar), moved to Bombay to escape political instability in the Konkan region. Others followed and soon the Company was recruiting Bene Israel volunteers from Bombay as well as the countryside, referred to in Company records as belonging to the "native Jew caste." Bene Israel Jews rose to the highest ranks for native soldiers and many received medals for bravery and outstanding service in the field of battle. Others found work in construction and shipyards, and as carpenters.

In 1796, Samaji Hassaji established the Shaar Harahamim Synagogue on the coast of Gujarat, north west of Bombay. The synagogue commemorated his close encounter with death when he was taken prisoner in the Second Anglo-Mysore War by the warrior king Tipu Sultan. The devoutly religious mother of the ferocious warrior had learned about Jews from the Qur'an; when she heard a few Jews had been captured, she asked to meet them. Having done so, she interceded on their behalf to prevent her son from executing them.

By the twentieth century, the majority of the Bene Israel had moved from their villages to Bombay, although some spread out to other cities in the Western part of the subcontinent—Poona, Ahmedabad, New Delhi, and Karachi—and as far away as Aden in Yemen.

Compared to the Bene Israel, who put their roots down in the villages and cities of Western India but lived in relative isolation from the rest of Jewry for almost two thousand years, mine was predominantly a traveling community that settled from the eighteenth to the twentieth centuries along the string of port cities stretching from Basra to Shanghai in the East, and to London in the West. They chose to remain apart from the culture around them but were very much a part of Jewish Asia.

Bombay was the place where these two distinctive and flourishing Jewish communities came together. Like the Bene Israel, my Baghdadi ancestors moved to Bombay in the eighteenth century. The first Baghdadi Jews arrived around 1730. Around 1832, David Sassoon, a wealthy Jewish leader from Baghdad moved his family to Bombay where he established an industrial empire. He and his family soon dominated Jewish life in the city, financing the elaborate Maghen David Synagogue, replete with an imperial clock tower. They also built many important secular, educational, and charitable landmarks in both Bombay and Poona.

Although both the Bene Israel and the Baghdadis contributed greatly to the city, there was little interaction between them because of cultural differences, divergent historical trajectories, and social aspirations. The Bene Israel had welcomed the Baghdadi Jews when they first arrived in Bombay, inviting them to attend services in their synagogues and to bury their dead in their cemetery, but a rift eventually developed based on racial and socio-economic considerations, and by the early twentieth century the tables had turned, with the Baghdadi Jews denying the Bene Israel certain rights in the Baghdadi synagogues and excluding them from charity trusts and burial grounds.

By the time David and I were growing up in India in the fifties and sixties, we both lived in predominantly non-Jewish worlds—the emigration of the Bene Israel and Baghdadi Jews to Israel, England, Australia, Canada, and the United States had begun by then, and our tightly-knit communities were dissolving. Baghdadi Jews emigrated mostly to England, Australia, and Canada in search of greater economic opportunities, while many Bene Israel immigrated to Israel, drawn by Zionism as well as uncertainties about their prospects in postcolonial India. In *The Walled City* David writes, "Most of our relatives, including our Bombay cousins, have left for Israel. We receive wedding invitations, announcements of births, deaths and engagements, New Year cards and Hanukah wishes, photographs of cousins in dresses, shorts, jeans, short hair and army uniform." By the time we were in high school, there were only some two thousand Bene Israel left in Ahmedabad and Bombay and barely two hundred Baghdadi Jews, if that, in Calcutta.

It was through writing and chronicling family histories that both David and I were able to make sense of who we were and to come to terms with our Jewishness. David has said that when she was growing up, "to have a Biblical name and say . . . prayers in Hebrew," made her feel "bewilderingly aware of her hidden difference" from those around her. Writing *Book of Esther,* a richly colored skein of stories loosely based on her family's legends, rekindled her interest in Judaism: "Being Jewish, and spending a long time running from my Jewish life . . . is what made me a writer. And then it was only in writing that I was able to understand myself, my family, and where I came from. I still cannot follow the religion like other Indian Jews, but, through research and a sense of history, I am now more spiritually Jewish."

As a young girl growing up in independent India, I, too, had wanted to run away from my community and its disengagement with all things Indian, a disengagement that seemed old-fashioned and out of place in postcolonial society. Both David and I were drawn to the stories of the strong-willed women in our families—women who, despite the strict mores of the times, challenged their circumscribed roles, sought and obtained education, and became professionals in their own right.

Afterword

When she was a young child David and her parents lived with her grandmother, to whom she was deeply attached. This grandmother kept the Sabbath and attended synagogue regularly. In *Shalom India Housing Society*, David wistfully recalls the high-domed Maghen Abraham Synagogue of her childhood, with its smooth marble flooring, glass windows, ancient crystal lamps, and wall of yellow stained glass in the women's gallery. She describes the marble plaques of the Ten Commandments written in Hebrew and Marathi, testament to the way in which Judaism is intimately intertwined with India among the Bene Israel.

At the age of seven, David moved with her parents across the city to live in the zoo her father had established. The zoo was her playground, filled with exotic birds and animals. Living apart from the Jewish community with a father who was fairly unobservant, "believing more in Darwinism than Judaism," meant that she grew up quite removed from the remnants of Jewish community life that still existed.

David and I both mark the histories of our ancestors in a more intimate and personal manner than the formal histories of our communities. We approach our cultural experience from the standpoint of women, and with a deep respect and appreciation for the courage of our foremothers. In *Book of Esther*, David pays tribute to her great-grandmother Bathsheba in a character in her novel also named Bathsheba, a woman who had the "courage to speak to her father-in-law about the desire to be in charge of the property. . . . She was certain that her decision to step outside the house would bring a lot of opposition from her own family and other Bene Israel families from Revdanda and Nandgaon." We have both relied on our memories of community, old photographs, and fragments of stories, recreating the material and spiritual culture to bring these personal histories to life. As I noted in my book, "I look back into a world I knew as a child; a world that no longer exists in Calcutta except in shadows, musty rooms, and the old, lined faces animated only by their memories."

The many intriguing characters that distinguish David's storytelling move seamlessly between Bombay and Ahmedabad, from India to Israel. As the numbers of Jews in India continue to shrink, there are few except David who could create such sweeping, multi-generational, multi-locational, and fable-like stories based on historical fact, family lore, and history. David embellishes tales handed down through the generations, enriched by her artistic eye, her sense of humor, and her ability to imagine the inner yearnings of generations of women. Her understanding and love for the city of Ahmedabad reverberates throughout this playful and subtly political book.

Shalom India Housing Society is set after the Gujarat riots of 2002, when for the first time in all the centuries they lived in India, Jews began to feel unsafe. They did so, not from fear of persecution, but rather out of fear of being mistaken for Muslims. Mass violence erupted that year when two carriages of a train containing Hindu activists were set on fire by what were believed to be Muslim militants. The Hindus had been campaigning to construct a temple to Ram, an important Hindu deity, on the site of a sixteenth century mosque destroyed by Hindus ten years earlier. Fifty-nine passengers died in the tragedy. In retaliation, Hindu mobs slaughtered hundreds of Muslims, raped and mutilated Muslim women, and looted and burned Muslim homes, businesses, and places of worship. Thousands of surviving Muslims were displaced, their lives and futures ruined. In the aftermath, the Gujarat government did not pursue the perpetrators of the violence, and in fact intimidated victims, witnesses, and human rights workers who called for the prosecution of those responsible.

Wary of the government's complicity and the seemingly endless cycles of retaliation, many Bene Israel decided to band together in a segregated housing society, much like the fictional Shalom India Housing Society. Because Muslims, like Jews, were circumcised, and angry mobs frequently used circumcision to distinguish a Muslim from a Hindu, Jews felt they needed to take themselves out of the crossfire between the two groups. Moving out of the old city to new quarters was a painful and precipitous move for families that had lived and worshipped in the old part of Ahmedabad for centuries. At the real housing society, as well as in the fictional one, there were two buildings, one for Jews and the other for Parsis and Christians—two other minority religions in India.

Shalom India Housing Society is Esther David's cathartic and deeply personal response to the riots, which she experienced firsthand. Her home in the old city bordered both a Muslim neighborhood dubbed "Mini Pakistan" and a Hindu area. In an interview, David describes a moment during a brief lull in the violence when she went out to stock up on food. On the road lay a naked corpse under a white sheet. It was the body of her neighbor, a Hindu woman married to a Muslim, who had been attacked with swords and left to die. Although she no longer felt safe, David continued to live in the old city for a while longer. As an artist, sculptor, designer, and writer, she drew inspiration from the cultures of the old city—Hindu, Muslim, Jewish, and Christian. And the home she had lived in much of her life, with its cool mosaic courtyard, carved stained-glass windows with star-shaped grills, and roof with terracotta tiles, was difficult to leave. Memories were everywhere. "The house in Dilhi Darwaza," she has written about one such memory, "would be filled with the fragrance of ripe Alfonoso mangos spread out on straw mats. Our lives revolved around mangos: pickled, raw, dried, ripe and over ripe."

The terror attack on Mumbai in November 2008 marked a new sense of uncertainty and created a palpable fear among India's remaining Jews. It was the first deliberate attack on Jews or a Jewish organization ever to take place in India. The attack seemed aimed at tourists and Westerners, with the Chabad House, a Jewish Cultural Center run by the Lubavitch sect, clearly a target. Afterward, for the first time in their history in India, several Indian Jewish communities, including the Bene Israel and the Baghdadis, felt compelled to appoint security guards to protect their synagogues.

At the beginning of the twenty-first century there are more Bene Israel living outside India than in it. Among the Bene Israel who have settled there, their pride and love for India is undiminished. Bene Israel Jews travel back and forth to India when they can and have a deep nostalgia for their homeland—its color, its tastes, its energy, and its warmth. In Israel, they eat Indian food, celebrate Indian festivals, are active in Indian clubs and associations, and enjoy Bollywood films and cricket, India's favorite sport. Many of the young women learn Indian dance.

Israel has been challenging for the Bene Israel. They have faced racism and their Jewishness has been questioned—especially in the fifties and sixties, when they were among the darkest of the new arrivals. They were subjected to differential treatment in housing, employment, and education, and were generally considered second-class citizens. One of the tensest debates in the history of the Knesset, the Israeli Parliament, occurred when the Chief Rabbinate questioned the right of a Bene Israel to marry outside the group. The Knesset denounced the rabbinical decree and threatened to limit the Rabbinate's authority if it insisted on using judicial power to discriminate, which also had a detrimental effect on efforts to encourage Jewish immigration. Now that DNA tests support the Bene Israel claim to be descended from the earliest Jewish priests, the *Cohanim,* the question of whether they are Jewish is no longer debated.

The allure and disappointment of Israel, the impact that emigration has had on the Jews that remain, and the struggle to define their place in India, are themes that run through David's fiction. In *The Walled City* she writes of "Oversized matrons with heavy double chins from the land of milk and honey, protruding stomachs stuffed into jeans and skirts or nylon saris with large geranium flowers . . . they wear gold bangles and necklaces. . . . They carry cameras and sling bags, and offer gifts of almonds, Scotch whiskey and kosher Magi soup cubes. 'Come to Israel,' they say, 'it is wonderful. Almonds and chicken, so cheap, so good.'"

In *Shalom India Housing Society* we get to know Rachel, a young woman who is determined to shake free of Bene Israel cultural expectations for women by starting a cyber romance with an Israeli boy. She hopes to emigrate, wear tight jeans and a tee shirt, work on a kibbutz, pluck oranges, and dance to Hava Nagila under the desert stars. We meet Juliet as she falls in love with Rahul, her Hindu neighbor. Their story charts their struggle to settle in Israel, their nostalgia for their families and the life left behind in Ahmedabad. Juliet writes to her uncle about her decision to return to India "because when you live in a country like Israel, which is yours but not exactly yours, you have to work harder. . . . Sometimes we also had fights because we were hungry and there was no food at home waiting for us. . . . I don't have to tell you how hard it is to keep a marriage going in the face of all odds. We feel perhaps we could organize our lives better in India."

Esther David has not only written fiction about the Bene Israel but has contributed to scholarly writing by documenting their clothing styles from ancient times to the present. The growing body of work by Indian and foreign scholars has rekindled an interest in India's Jewish heritage. Sophie Judah has, like David, created enduring fiction about her Bene Israel community. *The Girl from Foreign* is American Sadia Shepard's elegant memoir of her search to discover her grandmother's Bene Israel background, and Ruby Daniel's memoir, *Ruby of Cochin*, written with anthropologist Barbara Johnson, is an important documentation of the traditions and culture of Cochin Jewry. Artists like Siona Benjamin, a member of the Bene Israel, fuse Jewish and Indian cultural motifs, and musician Rahel Musleah has popularized songs of the Baghdadi Jewish community. The work of these women and others has placed the Indian Jewish experience on the map, ensuring that its culture and history are not lost to India or to the world. The special attention to the potent roles that women have played in the three major Jewish communities is especially important, allowing a more complete picture to emerge.

There have been few literary contributions about the small minority communities of India. Rohinton Mistry and Bapsi Sidhwa's novels depicting the Parsi community are now world renowned, and there are several other authors such as Thrity Umrigar, Meher Pestonji, and Dina Mehta who examine the experience of being a minority in such an imposing majority culture. Much of this literature deals with the issues that David so aptly explores: the ways in which a minority community copes with hegemonic forces, identity crises, and the struggle to create a viable space. One sees that many of the concerns of the Parsi community—declining population, brain drain, late or interfaith marriages, modernist versus traditionalist approaches to religion, and the existence of ethnic anxieties—are similar to the ones David explores in her fiction. Within this context, David is distinctive in coming to her work from a decidedly feminist perspective. Strong women characters dominate her writings, and she explores women's experiences from a range of class and generational perspectives.

Minority narratives have a special place in India today as forces of secularism are increasingly threatened by efforts to assert Hindu dominance. These narratives challenge contemporary histories that are being rewritten to serve political agendas. They stand as testimony to India's pluralistic past, where many communities thrived; they confound and enrich the present and are essential to imagining a future for India that honors its richly diverse history.

Jael Silliman

Bibliography

Abramov, S. Zalman. *Perpetual Dilemma: Jewish Religion in the Jewish State*. Rutherford, NJ: Fairleigh Dickinson University Press, 1976.

Daniel, Ruby and Johnson, Barbara C. *Ruby of Cochin: An Indian Jewish Woman Remembers*. Philadelphia: The Jewish Publication Society, 2002.

David, Esther. *The Walled City*. Syracuse, NY: Syracuse University Press, 2002.

———. *Book of Esther*. New Delhi: Viking Press, 2002.

Judah, Sophie. *Dropped from Heaven: Stories*. New York: Schocken Books, 2007.

Parfitt, Tudor and Egorova, Yulia. "Genetics, History, and Identity: The Case of the Bene Israel and the Lemba." In *Culture, Medicine and Psychiatry* 29 (2): 2005.

Rosenberg, Amy. "A Passage to Gujarat," *Nextbook*, June 4, 2008, http://www.nextbook.org/cultural/feature.html?id=779 (accessed July 22, 2008).

Shepard, Sadia. *The Girl from Foreign: A Search for Shipwrecked Ancestors, Forgotten Histories, and a Sense of Home*. New York: Penguin Press, 2008.

Silliman, Jael. *Jewish Portraits, Indian Frames: Women's Narratives from a Diaspora of Hope*. Calcutta: Seagull Books, 2001.

The Feminist Press
at the City University of New York

is a nonprofit literary and educational institution dedicated to publishing work by and about women. Our existence is grounded in the knowledge that women's writing has often been absent or underrepresented on bookstore and library shelves and in educational curricula—and that such absences contribute, in turn, to the exclusion of women from the literary canon, from the historical record, and from the public discourse.

The Feminist Press was founded in 1970. In its early decades, the Feminist Press launched the contemporary rediscovery of "lost" American women writers, and went on to diversify its list by publishing significant works by American women writers of color. Beginning in the mid-1980s, the Press's publishing program has focused on international women writers, who remain far less likely to be translated than male writers, and on nonfiction works that explore issues affecting the lives of women around the world.

Founded in an activist spirit, the Feminist Press is currently undertaking initiatives that will bring its books and educational resources to underserved populations, including community colleges, public high schools and middle schools, literacy and ESL programs, and prison education programs. As we move forward into the twenty-first century, we continue to expand our work to respond to women's silences wherever they are found.

For information about events and for a complete catalog of the Press's 300 books, please refer to our web site:

www.feministpress.org